When Hearts Collide

What Reviewers Say About Renee Roman's Work

Body Language

"The whole story is about self-confidence and learning to see yourself the way others—the others that matter—see you. It's about loving oneself and all aspects of oneself. I liked the body positivity message and how it translated into the sex scenes. …The chemistry is strong, and the fact that the characters keep being surprised at how much the other wants them adds to it. I quite enjoyed reading this book, and I'll have a look at the author's other novels."—*Jude in the Stars*

"Such a beautiful passionate story and so much more than I initially bargained for. Not only do I love the idea of this book and all the story promotes, it has a gorgeous cover that is super enticing and just made me want to pick it up without even reading the blurb, and I am so glad I did. The whole story was emotional, even if you have never been in either of the characters shoes, you can still relate, and I most certainly did. …I loved that Renee took such an everyday, sensitive subject that we all can relate to, no matter what, and delivered an engaging and exciting story that I totally fell in love with."—*LESBIreviewed*

Where the Lies Hide

"I like the concept of the novel. The story idea is well thought out and well researched. I really connected with Cam's character…"
—*Rainbow Reflections*

"[T]his book is just what I needed. There's plenty of romantic tension, intrigue, and mystery. I wanted Sarah to find her brother as much as she did, and I struggled right alongside Cam in her discoveries."—*Kissing Backwards*

"Overall, a really great novel. Well written incredible characters, an interesting investigation storyline and the perfect amount of sexy times."—*Books, Life and Everything Nice*

"This is a fire and ice romance wrapped up in an engaging crime plot that will keep you hooked."—*Istoria Lit*

Epicurean Delights

"[*Epicurean Delights*] is captivating, with delightful humor and well-placed banter taking place between the two characters. …[T]he main characters are lovable and easily become friends we'd like to see succeed in life and in love."—*Lambda Literary Review*

"Hard Body"

"[T]he tenderness and heat make it a great read."—*reviewer@large*

"[A] short erotic story that has some beautiful emotional moments."—*Kitty Kat's Book Review Blog*

Visit us at www.boldstrokesbooks.com

By the Author

Epicurean Delights

Stroke of Fate

Hard Body

Where the Lies Hide

Bonded Love

Body Language

Hot Days, Heated Nights

Escorted

Glass and Stone

Desires Unleashed

Decadence

Searching for Someday

Chance Encounter

Stranger in the Sand

When Hearts Collide

When Hearts Collide

by

Renee Roman

2026

WHEN HEARTS COLLIDE

ISBN 13: 978-1-63679-922-3

This Trade Paperback Original Is Published By
Bold Strokes Books, Inc.
P.O. Box 249
Valley Falls, NY 12185

First Edition: March 2026

Credits
Editor: Cindy Cresap
Production Design: Susan Ramundo
Cover Design By Tammy Seidick

Acknowledgments

When I first embraced these characters I knew my fur baby, Maisie, was going to take on an important role. I've been blessed by the sweet, intelligent, loveable, and adorable kitty you are.

Thank you to Tagan Shepard and Kimberly Cooper Griffin for being sensitivity readers and helping me represent autism in real-life settings. Also, thank you to Ali Vali for allowing me to reference *Carly's Sound*. It was the perfect story for this book.

For friends and family who cheer me on and understand the solitary house as a choice and a necessity, "Thank you" for being with me in spirit.

As my editor, Cindy Cresap has provided me a way to understand the intricate details of grammar, and I am grateful so many have stuck. To the Bold Strokes Books staff, readers, and behind the scenes individuals, my gratitude to each one.

And to Dutch, thank you for pointing out how to look at the world with a photographer's eye and showing me that there are so many adventures in life. And even more so, I am grateful and blessed by your love.

Dedication

There comes a time in life
when you realize you are perfectly you.

Hold on to that understanding.

Prologue

"Annie, it's time for dinner."

With a roll of her eyes, Annie Dawson put down the book she was reading and headed to the kitchen. The regimented routine her mother had helped her adopt was good for focusing. It was also a pain when she was concentrating on something she wanted to finish. She sat with a moan, wondering if she'd ever be in charge of her own life. Autism sucked. Her mother joined her after sighing.

"Do you want to go for a walk after dinner? Maybe go for an ice cream?" Her mother smiled with kind patience.

Being out in the world with her mother to help navigate the awkward moments she encountered in everyday life was a treat Annie never passed up. She knew her mother loved her. Autism, similar to its cousin, ADHD, was largely misunderstood. After the psychologist identified the reason why she had trouble focusing and reacted to the world in non-typical ways, she understood herself better, but knowing she would always be different from her peers kinda sucked.

"Yes. Can we go now?" Annie looked at the food on her plate. What was usually her favorite looked foreign and unappealing, similar to her feelings about school and having to deal with the looks from others who thought she was weird. Or crazy. Maybe both.

"Your mom said after dinner. She made your favorite." Her dad did his best to deal with her, but sometimes he only made her feel like a disappointment.

Annie had learned the coping mechanisms that helped her move through a society that feared and despised things that were misunderstood. Now, as a college student, Annie didn't worry about what others thought of her actions. She was confident she could be herself and make space in the world for her true self. The one she was still discovering.

❖

Harlen McGhee couldn't believe her luck. The required color theory class was led by a man whose monotone voice made her want to take a nap rather than take notes. Her coffee cup was nearly empty; any caffeine boost she was hoping for would have to wait another ninety minutes. Great. She pushed the cup aside and pulled her water bottle from her backpack. Harlen fought the urge to surf on the internet. If she failed this course she'd just have to retake it, and once was going to be more than enough. Hopefully, the rest of her curriculum was less theory and more practical. Understanding the why behind the choices she would make made sense; being bored out of her mind did not.

The lecture hall door squealed as a student made her way to an open seat near hers. The distraction might have annoyed her if it wasn't for the smile she received when the new arrival's gaze met hers. This was a distraction she could live with.

Try as she might, Harlen would have to rely on the course notes posted in the student resource section. Ever since the woman's arrival, Harlen had to keep pulling her gaze back to the lecturer. Beauty may be in the eye of the beholder, but she'd have to be blind to not see it in the woman. When the class ended, the woman began gathering her things, and Harlen took the opportunity she'd been looking for.

"Hi. I'm Harlen."

The woman glanced up. "I'm Chloe. Hope I didn't disturb you." Her cheeks pinked. "I hate these maps." Chloe waved the campus handout that students received during orientation. "Whoever came up with the idea that an ariel view was the best way to orient people must have been a pilot." She laughed nervously, her eyes sparkling.

"I know what you mean. I keep turning it until I find a landmark, but it doesn't help with finding what direction I should head in."

"Exactly!" Chloe stood, appearing in no hurry to find her next destination. "Thank goodness I have a break. Maybe I can make sense of it all before my next lecture."

Harlen gave a silent thanks. "I have a break, too. Want to get a drink and figure it out together?" she said, mentally crossing her fingers.

"That would be great. Thanks." Chloe led the way, all the while checking her map. Harlen only had to redirect her once when Chloe turned left instead of right onto one of the dozen intersecting paths.

That was the day Harlen fell in love. She didn't realize it at the time, but fate had brought her an angel and she wasn't about to let Chloe fly away.

CHAPTER ONE

Harlen moved documents between her three screens, mumbling under her breath. Family expectations meant she was destined to follow in the footsteps of her grandparents in their real estate business. All of the Forrest grandchildren were destined to participate in some way. She had chosen acquisitions, looking for homes without buyers. It wasn't what she wanted to do, but someday she wanted to take control of listings that were rundown or needed major renovations. That's where she would step in and feed her passion, designing homes for buyers or renovating fixer-uppers that were in high demand. Those projects were the type she wanted to do, even if it wasn't her own business. This worked for her…for now.

For now, indeed. Harlen sighed then coughed. The air in her semi-private cube was dryer than a popcorn fart. She chuckled. Did people still say that? She first heard it years ago from Grandpa Harry, half of the dynamic duo who spearheaded the company. When money was a luxury no one Harry knew enjoyed, he and Grandma Sam had worked hard to make *their* dreams come true.

The alarm chimed on her phone. The weight of her devotion settled like it always did, along with the sadness that never left. Harlen logged out of her computer before grabbing her keys and phone.

"Kell, I'm out for the day." The volume of her voice echoed in the large space. Her overwhelming sense of duty was Harlen's decision, but it took a toll on her, nonetheless.

"Best to travel in safety," Kell said in response from behind a nearby cube. The exchange between them had been playing out for almost two years.

She didn't remember getting into her car. Her head was not in the game, and like it or not, every day was just a game to her. She wasn't living. Hell, she barely existed. Her life was on perpetual hold. The drive to the hospital was an autopilot occurrence as well. Once inside the lobby, she pushed the up button. As the elevator rose, hope found its way to her heart that today would be the day. Stepping onto the eerily quiet Critical Care Unit, Harlen let hope slip away. It's not that she was giving up as much as she sometimes wished she could just walk away. Instead, she simply accepted the reality that was her life.

"Hi, Harlen." One of the evening nurses raised her hand in greeting.

"Hey, Patty. How was your daughter's recital?"

"She was a hit and remembered all her steps. That alone was reason to celebrate." Patty's five-year-old had been in the show last year and had stood on the stage crying until one of the teachers guided her to where Patty was waiting.

"Congratulations."

"Thanks." Patty's smile receded. "No change with Chloe."

All Harlen could do was nod before heading to the softly lit inner sanctum where her partner, Chloe, lay beneath a pristine sheet. Her thin and pale arms were supported by pillows. The ever-present hissing of the ventilator, along with the rhythmic beep of the monitor, were mere illusions of a living person. Chloe hadn't been alive since the day of the accident. Back then, Harlen had hung on to the slightest chance that she'd wake up. But she knew better than to keep the hope alive that Chloe would someday wake when the EEG showed no sign of brain activity after a week.

Like the ankle weights she wore when she swam, her legs were heavy before she lowered onto one of the two convertible recliners that had been brought into the room following the day the medical staff confirmed that Chloe was in a vegetative state and it was just, "A matter of time." Two years later, Harlen wondered if that time would ever come.

❖

"Shit, Shit, Shit."

Annie swore as she rushed around gathering her lunch, keys, and purse. Technically, she wasn't late by work standards, but she had to be there early. There wasn't a lot that she liked more than a quiet office. After years of learning to adapt to societal expectations, Annie was knowledgeable and confident, making her a formidable and competent employee. She put a lot of work into being capable and accepted for the woman she was, though it hadn't always been that way. Autism still carried a stigma of being "less than," a label she refused. Fortunately for her, she landed a job at the Society for Neurodiversity as the fundraising organizer. She gave the SFN her best, however, she had a life outside of work. No dream job was going to make her forget to take care of herself.

With a glance at the passenger seat to confirm she had what she needed, Annie got it into gear, so to speak. Part of her diagnosis played out in ways that were hard for others to understand. Like her need to stick to routines and be on time, if not early. She planned out predictable events because it helped keep anxiety from creeping in. Being late sent her internal clock into a tailspin. She disliked wasting anyone's time.

Prospective donors liked that about her. While waiting for the light to change, Annie thought about the report sitting on her desk, a snapshot biography she'd found on the internet of a potential donor she'd earmarked to pursue this month. Her initial research would be a deeper search where she would look for things such as negative publicity, their yearly donation amount, and if it was based on the business's profit margin or a reflection of their commitment to the community, regardless of their profitability. Her phone rang and she pressed the connection on her steering wheel.

"Hello?"

"Good morning, Annie." Michael, the executive administrator at work, greeted her.

"Hi, Michael. How can I help you?" Annie pursed her lips. The car in front of her was moving at a snail's pace. At this rate she would be late walking through the office door. Her pulse quickened.

"Ms. Goldberg wanted to let you know the initial feasibility of the target donor looked good on paper. She's on board with you pursuing support."

Annie wasn't an instant gratification kind of woman. She did, however, appreciate the society's president endorsing her picks. "Thanks, Michael. I'll be there shortly." *If this damn car would get out of my way.* She hung up and concentrated on the road ahead of her. Five more minutes and she might be okay. The car turned and Annie sighed in relief. The light changed and she inched forward.

Her car lurched at the impact and she stomped on the brake. Another delay. Annie took some deep breaths and counted as her thumb touched each fingertip on her hand. Where the fuck had that car come from?

Chapter Two

"Not again." Harlen sat back and killed the engine. The last time there'd been an accident that affected her was two years ago, though at times it felt like yesterday. Since then, she still hoped to get her life back on track. She took a steadying breath and focused on the present.

The driver of the other car banged her hands on the wheel. Unfortunately, Harlen's frustration with her life had affected another person, based on the other driver's actions. The good fortune this time was that no one was hurt. The point of impact where the cars had met wasn't huge, just a fender bender. Harlen grabbed her cell and insurance card. By the time she got to the other driver, the woman's door was open and she was rummaging through her console.

"Are you okay?" Harlen asked.

"I'm fantastic, thanks for asking." The woman pursed her lips before closing her eyes and taking a visible breath. "I believe I had the light." The woman exited her car and Harlen couldn't help admiring her full figure beneath the form-fitting fuchsia-colored dress. The bright blue flats were a surprise, as was how well the contrast worked.

"I'm sorry." She considered if she should say more. It wasn't her style to be candid with strangers. "I've had a lot on my mind and I wasn't paying attention." The driver studied her for a long beat, her fingers moving as though she was counting. "It's not an excuse." Harlen held out her license and insurance card. A foreign feeling moved inside her.

The woman took her information. "Harlen McGhee. That's unique."

She shrugged. The comment was one she often heard. "It's a combination of my parents' names." The woman was clearly frustrated with the morning's event.

"Fascinating." Using her phone, the woman took pictures of both items before handing them back. "I'm sure they thought they were being clever." She presented her cards, practically jabbing them into Harlen's outstretched hand.

Confusion coursed through her, joining the other emotions she hadn't identified. Could it be that she was being reminded of how life could change in the blink of an eye? Harlen's momentary lapses in concentration were increasing. The current situation was her fault.

"Annie Dawson." Harlen read the name out loud.

Annie glanced around. "That's me." She raised her hand and smiled, though it didn't reach her eyes.

"I know I've inconvenienced you. We'll get through this as quickly as possible."

Annie's arm moved to her side, her thumb lightly touching each finger in a pattern. "I don't like being late to work." Annie ran a hand through her thick, lustrous hair.

"I really am sorry."

"I don't think you planned this," Annie said as she pointed to where their vehicles met. "But I really need to go." Her face revealed nothing before she smiled again, but this time her beauty shined through.

"That's a shame. I thought we'd grab a cup of coffee and put this behind us." She hadn't meant to make light of the situation. Annie's discomfort became hers, though why she felt such attachment to a stranger was disconcerting.

Annie looked around, her fingers twitching as though fighting against an inner struggle. "I…" She swallowed hard.

"Sorry. Poor timing on my part." Harlen expected a rebuttal. Instead, Annie surprised her by laughing and she couldn't help joining in. The tension broke while traffic moved around in the background. When was the last time she'd had a reason to be amused. She handed Annie's documents back. "Have you called the police?"

"I'm not a fan." Annie rounded the front of the car and bent to inspect the damage. It was a good thing her dress was so tight, otherwise Harlen would have had quite the show. "Well, there isn't much damage on the tanker." Annie tipped her head. "How about yours?"

Granted, Annie's car was likely a decade old, but it was in good condition. Harlen glanced at the fender on her vehicle, unconcerned. "I don't see anything to complain about." The look Annie gave her unnerved her. "Besides, it's a company car."

"So that makes it not matter?" Annie studied her, and Harlen was surprised by the lack of judgment.

"Not at all. It belongs to my family's business. I'll pay for any damage myself, since this was clearly my fault."

Annie glanced at her watch. She looked like a woman who wanted to be anywhere but there.

For Harlen's part, she couldn't deny wanting to know more about Ms. Annie Dawson. Something about her was familiar, but she dealt with so many names in her line of work, it was likely her imagination. "Are you sure you're not hurt?"

Annie opened her driver's side door. "The only thing that's hurt is my impeccable reputation for being on time," Annie said, her face revealing neither anger nor annoyance. Before she could get in, Harlen held out her phone.

"Still, I'd feel better if you'd let me know that hasn't changed."

"That what hasn't changed?" Annie asked.

"That you're still feeling okay."

"If I do, will that make you feel better about the accident?"

"No, but at least I'll know you haven't been injured." Harlen continued to offer her phone. To say she was intrigued was an understatement. Annie snatched it and punched at the screen.

"I appreciate your concern," she said before doing the same with her phone. "For future reference, a better statement would be, 'Please message me later that you're still okay.' See how this makes it clearer?"

Again, she was pulled up short by Annie's demeanor. It was refreshing in so many ways Harlen wondered if that was causing her to have an overwhelming concern for Annie's well-being. Truth be told, she couldn't explain it. "Message heard loud and clear."

"Excellent." Annie got into her car and the engine caught before she rolled down the window. "You'll need to back up first. Cause and effect kind of thing. If I pull away, there will be more damage."

"Oh, sure." Harlen hurried to her vehicle and slowly backed away without touching the steering wheel. As soon as there was space, Annie pulled away. *What the hell just happened?* Aside from the accident, Annie was the only thing she was focused on. She glanced in the rearview mirror. The smile wasn't familiar, but it looked good on her. It felt even better.

"Michael, it's Annie. I'm about ten minutes away."

"Is everything okay? You're never this late."

A tune her mother used to sing to her when she needed calming began in her head. "Mama Said (There'd Be Days Like This)" hadn't come to mind in years; what it could mean spewed like a ticker tape parade. "No, I'm not okay. I'm late." That alone was enough to cause stress, never mind what else was going on with her. She'd examine her feelings later, when she wasn't taking advantage of the flex time that didn't interest her. "I'll tell you all about it."

Annie disconnected and took the first opportunity to pull into traffic. Getting to work was her first priority. "I'm okay. I'm not that late." At the next light, she replayed the exchange with Harlen. The accident had been stressful because it threw off her timeline and she'd reverted to stimming, a behavior she'd learned to avoid after high school since the general population saw such outward movements as an indication there was something wrong with her and others who were autistic. Annie considered if the familiar though long-absent butterflies were confirmation of her attraction to Harlen, or a by-product of the tailspin she was in for needing to already *be* at work. She glanced at her phone. Harlen hadn't offered her number, but that hadn't stopped her. Getting said number gave her a sense of control over the situation. Why the need was strong deserved a closer look, but not now. Right now Annie had to stay in the moment.

It was more like seven minutes before Annie walked through the door. Michael met her at the elevator with a cup of coffee and a look of expectation. He had the good sense to wait until she'd taken a sip and waved for him to follow. "Monday, rushing around. I'm finally on my way to work when some..." How could she describe Harlen McGhee? "Someone who wasn't paying attention rolled through a stop sign and into my car." Thank goodness Harlen hadn't been going any faster than she was. At least they were both okay. Annie might school her visible reactions, but that didn't mean she didn't care about people.

Michael's hand moved to his chest. "Oh, no. You're okay though?" He knew her dedication, meaning she might have come to work without seeking medical attention.

"I'm fine. I barely felt the impact." That was true. The collision was minor. What wasn't minor was the unwanted attraction coursing through her. Harlen, while masculine presenting and handsome, was also the person who hadn't been paying attention. Annie would not entertain her feelings for anyone who was careless by nature. Admittedly, she didn't know Harlen, but first impressions were important. She needed strict planning in her life to maintain her equilibrium. Harlen appeared to be distracted, even when she looked to be in the moment. Distractions were the one luxury Annie could not let creep into her orderly life.

"I'm glad you're okay," Michael said as his shoulders lowered. "How is your car?"

"A small dent that I can live with." The relief that followed after surveying the damage was the result of not having to deal with another institutionalized part of society where people sued over unavoidable outcomes. The collision wasn't unavoidable, but Harlen was a troubled woman who had a lot on her mind, obviously.

Michael stood. "That's a relief." He touched the snow globe on her desk. It was their way of giving an uninvited hug and she warmed at his caring nature. "If you need anything for the Forrest Enterprises meeting, let me know."

"Will do."

The door closed softly and she pulled the donor file from the holder. The color-coded folder had been changed by Michael from manilla to green, indicating she had approval to go ahead and pursue the company or organization inside.

"Well, Mr. Forrest, let's see how open your pockets can be."

For the remainder of her day, Annie focused on in-depth research to understand the value of the target company, its treatment of employees, and its donation history. She'd make notes under each column on the preprinted sheet in front of her, the top of which was completed in Michael's crisp penmanship. Annie couldn't ignore the visions of Harlen that replayed on a loop. There was something about her Annie wished she could put her finger on, but whatever it was, the notion remained elusive, and she wasn't about to waste her day fixated on a practical stranger. But even as the hours ticked by, Annie wanted to know more about Harlen McGhee.

Chapter Three

Harlen tossed her keys into the basket on the entryway stand, then tossed the day's mail on the coffee table. She pulled a beer from the fridge and dropped onto the couch. She could still hear the machines that were her only company when she saw Chloe. The weekly visits had become rote, driven by her inability to give up entirely on Chloe's recovery.

It wasn't lost on her that if by some miracle Chloe did wake up, she'd never be the same. The sad outlook hung over her on a daily basis, and part of her wished the waiting was over so she could accept the inevitable and move on, but she couldn't. She'd made a promise to Chloe and she intended to keep it. As the alcohol began to work its way through her system, she closed her eyes. She drifted toward sleep, wanting to forget how tedious her life was, when her phone rang. Maybe it was the hospital. She answered without looking at the display.

"Hello."

"Hey, Har, how are you?" Daniella's voice reminded her there was good in her life too, and she took a deep breath. Her best friend instinctively knew when Harlen's spirits were down.

"Hi, Dan." She took a swig of her beer and settled in for the long conversation that would follow. "I've been better." They agreed long ago to not sugar-coat things when they talked.

"Chloe's the same." Dan pulled no punches when it came to what was on her mind.

"Yeah." She blew out a long breath. "I was in an accident this morning, and before you go into full protective mode, I'm fine."

"Shit, Har. What happened?" Dan asked.

Harlen considered if she wanted to get into the whole story, but she needed to unload. "I was thinking about Chloe for the millionth time, lying there for no damn good reason, and wasn't paying attention to driving."

Dan slow-rolled her answer. "Chloe was in an accident, bro. You know she would have likely recovered if she was wearing a seat belt."

Fuck. Of course, Harlen had looked for reasons to be angry at someone—anyone—but Chloe. "You're right. I just…" Silence followed as her mind drifted to that night in the ER when her life had gone from complicated to dismal.

"You were wearing your seat belt, right?"

"You know I was."

"Good. Then I need to remind you that you wouldn't be with Chloe right now whether she was in a coma or not. She'd be gone from your life and you'd have moved on."

Anger flared for a hot minute. "I know, I know." The pulse pounding through her head meant she was still fighting against what was right in front of her. "I've tried."

"I can't imagine what the waiting feels like for you." Dan paused. Harlen knew there was more to come. "What I do know is that Chloe would not want you to live your life in limbo."

Dan was right. "It's not as simple as it sounds. Chloe is…" She swallowed the knot in her throat. "Was the love of my life. I never thought what we had would end." The volume of her voice was a whisper, as though if the world heard her, Chloe would vanish from Harlen's life. Even in the state Chloe was in, she still fantasized about how things would be when she woke up.

"I'm worried about you. Being like this for…what? Going on three years? How long can you keep existing without actually living? Because you're not."

How many times had she argued with herself about the foolishness of hanging on? Long before the accident, Chloe was restless. Harlen was miserable in her job and she hadn't noticed until Chloe sat her down and told her she wasn't happy and wanted out of the relationship. Of course, later Harlen realized there were tells, but she'd been too self-centered to pay attention. What she *was* turned out to be a lot of excuses about why she hadn't noticed they were in trouble.

"Listen, I get it, but nothing's going to change tonight. Can we revisit next time?"

Dan sighed. "For your sake, I hope there isn't a next time." After a beat, Dan went on. "As for me and my world, a solo vacation would be fantastic."

Harlen laughed. Dan and her partner somehow managed to have three children between them. One each from a previous relationship and one together. To say their lives were hectic was an understatement. "You chose your situation, bro." She wasn't convinced she came across as teasing. Every aspect of her life felt off kilter.

"Absolutely." Dan had the good grace to not mention the slight. "You know what sounds even better?"

Oh, this to be good. "No. What?"

"If my best friend went on that vacation, too."

She had to give Dan one thing. She didn't give up when she believed in a course of action. "Work is super busy."

"Your family runs the business. I'm sure they'd agree to let you go."

"What if something happens with Chloe?" Harlen would never forgive herself if she woke up and she wasn't there.

"Where do you think we'd go? Bora Bora?"

"With you I couldn't begin to guess." She smiled. Damn, she loved this woman for always knowing when to tag her.

Dan laughed heartily. "True. I was thinking more along the lines of the Virgin Islands or Aruba."

"Still." It got harder and harder to convince herself that no matter what, she still loved Chloe and couldn't walk away.

"I'm going to give you some time to think about it. Just remember wherever we go, there are cell phones. We'd be a plane ride away."

It was even harder to convince Dan that love kept her prisoner. What kind of love was that? "I'll think about it."

"That's the spirit! Get something to eat to go with that beer. Later."

"Dan?"

"Yeah?"

"I love you."

"Yeah. I know. Eat. Sleep. I'll call you."

Harlen smiled at the image of her and Dan at some party, goofy smiles at the camera like the two geeks they were. As she thought about what edible food might be in her refrigerator, Chloe's image drifted in front of her like a ghost. For a brief moment, Harlen wondered if she'd ever be able to say good-bye.

❖

"Maisie?"

Annie dumped her bags by the door and kicked off her shoes as she watched the hallway.

"Where are you, you little shit?"

By the time the second shoe dropped, her adorable and way-too-smart Maine coon was sprinting to greet her, the long fur of her pants swaying as she ran.

"There's my girl."

People could say what they wanted about her fur baby, but Annie knew they shared their own language. Each understood the other perfectly. Maisie often chose to take the two-year-old child attitude by ignoring her. Annie knew she did it because she loved attention, at times not caring if it turned out to include a scolding.

"Meow."

"What do you want?"

Maisie flopped over, exposing her belly. She was the one exception to all the cats Annie had known or owned. Cats, as a rule, did *not* like their bellies rubbed.

"You're such a little slut." Annie smiled as she squatted and rubbed the long, soft, light-colored fur. The familiar movement and the feel of Maisie's fur beneath her fingers reminded her she was okay. "You need a combing, little girl." She was grateful Maisie liked to be combed and brushed. The only difficult part was that her feline got easily distracted, making a game out of having Annie coddle and cajole her into coming back for more. The process could take over an hour and messed with Annie's evening schedule. Therapy cat or not, sometimes Maisie pushed a few too many buttons.

As she changed from her work clothes into leggings and a bright blue T-shirt, Annie chuckled. She had unwittingly pushed a few of Harlen's buttons. She could tell by the deepened hue of her blue eyes. As a general rule, people were unaware how much their features revealed. Annie had learned over the years to school her own because there were times when she crossed the line of societal expectations by reacting in ways that others misinterpreted.

That wasn't her only superpower though. Her uncanny ability to chronologically recall times and events had never failed her, however she was struggling with today's timeline. Annie remembered the various tasks she completed, but not the order of completion. Bats began to flutter in her stomach, a key indicator she was heading toward a bout of anxiety.

"Oh, no. Not after this morning's bullshit." She turned to call out, but she didn't need to bother. Maisie sat in the doorway with her head tipped and her bright gold eyes big and full of curiosity. As if she was wondering what Annie was in a tizzy about.

"Baby girl, Mommy's spinning."

Maisie chortled a trill sound and moseyed over to rub against her. Her therapist said she was gauging her tension, and that cats were very intuitive. To Annie, Maisie was the best therapy she'd ever had. Hence the eons-old belief that cats were mysterious and to be worshipped for their mystical powers.

"Hmm." Annie stroked her soft fur, then gave her a good scratching under her chin. The rhythmic purr vibrated to Annie's soul, that deep inside place that only Maisie could reach. "We need to eat, and when I say, 'We' I mean me. You can feed yourself."

"Meow."

"Indeed, I'd love your company." Together, they strode to the kitchen. "After dinner, I need to write out today's events." Sometimes the exercise worked well, occasionally not so much. Either way, the attempt to get her thoughts organized would help center her.

While she stared into the refrigerator, Annie's thoughts moved to Harlen McGhee. Good-looking? Absolutely. Intriguing? No doubt. What she was left wondering was why she looked familiar. Where had Annie seen Harlen before today?

Chapter Four

Thank you for agreeing to meet, Ms. Forrest." Annie offered her hand in greeting.

"Please. It's Jane." Jane gestured to the two comfortable-looking chocolate leather chairs. "Forrest Enterprises is happy to support our community, Ms. Dawson."

Annie disliked informal meetings because there was less control, but she adapted over the years. "Annie," she said before taking a seat.

Jane rounded the desk and sat in the vacant one. "Tell me about your organization and the reasons we should consider becoming a sponsor."

Ah, so not so informal after all. She had to give the woman props for getting to the crux of the reason Annie was there. During the first weeks of her employment at SFN, she put together campaign materials that highlighted the types of support and services it provided for its clients. The people who leaned on their services were often times without close family ties to help them navigate in a judgmental and unkind world. Others lacked knowing where to turn when a difficult situation arose. The society had a bevy of pro bono experts at their disposal. To keep those numbers up, there had to be a draw of some type. While it was true that some of their staff volunteered for purely humanitarian reasons, there was an equal number that were there for the prestige it would bring to their résumés, promoting their respective companies as a charitable entity.

Annie handed her the folder that contained a letter from the board describing the services offered on a sliding scale. Services were provided free when a client's resources were minimal. "The neurodivergent population hasn't grown over the last few decades as much as individuals are now being identified and professionally acknowledged. The Society for Neurodiversity took on the role of overview and oversight, providing much needed services such as counseling, life-planning, coping strategies, job acquisition, and much more." She took a breath. "Monies raised are used to pay for these services for most of our clients, as well as the development of programs that are often overlooked, falling under the realm of self-care, validation, and motivation."

"Motivation. That's a term I rarely hear from an organization."

"Unfortunately, but it's true. Organizations such as ours have the best of intentions, however, they often forget that without validation of clients' emotions and difficulties, programs are a Band-Aid approach. In order to truly help, we acknowledge that people with different abilities and needs suffer as a result of those differences, and the resulting low self-esteem leads to lack of motivation."

Jane leaned forward. "How so?"

"Imagine you go through life being looked at as someone who was less-than or incapable of holding a job, not to mention an upper echelon position because of their condition. After a while, you begin to believe that you're less capable than your peers, so you stop trying to be the best you can be. Our organization is there to boost self-esteem and prove to employers that just because we process information differently doesn't make us less capable, it makes us differently able."

Jane took the information in. It was clear she was mulling over the words and that usually meant a potential donor was interested. "You said we. Is that correct?"

Annie prepared for the worst and hoped for the best. "Yes. I was diagnosed as autistic when I was a teenager."

"The society did well hiring you to spearhead their fundraising." Jane smiled, then opened the folder and glanced at the introductory letter. It didn't hurt that there were a couple of lucrative companies represented on the board. She closed the folder. "I'll need to review these documents and bring it to the board at our next meeting."

"Thank you for your consideration." Annie stood. The initial meeting was coming to an end. She didn't believe in brow-beating the person she spoke with to get them on board. She held out her hand. "If you have any additional questions, please reach out to me."

"You know your employer well, Ms. Dawson."

"I do." Annie took pride in the work she'd done to this point and she had no plans to change her work ethic or her approach. The organization needed money, and she wanted to make sure they got it.

"Excellent. You'll be hearing from me within the month."

Until then, Annie would do more research on Forrest Enterprises. It might take a bit of digging to uncover any impropriety, but if there was a red flag to be found she wouldn't hesitate to inform Allison. She strode through the floor of interior cubes and the perimeter offices that had windows. When she made eye contact with the staff, Annie made sure to smile. Whether she felt like it or not, she understood the importance of representing her employer in a favorable light. She glanced at the well-lit and surprisingly bright work environment. If Forrest cared this much about its employees by making the space warm and inviting, perhaps she had found a gem among the ethically questionable businesses she'd bypassed contacting.

She pushed the down arrow and waited, telling herself the moving box she was about to step into would not plummet the eleven floors below. Annie studied the carpet of intricate geometric symbols and began counting. The elevator doors opened. Things did not often surprise her, but she was so caught off guard, her jaw dropped.

"Annie?" Harlen asked.

"Hi," she said after regaining some of her equilibrium. She glanced around, checking the large sign on the wall. Annie was sure she'd been swept into another dimension. What were the odds of her and Harlen meeting twice in the same week?

"Are you okay?" Harlen stood a few feet away looking as confused as Annie felt. "Were you looking for me?"

"No. I'm here for work."

Harlen waved to a staff member who greeted her from across the room.

"What are you doing here?"

"I needed to stretch my legs and went for coffee." She held up the to-go cup that Annie hadn't noticed.

"This is where you work?" Annie asked. What were the odds that the person who hit her car worked at the lucrative company she was wooing for sponsorship.

Harlen's cheeks turned pink. "Forrest Enterprises is my family's business."

"Oh." Annie's mind was working double time. "So when you said the car you were driving was a company car you meant it belonged to your family?"

"Yes." Harlen glanced at the staff moving about. She gestured to the waiting area just off the lobby. "Are you okay? From the accident?" She shoved a hand in her pocket in a tell that said she was more nervous than when she'd last seen her.

"I'm fine."

"You didn't text me."

"You didn't bother to text me either."

Harlen laughed. "Will our conversations always turn into a witty banter?"

Annie studied Harlen. Aside from their recent meeting, Annie still couldn't shake the feeling she knew her from somewhere. "Are you under the impression we're going to become friends?"

"People meet in lots of ways, Annie, though ours is a bit unusual." Harlen grinned.

Annie wondered if she was making fun of the awkward situation. It was difficult to tell.

"What kind of work do you do?"

The fact that Harlen had chosen to ignore her remark about becoming friends led Annie to believe it was a stretch or the outcome she was interested in. "I'm the fundraiser for the Society for Neurodiversity."

"Ah, gathering intel." Harlen smiled. This time Annie knew Harlen was teasing and tingles coursed through her.

"Actually, I already did the research. I met with the financial officer this morning."

Harlen chuckled. "Then you met my sister, Jane."

"Is she a Forrest?" Annie calculated the various ways that Harlen and her sister were connected to the business.

"No. She's a McGhee, but she doesn't correct people if they happen to assume she's a Forrest. It gets complicated, since most of the workforce are relatives."

"Are there any more McGhees that I should look out for?" Annie's mind raced. She hadn't prepared for an office full of McGhees. How would she have known? The family resemblance was obvious in the color of their eyes and full lips. Not that she noticed before now.

"A few, though the Forrest members outnumber the McGhees."

Annie wanted to spend more time getting to know Harlen. "Thanks for the heads up." Nervousness wasn't an emotion that Annie had to deal with very often, and she didn't like it. "I'd love to chat for hours, but I'm expected back at the office."

"Of course." Harlen's gaze moved quickly to her lips and back before she held out her hand. "I'm glad you're alright."

After a brief hesitation, she took Harlen's hand. "Thank you." It had taken years to get past her aversion to touching a stranger even if it was only for a handshake. Intimacy was another story. One that she'd also overcome with the help of a kind and loving person who showed her what she was capable of.

"Maybe we'll see each other again."

"Likely not, unless you plan on driving into my car again." Annie didn't want to be with anyone who threw her off kilter.

"I meant here. Unless you're a one and done kind of woman." Harlen's face reddened.

Misinterpretation wasn't a mistake she often made. Being around Harlen made her do things she wouldn't usually do especially when she was working. "Did we meet before the accident?" She'd tried to shake the déjà vu of recognition, but she couldn't. Harlen stared at her, and Annie's lower region tightened under the scrutiny.

"I would have remembered if we did."

Annie took a quick breath. What did that mean? Why was she questioning herself when she had a handle on her actions, having thought through every possible scenario and the implications of each. "Have a good day, Harlen." She needed to escape the sparkling, ice blue eyes boring into hers.

"You as well, Annie. I hope we can help your organization." Harlen headed into the sea of cubes.

She pushed the button a second time and willed the elevator to arrive. She felt Harlen's gaze as she waited, surprised that pleasure coursed through her in equal measures of excitement and trepidation. It had been a while since anyone had looked at her with something other than confusion or disgust.

The ding brought another emotion—relief—and she stepped into the elevator. When she turned, Harlen stood in the center of the lobby, smiling at her and waving good-bye. Her cheeks heated before the door closed.

CHAPTER FIVE

"Hey, sis."

"Good morning, Harlen. To what do I owe the honor of a visit?" Jane set her glasses on the desk before she picked up her steaming mug. They were both coffee hounds.

"Can't I drop by to see my favorite sister without a reason?" Harlen dropped into a chair wishing she had another cup of coffee, too.

"You mean your only sister and, yes, you only stop when there's something you want info on." Jane smiled.

Harlen considered her sister's words. "You're right." She leaned forward. "I'll work on that."

"Uh-huh." Jane sat back, ignoring the ringing line on the phone. "Now that we've gotten that out of the way, how can I help?"

"Did you have a meeting with Annie Dawson?" She wasn't one to pry into the finances of the company, but she couldn't help that her ongoing curiosity about Annie needed to be stoked.

"I did." Jane tipped her head. "You've never asked about the support Forrest engaged in before. What gives?"

"I had a minor accident a few days ago and Ms. Dawson was the other driver."

Jane sat up. "Is she going to sue you?"

"No." Harlen hadn't thought about that possibility. "At least I don't think so. I'm curious what your impression of her is."

She chuckled. "So you're on a fact-finding mission."

"Kind of."

"Ms. Dawson is intelligent and the perfect spokesperson for her organization."

Harlen nodded. Since Annie had disappeared in the elevator a couple of hours ago, she hadn't been able to get her off her mind. If Annie believed they'd met previously, Harlen was sure she likely had, though the feeling wasn't mutual.

"What's going on with you?" Jane's concern wrinkled her forehead.

"Nothing." When Jane wasn't convinced, she tried again. "I like her, and I'd like to find out more about her without being stalkerish."

"Oh, now I get it." Jane chuckled. "You've always had an attraction for women who didn't fit the mold."

It was true. Chloe had an unconventional style and a bohemian way of dressing. Harlen's heart was heavy. When they first met, she had no doubt they would be together for a long time, but the hand of fate was dealt without her permission. Chloe hadn't been happy, and no matter how much Harlen believed in happily ever after, perhaps there was no such thing.

"I guess so, but hooking up with Annie Dawson isn't going to happen." Whatever motivation was at play Harlen was certain of one thing. She wasn't ready to get involved. Whether Chloe remained in a coma for another month or another year, she would continue to fight for her right to die with dignity. Until then neither she nor Chloe would find peace.

"Har, I can't imagine what being in limbo feels like, but I do know that clinging to the hope that Chloe wakes up isn't good for you." Jane was a kind person, but she was also pragmatic.

She waved her hand. "I gave up on Chloe waking up a long time ago. That doesn't mean I can walk away. She told me she didn't want to be forced to keep existing, Jane." Harlen didn't want to have this conversation. Not again. She took a deep breath and ignored the sympathetic look from across the desk. "What company does Annie work for?"

"The Society for Neurodiversity." Jill handed her the folder about the organization. "It's a nonprofit with a wide array of sponsorship."

Harlen read a few paragraphs to get a sense of what type of support services the organization offered. "Not that it matters, but do you know how long Annie's worked there?"

Jane shook her head. "We kept our conversation on sponsorship and services." Jane quietly studied her in the way that only a sibling could, and Harlen fought the urge to squirm. "I'm assuming you're asking because you want to pursue her for personal reasons."

It was Harlen's turn to smile. "I know it's not an ideal way to meet someone. It's been a while since I've had an urge to even consider dating." What would it be like to be in another relationship? Did she want to find out what Annie was like when she wasn't in an awkward situation? "So, does she have our support?"

Jane held her mug and stared into the rising mist. "I'll have to take it to the board for approval after I check where our donation level is for this quarter. I like Ms. Dawson and the organization looks to provide much needed services."

Though she itched to ask more regarding her sister's impression of Annie, doing so would further Jane's curiosity. Harlen thought it best to let it go. She stood, handing the folder back as she did.

"I'm sure they'll agree to whatever you recommend." Harlen's mother, Lenore, tried to get her to take the family representative seat on the board last year, but she had no interest in arguing moot points with people who would never understand seeing things from her perspective. The company's board was only interested in the bottom line and remaining in the black.

"You've always believed I could sway the board."

"Because you can." Harlen had no doubt they would listen. Jane was responsible for restructuring the company, based on financial projections. Her recommendations saved the business from financial ruin when the economy tanked and property prices plummeted. "I'll see you later, sis."

"Hey." Jane came around the desk and put a hand on her shoulder. "I'm not sure what's going on with you." She searched Harlen's eyes. "Whatever it is, promise me you'll make yourself a priority for a change."

Doing what Jane asked would be a tall order. "I'll try."

"Liar." She laughed, then Jane pecked her cheek. "Get out of here. I've got work to do."

As she headed to her cubicle, Harlen replayed the conversation. All the while, she hoped she'd be able to do as her sister asked. At the same time, the vision of Annie took center stage, and Harlen pushed it away. She had no room in her life for another complication.

Annie drummed her fingers on the pad of paper in front of her. She was supposed to be mapping out the formal proposal of sponsorship for Forrest Enterprises. Instead, her mind conjured the vision of a naked Harlen McGhee. She didn't often entertain sexual fantasies while at work, however, she hadn't been able to shake Harlen from her thoughts.

When she first pulled up her list of potential sponsors and had been drawn to the Forrest name, she had no idea how much of a presence it would have in her personal life. Well, not the company as much as one staff member in particular. She knew better than to let her professional life seep into her personal one, a rule all of the counselors she'd seen over the years had hammered home, and a decree she'd agreed to follow years ago. But she couldn't deny it was more the other way around. And if she wasn't mistaken, Harlen had intentionally delayed Annie's departure from Forrest Enterprises. At the accident, Harlen appeared in no hurry to leave and get on with her day. Was Harlen's behavior simply a reflection of Annie's imagination, conjured up from her desire to socialize with a woman other than Char, or something more?

The unfinished thought resonated through her. She hadn't been this caught up in an attraction in a while. She had to get a handle on her wandering mind before stress forced her to return to old habits she used before she understood her autism. At the moment, her neurons were firing in ways that made thinking jumbled and the discord made it impossible for Annie to concentrate.

"Maybe a cup of tea," she mumbled.

Annie walked to the breakroom with purpose in her step. As much as she liked her coworkers, she was happy to have the space to herself. She followed the routine for making tea she always used, finding comfort in being able to stay on task.

The first tentative sip was accompanied by a loud moan of pleasure. Maybe now she'd be able to get on with the sponsor letter. A voice startled her from overthinking.

"Hi, Annie." Michael strode toward her like he walked without touching the floor. The smooth cadence of his steps was a characteristic that Annie admired without envy. Everyone had their own way of moving through the world.

"Good afternoon, Michael."

"I didn't have a chance to ask you how your meeting went with Forrest." Michael had access to her calendar so she wasn't surprised at the inquiry, although his timing was a bit of a nuisance.

"I'm confident they'll be on board." A beat passed between them. Michael waited for more information. "The only question is how much." She took another sip of the aromatic organic tea. "I'm headed to my desk to draft a letter."

"Cool." Michael smiled and disappeared into the breakroom.

She was relieved at not having to answer any more questions, though being annoyed with work wasn't a feeling she was accustomed to. Her critical thinking was out of whack, and she needed some time alone to meditate. As she closed her office door, gratitude flowed through her. She would not have been able to take this job if she was part of a cube farm. Distractions were not kind to her thought processes, which was another reason she had to get her preoccupation regarding Harlen under control.

While the tea cooled, Annie sat with her feet flat on the floor, hands resting palm-up on her thighs and closed her eyes, focusing her attention inward. She used a vision of herself as a focal point. "One." Annie breathed in as deeply as she could and held the oxygen-rich air to the count of six before slowly releasing for six beats. "Two." This was the pattern that she found worked for her in most instances. On the fourth count, Harlen's bright blue eyes drifted into her consciousness, and she neither clung to the vision nor acknowledged it. Instead, she let the vision fade as she exhaled. When she reached ten, Annie turned her palms down and over her thighs before slowly opening her eyes to orient to where she was.

The overall feeling of well-being was a welcome one. After a few sips of her perfectly drinkable tea she pulled up the form letter she'd created to use as a basis for all potential corporate sponsors. Annie would reiterate what services the funds would be used for, outline how many people could benefit from them, and what the bottom line would be. The initial asking amount was based on a particular company's donation track record and tailored to an amount the organization was likely to accept. For a midsized, local company such as Forrest Enterprises, she would ask for an annual amount of five thousand for five consecutive years, or an alternative amount of ten thousand for a one-time donation. Of course, if the sponsor chose the one-time donation, she would contact them again in two years, especially if their bottom-line profit increased by at least ten percent.

She was good at number games. A lot of people with autism had unique abilities when it came to math, she was able to do calculations in her head. Annie was one of the lucky ones and did not suffer from dyscalculia like many of her acquaintances.

With the research folder open and the public access information in front of her, Annie took into account the Forrest profit margin and the housing market as it stood today. Using a few resources to predict future sales, she believed Forrest could match her suggested amount without SFN appearing to ask for more than was reasonable.

The letter was solid, though only a first draft. She would read it again and tweak the fine points until she was satisfied, then she would pass it on to Michael. He had a knack for finding small, obscure errors in punctuation or syntax, and Annie appreciated his sharp eye. By tomorrow, the letter would be ready to send. She clicked her tongue on the roof of her mouth, a childhood tic that occasionally carried over in adulthood. Her next decision was purely self-satisfying, though she didn't feel one iota of guilt for indulging in it. She sent the file off to Michael and headed for his desk.

Michael glanced up, his typical smile in place. "I got your funding letter. I'll send it back after I give it the once-over."

Annie well knew that the once-over was more like ten-over. Michael was meticulous about communications. "I'll want it printed out on letterhead. I'm going to hand-deliver it."

"That's unusual."

"It's a family-run business and I believe a personal touch would go a long way." If she happened to coincidentally run into Harlen, she wouldn't complain.

Michael studied her with the scrutiny of a scientist peering through a microscope before responding. "That makes sense." He smiled. "I'll have it back to you by tomorrow, if that's okay."

The break between visits would help her avoid appearing too pushy. Along with the letter, Annie would provide a copy of SFN's annual report. It listed both individual and corporate donors. The information could help Jane convince the higher-ups that a lot of good could be done by agreeing to join the list of supporters.

"Sounds good." She tapped the counter in front of Michael and nodded. Either way, she hoped that Forrest would be on board for this year at least.

With nothing else to do regarding Forrest Enterprises, Annie returned to her office and pulled the next file on a potential supporter. She never ran out of things to keep her busy and her mind occupied. She also wanted to pitch to the organization's president, Allison Goldberg, the idea of having a fundraiser gala. People liked to mingle with members of the business world and the affluent connections that could be made by SFN and its supporters. It made perfect sense to propose what might turn into an annual event. Now, if she could only keep her mind on the tasks at hand instead of the blue-eyed hottie she couldn't stop fixating on. Yes, if only…

Chapter Six

"I'd say let's hit the dance floor, but I doubt anyone would want to cut in." Dan drank half the cocktail in front of her, then slapped the counter. "Woo, that's got a bite."

Since they arrived, Dan had been trying to lift her spirits, but nothing seemed to help these days. The only time she remembered smiling was when she'd run into Annie at the office. The unexpected surprise had stirred her into a moment of reminiscence of the feeling she'd experienced when she first met Chloe. While it was true that Chloe and Annie were vastly different in both looks and demeanor, both had sent shock waves of instant attraction through her.

"Gee, you're so much fun tonight." Dan elbowed her enough to get her attention. "What's up with you?"

"Sorry. I'm a little distracted." Harlen drank some of the warming beer she had ordered when they arrived.

"I can see that." Dan moved closer, ducking into her field of sight. "It's me. You can tell me anything and I won't judge."

Dan's words were true. She'd been the one friend who had never made her feel foolish regarding her emotions and her commitment to Chloe.

"I know." Harlen let out a long, deep breath. She really needed to share. "I've met someone."

Shock registered on Dan's face. "Like an attraction kind of meeting?"

"Yes. No." She shook her head and took a sip, then pushed away the unappealing drink. "Fuck. I don't know." Harlen cleared her throat. "It's nothing really. Just a passing fancy."

Dan grabbed her shoulder and the stool she sat on turned. "Stop kidding yourself. If you mentioned it to me, it's more than a passing fancy, so give."

With a sigh and a motion to the bartender for another round, Harlen gave in. "Okay, but don't go all bat-shit crazy with enthusiasm. Promise?"

"Yeah, yeah." Dan waved her hand. "Promise."

"Remember the fender bender?" Dan nodded and she continued. "The other driver, Annie? She came to the office the other day."

"Holy shit. Did she track you down to sue you?"

Harlen punched her arm. "You can be such a jerk."

Dan grinned. "Which is why you love me. But I digress. Go on."

She took a swig of her fresh drink. "She works for an organization. I think it's called the Society for Neurodiversity, and she met with Jane to discuss Forrest becoming a sponsor or donor, or whatever."

Dan was silent for a few minutes, giving her a chance to think about how to explain the feelings she was experiencing. Maybe she just needed to have sex and Annie was a convenient choice.

"Okay. Just so I have the facts. Car accident with Annie. Then you run into her at the office."

Harlen nodded knowing full well that Dan was far from done.

"And?"

"Nothing. That's where the story ends." Or did it? They had each other's phone number and knew where each other worked.

"You're pathetic, my friend. If you're attracted to her, let her know."

Harlen rubbed the back of her neck. "It's not that easy." She swallowed around the lump that began to form. "There's still Chloe."

"Har, Chloe's gone. We both know that." Dan rubbed her hand over her shoulders in an attempt to comfort, but all it did was remind her how long she'd gone without a woman's touch. Her eyes blurred as she fought back the tears.

"I promised her."

"Dude. Chloe was leaving the relationship before the accident. You said the two of you discussed this kind of scenario, but she never filed a directive. You've done all you can."

As much as Dan's reasoning was valid, so had been her hope that the situation with Chloe would change for the better. She replayed the conversation they'd had months before the accident.

"Did you hear about Zack?" Chloe stirred the concoction in a sauté pan that she threw together with leftover items from the fridge. Whatever it was, Harlen knew it would be good.

"All I've heard is that he was in an accident a few weeks ago."

"Greg told me it was a rollover. Zack's in a coma." Chloe shook her head. "Greg said Zack never made out a legal healthcare proxy directive and the hospital is legally bound to keep him alive."

Harlen couldn't imagine what Greg was going through. "That's rough. Zack's been estranged from his parents since coming out to them. Is Greg going to petition for rights?" Greg and Zack had been together since high school.

"Unfortunately, he can't."

"Why not?" Harlen made a mental note to reach out to Greg. The four of them would occasionally go out together for social events or to see a play. Harlen poured wine into their glasses and brought them to the table along with the bowl of salad that sat on the counter.

Chloe brought a steaming platter of pasta and joined her. "The lawyer said because they weren't legally married."

"That sucks," Harlen said as she scooped servings out.

"I know. What complicates the matter is that Zack never filled out a health care proxy document with his primary. There's nothing that Greg can do."

Harlen considered the laws in their state. “And domestic partnership doesn’t carry over into the health care realm.” She shook her head.

Chloe was quiet for a time. “I wouldn’t want that for either of us. Coma, brain dead, whatever. I don’t want to have some machine breathing for me if the best outcome is a vegetative state, or worse.”

“I couldn’t agree more. We need to at least do the proxy thing.” Harlen made a note to herself to do it soon.

Now, here she was trying her best not to let the depression that threatened to take hold settle even deeper. Greg had finally moved away, leaving Zack behind in a sterile hospital room, alone and comatose. He said he had to remember that Zack had died more than five years ago. Harlen couldn’t fathom enduring the soul-wrenching torture that three more years would bring. She’d consulted her mother, who practiced family law, after the doctors made it clear that Chloe’s prognosis was likely not going to improve. Her mother reiterated what she already knew.

“I cherish your friendship, but you don’t know what it feels like to abandon someone you love.” Harlen thought about the weeks prior to the accident when Chloe had begun to pack. No one would blame her for walking away from the dire situation. As much as she wanted to move forward, leaving Chloe in the hospital felt like a betrayal of the love she still clung to.

Dan studied her. “You’re right, I don’t.” She sipped her drink. “However, I do know that you have been devoted to Chloe’s well-being for far too long. Don’t punish yourself for wanting a life without Chloe.” Dan stood and tossed some bills on the bar. “Let’s plan dinner together. I’ll pick up Chinese and we can binge on a show.”

Harlen almost turned the offer down. “I’d like that.” She could use a night of not being alone with her inner turmoil. Maybe she’d talk about her attraction to Annie, though she doubted it. For reasons she cited on a regular basis, her heart wasn't ready to love another.

❖

The bed beneath her was soft and comforting, but it did little to block out the obsessive ruminations in Harlen's brain. Since coming home to a quiet house and not wanting to face another night of staring at the TV only to have no clue what she'd watched, Harlen had opted for a hot shower and bed. She managed a few pages of the book on her nightstand before it registered she'd read the same paragraph over and over, her mind constantly returning to flashes of Annie's bright smile, followed by Chloe lying in the hospital bed covered by the sheet tucked under her arms.

Chloe had already decided there was no reason to stay together. She was unhappy and wanted them both to move on with their lives. Harlen wasn't ready to give up. The last time they spoke before the accident, she asked Chloe to consider couples' therapy. Okay, so it was more like she begged, but Harlen would do everything she could to keep the relationship intact. That's how much she loved Chloe.

"Why can't you let go?"

Her words echoed in the quiet of the night, and she wasn't sure if she was directing the question to herself or to Chloe. An affirmation from either would result in release from the commitment she was determined to hang on to. For what end, she didn't know. How many times would she attempt to walk away, telling herself this was the day she stopped obsessing over things she couldn't change? What she could change was hanging on to the idea that Chloe would wake up, her former decree that it was over between them just a forgotten memory.

The sigh that she released should have been cathartic, but once again, the peace she sought eluded her. She flipped onto her side and fussed with the pillows in search of a position that would lead to sleep. Harlen focused on her breathing by taking in a slow, deep breath and holding it for a count of five before letting it out. After a few minutes, she felt herself drifting toward the place of nothingness that was sleep. The last thing she remembered was watching Annie walk into the elevator and wondering if she would see her again.

❖

"Mommy's home!"

Annie's announcement was part of her daily routine. She liked the consistency almost as much as she liked watching Maisie trot toward her.

"What have you been up to all day?"

Maisie trilled as she flopped over, exposing her white belly. Annie stroked her long, soft fur and Maisie purred loudly.

"It's been quite the day, my girl. How about I change and we have some love time?" The chortle she got in return made her chuckle. Maine coons were known for their expressive communication and intelligence. Sometimes Maisie was too smart, but she also had a wonderful personality that suited Annie's emotional support needs well.

Changed into her favorite after work loungewear, Annie began to relax, comforted by the soft cotton against her skin. Maisie sat on the edge of the bed watching every move she made. Rubbing the cat's neck and chin, Annie acknowledged, not for the first time, how much she adored her fur baby's companionship. It wasn't the same as the cravings she had for human company, but the quiet presence and steadfast adoration of her beloved Maisie helped fill the gaps when there was no romantic person in Annie's life.

Which was another thing that both fascinated and annoyed her about her recent fixation on Harlen. While it was true that Harlen had been open and friendly during their last encounter, Annie wasn't sure there was anything more to consider other than her actively engaged libido. Maybe she should talk with Charlie and share her preoccupation about Harlen. It's not that she didn't think Maisie could understand her ramblings, but without dialogue, sharing her feelings with a nonverbal entity wouldn't help her suss out what was going on in her head.

She filled the dishes her pet led her to and decided a glass of wine was in order. Charlie would be full of questions and she wouldn't be deterred from getting answers. Settled into her favorite chair, Annie put Maisie's blanket on her lap, knowing she'd settle there once she had her dinner.

"Hey, Annie. How are you?" Charlie asked.

"Mentally exhausted and physically fit." She chuckled.

A grunt from the other end of the phone meant Char had dropped onto her couch. They'd started these sessions years ago and had continued them until this day whenever the need arose. For her particular manifestation of autism, Annie needed the understanding that another person who could relate to provide a sounding board from time to time. They were there for each other when an in-depth discussion was necessary.

"Okay. I'm ready. Lay it on me."

"Last week, I was involved in an accident."

"Oh, no. Were you hurt?"

"Like I said, physically I'm fine."

It had been about two years since she'd lost control on a patch of ice and headed for a car traveling in the opposite direction. The car was going way too fast for the conditions, and when the driver reacted, their car flipped several times before coming to a stop at the edge of the tree line. Annie had called for help after regaining control and pulling to the side of the road. Her calm demeanor had masked how much the accident scene overwhelmed her ability to engage. She hadn't been able to move from her car to help the driver. She later found out on the local news channel that the driver hadn't been wearing a seat belt and was seriously injured, resulting in major head trauma and ending up in a coma. There was likely nothing she could have done.

"I'm not alright, Char." Annie patted her lap when Maisie sauntered in and began to stroke her luxurious fur once she curled into a ball.

"Right. So, tell me everything."

Annie hesitated. Not because she didn't want to talk about what was going on with her. The real problem was she had a hard time identifying exactly what the issue was. "It's internal."

"Uh-oh. You have the hots for someone," Charlie said, matter-of-factly.

"I do, but that's not the whole reason I'm distracted." She counted to ten as she continued to stroke Maisie.

"A compound conundrum. Tell me more."

She could practically see Charlie clapping in anticipation. "I've met her before somewhere."

"Who is *her*?"

"Harlen McGhee." Even saying the name out loud sent vibrations through her. "The woman whose car hit mine."

"The plot thickens." Charlie chuckled.

"You know I called you for help, right?" Annie smiled.

"Oops. Sorry." Charlie slurped. "What part are you looking for help on?"

Annie sighed. Trying to put her finger on the pulse of her anxiety was never easy and even more so when her body's untimely reactions came into play. "Harlen's actions lead me to believe she was flirting. It might be wishful thinking on my part."

"Is she the type of handsome you're drawn to?" Charlie had witnessed her sexual attraction and sometimes voracious appetite for physical pleasure. She wasn't surprised Charlie went there.

"Yes. Big blue eyes and masculine mannerisms." Not to mention a body to match, from what she could tell without seeing her naked. Annie's clit jumped.

"Well, it's not surprising that you're interested. What makes you think it might be mutual?"

This was why Annie called her bestie. She helped her eke out the whys of situations because of her non-involvement. "She gave me her phone number after the accident even though I was obviously fine." She pinched the fleshy part of her hand between the thumb and forefinger to keep from getting worked up while talking about Harlen.

"She could have just been concerned."

"Don't burst my bubble." The rebuke included a smile. "I'd like to think my charming ways caught her attention."

"Shit. Did you drop the autism bomb on her?" Charlie had warned her shortly after they met that the general population of neurotypical people didn't understand the characteristics of someone with autism. Their brains processed information differently, and they sometimes said out loud what was on their minds without the social construct that others followed.

"Of course not. Why would I?" While Annie believed the best way to educate others was to be upfront about her diagnosis because, in truth, she knew there were a lot more neurodivergent people in the world than naysayers would have others believe. But what defined normal was societal expectations, which she learned over time if she wanted to function in the world, she had to learn what was considered acceptable behavior. "Besides, when I saw her again…"

"You saw her again? When? Where?"

"Char, take a breath." Annie shook her head. Sometimes Charlie's brain was like a runaway freight train. "I saw Harlen coincidentally. One of my potential sponsors is her family's business and when I went to meet with the financial officer I ran into her."

"Funny that first she ran into you, then you ran into her." Charlie laughed heartily.

"Not funny, but interesting."

"You're such a buzzkill sometimes."

"It's one of the many things you love about me. Can we get back to why I called? Please?"

"Fine." That one word meant Char was refocused, which she really needed her to be. "What happened next?"

Annie could still feel Harlen's hand holding hers. "She asked why I didn't call to let her know I was okay." Hope that there was a spark between them lingered.

"I guess it's a good sign that Harlen is interested."

"Which is the reason I called. It felt like she wanted to ask me something more than common courtesy would warrant."

"What do you mean?" Charlie crunched on something, likely chips, and Annie rolled her eyes. Whenever they had an intense conversation, Charlie ate.

"Like she wanted to ask something but changed her mind."

"Was your observation a hope or reality?" Charlie asked.

Much like herself, Charlie rarely sugarcoated the point she was trying to make. "Both," Annie said.

Chapter Seven

"I'm not sure if you ever had Chloe's best interests at heart." The words Margaret Williams, Chloe's mother, spoke cut through Harlen like a saber.

"I loved your daughter enough to try to honor her wishes, and nothing can change that." She fought to keep the tears caused by the pain and the depth of her devotion from failing. The Williamses were being ruthless and refused to listen to anything she had to say.

"Ah. There it is." The smirk on Margaret's face turned her heartache to fury.

"What are you talking about?"

"You said 'loved,' meaning you don't love her now." She patted her lifeless daughter's hand. "I don't believe you ever had the conversation you claim where Chloe said she didn't want to be kept alive by any means necessary."

For the entire time Harlen had been coming to the hospital, she had bitten her tongue in an attempt to win Chloe's parents over so they would accept what she said as the truth. "I used the past tense because your daughter is medically dead. Why you insist on keeping her a prisoner in an empty shell is heartless and selfish on your part."

"I think it's time for you to go, Harlen." Jason, Chloe's father, was a reasonable man. However, when it came to dealing with his wife he bowed to her fervor. Harlen couldn't blame him, except this time.

Harlen wanted to rage at them both. She wanted to tell them they were torturing Chloe for no reason other than to prove that in their eyes, Harlen had no recourse, and any and all decisions about their daughter's care was up to them.

"Get out." Margaret moved closer, invading her personal space. Jason stepped in between them.

"Please, Harlen. It's for the best." Jason's hand on her shoulder let her know he sympathized with her plight. She turned to leave knowing more arguing was useless.

"Don't come back!" Margaret yelled vehemently. Jason held his wife back from following her. "Chloe doesn't want you here and neither do I!"

Jason's sympathetic look did nothing to tamp the anguish rising inside her. Even as the door shut behind her, Harlen heard Margaret's raised voice. Her vision grew blurry as she fought to keep her composure. Staff who knew her stared at Chloe's room and shook their heads. Harlen believed they'd dealt with Margaret enough to have witnessed her outbursts, some of which had probably been directed at them.

Harlen took to the stairs. She couldn't share space with anyone when she was barely hanging on. Once she was out in the cloud-shrouded evening, Harlen leaned against the building, and took in one deep breath after another. Visions of the hospital scene after the accident played on the inside of her lids like a slide show.

The phone call that brought her to the emergency room was accompanied by panic. She had to have Jane drive her. She was in no shape to get behind the wheel. Racing through the doors, Harlen had practically shouted at the ER nurse behind the glass. She couldn't see Chloe. Harlen was told a message was left for her parents to call the hospital. All Harlen knew was they were in Africa on a safari. The wait had been excruciating. Jane had insisted on staying, but Harlen didn't want anyone to see her break down. In her heart, where Chloe resided, she knew the situation was dire. Four hours later, the doctor finally came out.

"Is anyone here for Chloe Williams?" His serious expression spoke volumes.

Harlen met him on rubbery legs. "I'm Chloe's partner, Harlen McGhee."

The doctor's features softened. "I'm very sorry. We've done everything we could." He placed a hand on her shoulder.

Tears formed and her throat tightened. "She died?"

"No. She sustained traumatic brain injury due to not wearing a seat belt. She's in a coma and on life support."

Harlen nearly crumbled and the doctor helped her to a seat. She wasn't surprised by Chloe having not worn the mandated seat belt. Harlen had to remind her every time they rode together.

"I'm sorry to have to ask this. Do you know if she has a healthcare directive?"

She shook her head. Even after the conversation they had, Chloe never got around to filling out the paperwork to give to her primary physician. It was on the long list of things Chloe meant to do but never got around to. "She talked about it, but no."

"Are you married?"

At one time, Harlen had bought a ring and began to plan her proposal. That was shortly before Chloe told her she wasn't happy with her life and they needed to end the relationship. She hadn't returned the ring in the hope Chloe would see they could fix whatever was wrong.

"No."

"Then we'll need to wait for her parents before we take any further action."

"It could be a few days. They're abroad. I don't even know if they've gotten the message yet."

"There's no rush. Chloe's condition isn't likely to change." He reached into his pocket and pulled out a bent business card. "I'm the neurosurgeon on Chloe's case. If you have any questions, call that number." He pointed to the handwritten digits.

"Thank you." Harlen stared at the print. Douglas Pritchard, MD. "Can I see her?"

Dr. Pritchard rubbed his scrub cap. "Give us some time to get her settled in a room."

Harlen nodded and dropped into the chair. She should make some calls. Tell Jane and Dan the grim news, but she didn't want to talk to anyone. While she waited, Harlen replayed past memories of her and Chloe. The last one that stuck was her promise to not let her vegetate in a sterile hospital.

Tonight, when she walked through the hospital room door, Harlen had no idea it might be the last time she ever saw Chloe. As she walked to her car her tears fell. She thought she had prepared herself to someday say good-bye. Now that the decision was out of her hands and the day had arrived, she realized she wasn't prepared at all.

"Good morning, Allison." Annie greeted the organizational president for their biweekly meeting.

"Good morning. First, let me say how pleased the board is with having you on our staff. Since you took on the role, we've seen an uptick not only in online hits, but also emails asking about services and funding. Bravo."

Inside, Annie beamed. "Thank you. It's a worthy organization and I'm looking forward to having additional opportunities to bring about public awareness." This was the perfect time to pitch her idea of a fundraising gala.

"We are delighted by your enthusiasm." Allison pulled her file closer and dated the lined page. "Do you have any concerns with your coworkers, management, or board members?"

She thought about her friendship with Michael and smiled. "Everyone is courteous and helpful. Michael is the best assistant I've ever worked with."

Allison sat back and returned the smile. "I couldn't agree more. He has a flair for knowing what is needed without having to ask." She jotted a quick line on the paper. "How has the response been for corporate support?"

How this group had stayed in business with a small state grant and the few donors they had when she arrived was nothing short of a miracle. "I'm happy to report that Forrest Enterprises has agreed to a multiyear donation above my asking amount." She pulled the binding agreement from one of the manilla folders from the stack on her lap. The tab displayed the company name, a blue dot that had designated it as a potential donor, followed by a green dot, signifying the donor had agreed to support the organization. "Forrest will donate ten thousand dollars for the next three years. They requested a yearly report and scheduled a review at the end of the term."

"Excellent. Well done, Annie." Allison jotted a few lines and looked up expectantly. "Any other potentials in the works?"

Annie relayed the three upcoming meetings she had over the next month with corporations who might potentially give a substantial one-time donation. Large corporations were bound by stockholders and thus, making promises they might not be able to keep made holders nervous. By the end of the meeting, Annie felt endorphins flooding her senses. She liked Allison as a person. She liked her even more because she was good at making sure employees who were an asset to the organization were rewarded in some way. While for various reasons that did not always mean a bump in pay, there were other perks to be had. She held two tickets to a concert for a regionally acclaimed musical group. A number of businesses donated tickets or items of value, and since the upper echelon saw it as a conflict of interest, the donors were delighted that the staff would see the benefits of their generosity from time to time.

"How did it go?" Michael stood as she walked toward her office.

"Great." She didn't brag about the perk she received. It was unseemly to rub the tickets in another employee's face, but if Char couldn't go she would ask Michael. "Any messages?"

"No," Michael said without needing to look. He remembered everything that passed his desk without having to make a list or set reminders. She envied his quick mind but liked him all the more for his organizational skills. "But this came for you via currier." Michael gave her an envelope with her name on it in bold lettering.

Annie looked up. "Who's it from?"

"I have no idea, but it goes with what's in your office."

She glanced between the envelope and Michael several times.

"Go see what it is. We'll talk later."

"Okay." Annie didn't remember the short trip to her office as she jotted on the large sticky affixed to the file stack she carried. There was no missing the large, colorful bouquet of the most beautiful flowers she'd ever seen, the most striking of which were the two birds-of-paradise. Stunned, she looked for a card but didn't see one.

It wasn't her birthday. Annie checked her electronic date book. Nothing significant there. She tapped the stack of files. The envelope with the striking penmanship glared at her like a neon sign. Her hands shook as she opened it.

Dear Ms. Dawson,

I hope this finds you well. Even though you have assured me you haven't suffered any lasting effects from the accident, please accept the flowers in appreciation of your not making the collision to be more serious than it was.

It would also be an honor if you would allow me to take you to dinner. If you agree, please text me your acceptance and we will find a time in the near future that is suitable for us both.

With sincere gratitude,

Harlen

Annie didn't realize her hand was on her chest or her heavy breathing until she looked up. Harlen sent the flowers. She looked at the bouquet again, inhaling deeply of their intoxicating scent. After reading the note again, she dropped into her chair and glanced around her well-appointed office. While it was nicely decorated, the flowers added a personal touch she hadn't noticed was missing.

She appreciated that Harlen's gesture, and the ensuing invitation, left the decision to enjoy one or both up to Annie. In general, people assumed a lot about others and how they would respond to attention. Clearly, Harlen was not in that group. Annie remembered the day at Forrest. Harlen had acted as though there was more on her mind than wondering if she was okay. Had she considered asking Annie then but had refrained? That seemed a plausible explanation for the hesitation in letting go of Annie's hand. Maybe Harlen had thought it too forward to ask her on a date when she was there conducting business.

"Oh, God."

Annie jumped up, whacking her knee on her desk and ignoring what would be a bruise by morning.

"What do I do?"

Talking out loud was another coping mechanism when she had to weigh difficult options. Granted, she was attracted to Harlen. She'd have to be blind not to be enamored by her good looks, and her pleasant, attentive manner. Conversely, there was the matter of whether or not Annie could contain her traitorous body into behaving. She knew herself well. After an interesting conversation and dinner, there would be the notion that they would have sex. Amazing sex, if her recent fantasy was an indication of the reality to follow. She couldn't do that. Could she? Wouldn't it be unethical to go out with an employee of a sponsor? She didn't remember reading anything in the policies about prohibited behaviors with a sponsor, only with coworkers.

She glanced at her desk phone. If there was anyone who would know, it would be Michael. Dare she involve him in this?

"It's not like he doesn't know that something's up." Annie reasoned in the empty space.

When she got the job at SFN, she'd been given an employee handbook and she'd dutifully read it, but that was a while ago and she couldn't be certain she had total recall on the corporate sponsor item. Her copy of the manual was at home. It made perfect sense for her to ask someone. What difference did it make if she asked Michael rather than the HR person?

"Hi, Michael. Would you stop by my office when you get a chance?"

"Sure thing, Annie."

She paced the inner sanctum, happy that she rarely had visitors, including other staff. Annie took her notebook to the small round conference table. The center held the plant she'd bought herself as a kudo for landing her dream job. It thrived in the fluorescent lights, and the sun reached it during the winter months. A rap on the door drew her attention away and she waved Michael in.

"Hi," Michael said. The faint forehead crease told her he was concerned.

"Please." Annie waved to the chair facing her. "I need some information and since you're my go-to person, I thought it best to ask you." She smiled, hoping to dispel his obvious discomfort.

"Oh." Michael's shoulders lowered. "What do you want to know?" His pen was poised over his legal pad.

"You won't be needing notes."

Michael glanced at her book before setting his pen down.

There was no sense delaying. Stalling would only serve to make them both anxious. "Is there a policy against staff seeing a donor employee?"

"I'm not sure what you're asking?" Michael sat back and studied her.

Annie fought the urge to tap. She sighed, put off by not only her hesitancy, but by circumventing the real issue. "I meant to say, would it be against organizational policy if I saw a donor's employee outside of a business framework."

Michael tipped his head. "You want to date an employee of one of our donors?"

"No." Annie remembered to breathe. "Yes." She shook her head. "It's complicated."

Michael smiled. "Annie, I think it's fine if you want to see an employee of a donor socially."

Still, she wondered if that would hold true if it went further than socially. "It likely won't be a date."

"Then why are you asking?"

In the time she'd known Michael, his ability to read any situation still amazed her. "Wishful thinking." The smile she was compelled to share did nothing to quell the butterflies that fluttered inside.

"It's up to you to turn it into a dream come true." Michael rose, then quietly shut the door behind him, taking with him any argument against accepting Harlen's invitation. She scrolled through her contacts until she stared at Harlen's name. This was a bad idea. A very bad idea. She pressed the call icon and hoped she was wrong.

Chapter Eight

Harlen wiped a light layer of sweat from her upper lip. She wasn't nervous as much as she was anticipating seeing Annie again. When she saw Annie's name flash on her screen, she prepared for a thank you for the flowers, but rejection for her invitation to dinner. Annie went directly to the dinner invitation with a simple yes. It had taken Harlen a long beat to respond, and she replayed the moment.

"I'm glad you're up for dinner, Annie." Harlen cringed.

"Yes, well…I need to know what it means," Annie said.

"Uh…I'm not sure what you're looking for?"

Annie made a noise she couldn't decipher. "Is this a simple dinner meeting or a date?"

Oh. "The invitation wasn't work related, so it's safe to label it a date, if that's what you're looking for." She held her breath, hoping that clarifying the event wouldn't change Annie's mind.

"Okay."

She cleared her throat. Now she was confused. "It's okay that it's a date?"

"I'm glad it's a date."

Harlen blew out her breath. Her vision tilted and she gripped the edge of her desk. "Good. That's good." Jesus. She was so out of touch with how a simple conversation with a woman should go. "Is there an evening this week you're available?"

"Thursday at seven." Annie never hedged and it was a characteristic she admired. With only three days to prepare, Harlen had to decide where to make reservations.

"Is there a cuisine you don't like or are allergic to?"

"No allergies that I'm aware of." Annie paused again. "I wouldn't eat much if we went for sushi or anything raw."

Harlen chuckled. "That's not high on my list either."

"Okay. I'll see you Thursday."

"Annie?"

"Yes?"

"Could you please give me your address? I'd like to pick you up."

"I'll text it to you. Bye."

The line went silent and Harlen stared at the wallpaper of a night sky dappled with stars. She broke out in a full belly laugh. Annie never failed to surprise her in the no-nonsense way she had since the first day they met.

"Well, that's that then."

Harlen thought about the wide variety of local cuisine. She was fond of seafood, but that might be too close to sushi for Annie's taste. She needed a safe choice, and pressed a name in her favorites.

"Hi, Har. What's up?" Jane had her on speaker as she rustled papers, then tapped on her keyboard.

"I need a recommendation for either a French or Italian restaurant. Somewhere local."

"Wait. Does that mean you're meeting someone for dinner?"

She would have deflected the question, but her sister wouldn't be easy to divert from answering. "It's not a big deal, so don't make it one. Okay?"

Jane harrumphed. "Fine. Don't expect me to let you slide after the non-date, date." She made several suggestions, all within twenty minutes of downtown.

"Thanks."

"Harlen?"

She silently sighed. "Yeah?"

"Remember to have fun."

She eased her shoulders down. "Okay."

"Love you."

Her heart swelled. Family had always been an important part of her life. There wasn't one time she could remember not having their support and encouragement. "Love you, too."

She wrote the two words that stuck out in large, perfect print. *Have Fun!!* All she had to do was remember those words on Thursday.

❖

Thursday arrived a little too fast for Annie's liking. She had picked today because she bused on Tuesdays and Thursdays to do her part in reducing her carbon footprint. That wasn't the whole reason though. Working the next day would help keep her from fixating on what did or didn't happen on her date with Harlen over an entire weekend.

The reflection in the mirror didn't appear to be that of a woman looking forward to a much-anticipated date. Instead, Annie's face was contorted into a grimace from all of the uncertainty and unknown she had little control over.

Harlen was picking her up. Harlen picked the restaurant. Harlen hadn't told her where they were going. Would the evening end in a kiss? Would she ask her inside after dinner? If she did, would the implication be a promise of sex? So many unknowns.

"Stop." Annie admonished the reflection. "This isn't the first date you've ever had." At least that much was true. Fact was, Annie had dated a lot over the last decade. What she didn't have was a lasting relationship with any of the women. She didn't blame her condition for her solitary life. She was who she was. If a woman couldn't deal with her quirkiness then there was no place for her in Annie's life, or her heart.

But Harlen had sought *her* out. She'd made a point of exchanging phone numbers. If that wasn't enough proof of her interest, all Annie had to do was look at the flowers on her desk to realize that maybe this time things would end differently.

She smoothed the clingy material of her knee-length, royal blue dress before attaching the peacock pin on her shoulder. The dusting of eye shadow and mascara meant this was an "occasion." Her hair was more of a tousled mess than usual. The result of fussing too much with the already unruly waves.

"So be it."

It's not like she was trying to impress Harlen. That wasn't something she did. It wasn't in her nature to try to win people over, though that was exactly what she was doing, and admitting it only brought more anxiety. A glance at the clock revealed she had no more time for primping. What was done was done.

She grabbed the black cardigan from where she tossed it on the bed and slipped her feet into dark purple kitten heels. The small bag that would hold her keys, ID, and bank card matched her shoes. Having her bags complement her shoes was a fashion statement she'd embraced in school and part of her signature wardrobe. Luckily, her employer made no mention of her style of dress at her three- and subsequent six-month reviews. Being accepted for who she was and how she moved through the world made her happy.

"Meow."

Annie put her hands on her hips and stared at Maisie. "Have you nothing better to do than sleep when I need you?" When Maisie jumped on the bed and chortled, her heart melted. "I know. You're always here for me." She gave a good scratch under her chin, careful not to cover herself in the flying fur. Annie loved Maisie's long fluff, but no matter how much she combed her, the hair flew everywhere. If only Maisie could vacuum!

"Mommie has a date."

Maisie's head tipped while she purred loudly.

"I don't think you'll get to meet Harlen. I don't know if she likes cats." A chill ran through her. She couldn't imagine anyone not finding her beloved fur baby sweet. It would be a deal breaker no matter how well she got along with a date.

The doorbell rang and her pulse spiked. "If you want to get a glimpse, this is your chance." Annie tossed her items in the purse and walked briskly to the door. Maisie followed like the faithful canine she thought she was. Annie swung open the door.

"Hi." Harlen smiled. She wore black slacks and a gray pinstriped shirt. The paisley black and white tie lent a touch of eccentricity to an otherwise sedate ensemble. Her shoulders relaxed.

"Hello. Would you like to come in?"

Harlen glanced behind her. "We have a reservation, but I'd love to meet your kitty."

Annie turned to find Maisie sitting a few feet behind her. "That's Her Highness, Maisie," she said as she moved to the side. "Maisie, say hello to Harlen."

Harlen stepped in and crouched low. "She's gorgeous." Harlen held out her hand and Maisie nudged it with her head, signaling she wanted a pet. "And friendly."

"She's also totally spoiled." Annie couldn't help smiling. Maisie was well-behaved and well-trained, even when she pretended to be otherwise simply to annoy Annie.

"Well, beauties such as her should be spoiled." Harlen rose and held Annie's gaze. They seemed to be sizing each other up. "Perhaps I can give her more pets later. We should go."

Maisie chortled, and the spell was broken. "Of course." She grabbed her things. "Be a good girl. Mommie will be home later. Stay." The cat had only escaped once since moving, but that was enough to rattle her into training Maisie to stay back when the front door opened. She turned to find Harlen's gaze drifting from somewhere below her waist before meeting her eyes. "Is something wrong?"

Harlen shook her head as the haze-filled expression dissipated. "No. Everything is good." Harlen turned and opened the door while checking to make sure Maisie wasn't going to dart. Annie's heart melted a little more at her being mindful about her fur baby.

She followed Harlen and threw a fingers-crossed gesture behind her, quietly chuckling. While she and Maisie definitely had a language of their own, Maisie had no idea that Annie hoped the evening would be anything but awkward. Not like the last few minutes. But maybe it was mutual nerves between her and Harlen rather than awkwardness. Maybe the evening ahead wouldn't be a total bust after all.

❖

Annie looked anxious, throwing Harlen. If Annie had one characteristic that stuck in Harlen's mind, it was her confidence.

"How long have you been working for your organization?" She sipped her raspberry limontini.

Annie chewed the last of an arancini ball. "About eight months. It turned out to be the perfect fit for me."

"You seem to be doing well. The portfolio you left showed a promise to sponsors that their support is going to a wonderful cause."

Annie nearly sputtered her wine but managed to hang on. Her eyes wide when she glanced up. "You read it?"

"Of course. The family members who work at Forrest share everything that affects the business. Jane distributed the information at the last staff meeting and recommended a motion to the board to provide financial support."

"I didn't think this was a business dinner." Annie took another sip of wine.

Harlen pulled back slightly before remembering Annie said what she was thinking. Without any guesswork involved, she smiled. "It's not."

Annie licked her lips. "Good." Once their entrees were served, Annie met her gaze. "The board must have voted because we got a notice of sponsorship."

"I'm glad they did." Maybe the alcohol was helping to quell the uneasiness she sensed from Annie. She came across loud and clear that she didn't want to talk business with Harlen. She hadn't meant to bring up her job, although it was one way she could get to know Annie better. What she really wanted was to get a sense of who Annie was as a person, not a representative of a company. Perhaps even more so, Harlen wanted to know what made Annie… Annie.

Harlen cut a small slice of beef from her prime rib, but paused the bite halfway to her mouth. "Annie, I want to know you." There, she'd said what she'd been thinking for days. Harlen McGhee was showing interest in a woman other than Chloe. She wasn't about to waste the opportunity. She'd done enough wasting time. Besides, she couldn't see Chloe anymore, so what difference did it make? When Harlen finished the internal dialogue and swallowed, her eyes found Annie's and her heart began to triple beat. For a brief instant, she hoped the heart attack wasn't real. Just a reality check to let her know she was alive, and deserved to live. "I'm sorry. Did I say something wrong?"

"No…" Annie's voice cracked. Her hand trembled ever so slightly as she brought the water glass to her lips. She took several slow sips, her gaze never leaving Harlen's. How she managed to return it to the original spot, Harlen had no idea. "No one has ever wanted to know me."

Her curiosity about how Annie saw the world grew. She wanted to know what her childhood was like. How many times did she move as an adult? Where did she go to college? How had she learned to navigate in such a tunnel-vision laden society? All of it. Harlen wanted to know it all. "Well, Annie Dawson, I do." Oh shit. "Uh, I uh…" This was why she didn't date. One of the reasons anyway.

Annie burst out laughing. Not loud enough to be considered outrageous. Annie's laughter was pure and unrestrained and beautiful to witness. A small tug on Harlen's lower abdomen filled her with melancholy, reminding her of what it felt like when she'd gone on her first date with Chloe. Annie's voice brought heat to her face. What the actual fuck was she doing?

"It's alright, Harlen. I didn't take it as a marriage proposal." Annie's eyes sparkled as she slid her fingers over her hand. Harlen looked down.

"Annie, I'm sorry. I'm not very good at dating. It's been a while." She wanted to be somewhere else. She wanted to be with Chloe. Not the one that only existed in Chloe's parents' minds. Harlen remembered the time before Chloe became sullen. When they enjoyed each other's company. When they still loved each other. She wasn't ready to give up. Maybe she never would be, and Annie deserved better. She slid her hand away. The awkwardness had returned.

"You and I together definitely suck at dating." Annie looked at their barely eaten food. "Let's agree to enjoy the food, keep the conversation light, and we'll play the rest by ear." Annie picked up her fork.

Maybe she could feign illness, beg forgiveness. She'd already withheld the fact that she still loved Chloe. "I couldn't agree more." She pushed out a smile and picked up her utensils. "So, where were we?"

Annie began to giggle as she retold the almost proposal, or whatever the hell Harlen had let fly out her mouth.

Harlen nodded and waved her off. "Okay. What do you consider light conversation?" When Annie tipped her head the same way Chloe did when she was giving a topic fair consideration, Harlen nearly threw up.

Annie's mouth opened. "That would—"

"Excuse me. Hold that thought," she said, pushing back her chair. She didn't wait for Annie's response. If she didn't get to the restroom she might lose her appetizer on the floor. She turned to the short hallway and stopped. The line for both unisex rooms was four people deep. A few "Pardon mes" later, Harlen was bent over and leaning against the outside of the building, gulping in large quantities of air. She had to get her shit together and go back inside. Annie hadn't done anything wrong. Even if this was the only date they had, Harlen wasn't *that* kind of person. She'd faced worse. One last big breath and Harlen planted a smile on her face.

CHAPTER NINE

What the hell was that all about? Annie watched Harlen head to the hallway marked "Restrooms." Oh. She understood urgency. After her cholecystectomy, she learned what foods she could tolerate and what she couldn't. She ate what she wanted at home and dealt with the brevity of some of her choices. She chuckled. The sea bass was still warm, if not hot, with a small portion of risotto. She glanced up in time to catch Harlen darting out the front door.

"Huh." Annie kept her comment low, but a waiter was passing by at the same time.

"Is everything alright, ma'am?"

Annie had given up on being annoyed at the label of ma'am after she turned thirty-five. To anyone under thirty, she was matronly. A giggle escaped and the waiter's brows knit. "My date seems to be not feeling well. She went outside. Would you check on her?" She took a drink of wine and smiled. Perplexed didn't begin to describe the waiter's expression.

"Certainly." He hesitated a second before moving.

Annie shook her head. Just because she didn't act like there was a three-alarm fire happening under the table, didn't mean she wasn't concerned. She'd find out soon enough how Harlen was without all the fret that goes with worrying. Sometimes people felt sorry for her, but who had the simpler, calmer life? Simpler except for those occasions when her orderly world fell into disarray.

Harlen slipped onto the chair across from her. "Sorry about that." Her eyes were wary.

"Was your disappearance something you could have avoided?" Annie took another bite, savoring the sweetness of the flaky white flesh.

Harlen sat up. "No. I don't believe so."

"Don't apologize then." Annie took inventory of her plate. She'd left approximately a third and was pleased she'd have room for one of the decadent desserts she'd seen on the menu.

"You are the most unpredictable woman I've ever met."

"Is that a compliment?"

"Yes, it is." Harlen carved a slice and ran it through the jus on her plate. Everything was cold by now.

"Do you want your dinner warmed?" She planned on taking her leftovers with her. Lunch tomorrow would be top rate.

"No." Harlen pushed her plate away. "I want coffee and dessert."

The evening was looking up. Uncomplicated was the way to go when Annie wasn't sure how her date would end. After thinking she might have been left at the altar, she wasn't going to leave without a sweet treat to finish the meal. "Sounds about right." She pushed her plate away as well.

Harlen chose a triple crème brulee and Annie picked the chocolate lava cake with vanilla gelato. She might regret the choice later. In the moment, it was the divine way to go, along with a cup of Belgian dark roast.

"Can we go back in time?" Harlen asked.

"Do you have a time machine?" Annie watched as the corners of her mouth moved into a smile.

"No."

"Then refresh my memory." She stirred cream into the darkness of her brew and was delighted when it lightened to the shade of brown that made her think of those little squares of caramel wrapped in clear cellophane.

"I asked you to clarify what light conversation was."

Pleased that Harlen had been paying attention, Annie thought about the question. "Family. Pastimes and hobbies. Sex."

Harlen got her napkin to her mouth in time to catch what she might have spewed across the table. Once she recovered with only a minor cough, she shook her head. "Again, an unexpected response." After a few sips, she cleared her throat. "Let's stick to family for now."

"Both parents are alive and well, living in a cozy A-frame in Maine. I have a younger sister, Laura, who lives in England." Not for the first time, Annie thought at some point she should visit Laura. The only thing that stopped her was her intense dislike for travel. Public transportation was notorious for running late, and repeatedly fucking with Annie's inner clock was stressful. She took the bus twice a week, her part in trying to not harm the climate any more than her species already was. That, along with stringent recycling, helped. She wouldn't be bullied into feeling guilty for not doing more.

"Have you been to England?"

The question came up frequently and Annie knew the drill. "I dislike public transportation due to its unreliability." She glanced at her plate, disappointed to find only streaks of dark chocolate. She wiped her mouth. "What's your family situation?"

"Mom is a family lawyer, Dad corporate. A younger sister, Jane, whom you've met, and an older brother, Peter, who isn't an employee of the business at this time."

"That sounds a bit mysterious. About your brother, I mean." Her normal speech pattern was off. Another sign she was not fully comfortable in the moment. Her mind kept playing scenes of a naked Harlen; her imagination filled in the parts she couldn't see.

"He's the rebel of the family." Harlen grinned. "He has no interest in real estate, though he does want to help in some way. He's currently employed at an advertising firm and does our promotional work."

"All in the family," she said, watching Harlen's reaction.

"You could say that." Harlen's easy smile faded.

"Is that where your loyalty rests?" Annie asked the simple question because if this was going to work—whatever this was brewing between them—she had to be able to trust her. Harlen might have been looking at her, but her gaze was focused someplace in the distance.

"Yes, but not just family."

Harlen's intense eyes locked on her. This would be a time Annie imagined others would squirm. She wasn't a squirmer. "Is this a first or an only date?" There appeared to be an internal battle happening with Harlen. Annie had similar struggles centered around timelines, due dates, and her need to remain on schedule to keep her anxiety at bay.

Harlen quietly stared into her coffee for a long time. "I'd like it to be the first."

"But," Annie said, leading Harlen to explain why she was uncertain. She had a lot of experience with the "but" that often followed people's reasons for their actions.

"It's complicated."

Unsurprised by the response, Annie pinned Harlen with her gaze. "No, it's not. You either want to date or not." The butterflies had returned. For the first time since landing her current job with SFN, Annie wanted to experience affirmation in her personal life. There was still the mystery about where she recognized Harlen from, but it wasn't a reason to not date.

"I want to see you again."

"Okay." The waiter cleared their table and brought the check, setting it strategically between them. "Are we paying Dutch?"

Harlen pulled the folder closer. "Chivalry isn't dead." She smiled softly; her mouth quirked into a half smile. "I asked you to dinner." She slid her hand over her side and into the back pocket of her pants.

Annie's vivid mind felt the path Harlen's hand followed on her own body and shivered. The fantasy didn't stop there. Her eyes fluttered close and she let the scene play out, revealing where she wanted Harlen's hands and mouth.

"Annie?"

"Yes?"

"Are you okay?" Concern laced Harlen's voice, her creased forehead a visible sign.

"I was…" Annie didn't hedge and she didn't lie. "Thinking about what dating you would look like."

Harlen handed the bill folder to the waiter. "What did you decide?"

She took a deep breath. "Have you ever dated someone like me?"

"I've never met anyone like you, Annie." Harlen signed the printout and stuffed it back into the folder. "I find you refreshingly honest, intelligent, and sexy." Harlen leaned closer. "That's why I'd like to date you, Annie."

To her thinking, Annie didn't see that much of a difference between neurotypical and neurodivergence except for the way she processed information. That was, if she didn't include societal expectations of what "normal" looked like.

"As long as we're clear there are no expectations for either of us, I'd like to see you again." *In my bed.* Annie kept that little detail to herself. She didn't know Harlen well enough to invite her into her bed though Maisie had warmed up to her rather quickly.

Harlen stood and held out her hand. "I'm glad you're open to getting to know each other better."

Annie took her hand and smiled. Harlen leaned closer.

"There are a couple of safe topics we haven't discussed yet."

Her insides turned to jelly. She wouldn't let Harlen see how much she was affected by the seductive tone. Neither would she shy away from discussing sex, if that's where the conversation led. She needed to talk with Charlie as soon as possible.

Chapter Ten

"Did you kiss her?" Dan asked as she slapped a slice of pizza on her plate before putting her feet up on a corner of the coffee table.

Harlen took a bite and chewed. The stall tactic was more than the inner turmoil that had reared its ugly head. She didn't want to question her motives for not doing more. "On the cheek."

"Dude. What the actual fuck."

She sighed. "I know. It's just…I couldn't."

Dan drank from her bottle of beer. "So you aren't sexually attracted to her?"

"That's not it at all. She's got great curves and an exquisitely kissable mouth." The physical attraction between them sizzled whenever she saw Annie or thought of her. Harlen was pretty sure it wasn't one-sided, but when she thought of being in bed with someone for more than a night, Harlen had panicked. "I felt guilty."

"Oh, come on, Har. How long are you going to be committed to Chloe? She'd already made it clear your relationship was done."

"I don't know."

Harlen closed her eyes as she chewed. The last conversation she and Chloe had was easy to recall. It was the night any hope she had for a reconciliation had died. She'd suggested couples counseling, which Chloe had turned down.

"How can we fix what isn't broken?" Chloe took her hand in both of hers. "I'm not happy."

"Then let me help you be happy." Harlen pleaded with not just her words, but with her entire being.

"You can't. It's not for you to fix, babe." Chloe glanced at their joined hands. "You haven't done anything wrong. At one time we wanted the same things and now we don't." Chloe slipped away. "I love you, Lennie. I'm not *in* love with you."

She hadn't been able to breathe. The overwhelming emotions that coursed through her that night still assaulted her at times. Hearing there was nothing that would change Chloe's mind didn't relieve her of the sense of duty she still carried with her. Chloe's planned departure didn't change the fact that lying in a hospital bed and plugged into life support wasn't making her happy either. If she knew that's where she'd spend the next two years, Chloe would have pulled the damn plug herself. She set her plate down firmly. "Chloe's still lying there and I promised her." The boulder that formed in her throat was a constant reminder of the promise she failed to keep.

Dan set her plate down and scooted close enough that Harlen had to look at her. "It's out of your hands. Chloe didn't do what she needed to do to make sure her wishes were carried out. There's no one to blame but Chloe for the Ground Hog Day scenario."

She dragged her fingers through her hair. "Her parents won't listen to me. They told me to stay away."

"If the situation was reversed, what do you think your parents would do?"

"I have a health directive." Following the conversation about their friends' predicament, Harlen had her mom draw up the proxy papers and had them notarized and filed with her physician. Chloe hadn't taken the time to follow through on her end. Just like not wearing a seat belt, Chloe didn't make practical decisions. She was more of a spur-of-the-moment kind of woman. Nothing like Annie. Maybe that was part of the attraction. Except Annie had made a gesture at dinner that had sent Harlen in a tailspin, so maybe they were more alike than Harlen wanted to admit.

"You know what I'm saying. Stop with the literal. You aren't responsible for Chloe's current state of nonexistence, and the only people who can change it aren't ready to let go."

Of course, Dan was the epitome of logic. She wasn't stuck as much as she refused to give up. "That argument makes sense to everyone but me."

Dan stared at her, compassion and understanding clearly written on her face. "What I know is you deserve to have more in your life, and I want you to want that, too." Dan squeezed her shoulder before reclaiming her original spot on the couch.

The movie played on. Harlen drank her beer and pretended to be chill. Snapshots of her date with Annie flashed through her mind, including the panic attack that was so intense, she had to leave the table. As tempting as it was to be all-in where Annie was concerned, Harlen would not shortchange their budding relationship. Not while she acted like a drowning victim holding on to a lifesaver. A plan percolated. If she had any hope of letting go, Harlen needed to say good-bye to Chloe, knowing all along she should be fully covered by a shroud.

"No." Annie tapped on her keyboard. She had work to do. There wasn't time for her to lament. "There was no kissing." No one in their right mind would call that lip brush on her cheek a kiss. At least, not in her mind. It didn't matter that Annie's body responded as if Harlen had slipped her tongue inside Annie's wanting mouth. Fuck.

"What went wrong?" Charlie asked. Bless her heart, she was trying to help, but the reality stung. Annie had no idea what had happened.

"One minute, we were fine, talking about what our safe subjects were, and the next, Harlen's excusing herself from the table." Annie didn't want to tell Char her first thought of being abandoned at the restaurant. The food was good, from what little she had, and she wasn't about to leave. When she watched Harlen dart outside, she swallowed hard and shrugged. "She came back, of course." What the hell was she doing? She didn't defend her dates to others, especially not her best friend.

"Well, that makes it all better." Sarcasm flowed from Charlie's words. She blew out her breath. Yay.

"Char, I could use some support here." It was times like these that she loved how honest Char was with her. Others might look at her and not see the internal struggles her autism brought, making life harder at times. Her life wasn't perfect, but she was okay with how she lived it. All she wanted was to figure out what had happened on the date that had started with so much potential before fizzling out.

"Sorry, not sorry."

Annie rolled her eyes. Making faces and eyerolls that she couldn't help were reasons Annie didn't like video calls. She was human after all.

"I love you and you aren't afraid to go after what you want. You're my hero."

Her heart melted.

"Don't let anyone fuck with you. Okay?"

"Absolutely not." This was nice, but she was no closer to figuring out why Harlen had run away or left her wanting more at the end.

"Maybe she saw a ghost!"

Charlie was Annie's knight in shining armor. Bless her soul. "That's ridiculous." The more she thought about it, maybe Charlie was on to something, and not for the first time either. "Char?"

"Yeah?"

"What if it *was* a ghost?"

"Aww. Annie, I was only kidding. You don't honestly think Harlen saw a ghost, do you?"

Annie stood and began to pace in her particular rhythm. Five steps up, turn, five steps back. "What if Harlen's past—her ghost—came knocking at dinner?" She stopped with a jolt. She had no idea what step she was on. One more reason she couldn't get Harlen out of her mind. She had the unique ability to throw off her equilibrium.

"That would be good news for her, because then I wouldn't think she was a total jerk for leading you on."

"Hey, you know a little kindness goes a long way."

"Peace. So, what kind of a ghost do you think it is?" She could picture Char rocking side to side as she worked the possibilities out in head.

"I don't have—"

Char gasped. "What if she's married?"

"What? No." As she spoke the words, Annie focused on replaying the conversations they had prior to tonight.

"Are you sure? You don't sound sure," Char said.

She couldn't think with the bombardment of questions, but there was still the question of where to go from here.

"What are you going to do?"

It was kind of creepy how in sync their thoughts often were. "There's only one way to find out more." Details began to click into place and Annie enjoyed feeling more like herself. "I'm going to make sure there's a second date." She refused to start analyzing all the reasons she should take the hint and walk away.

Chapter Eleven

"Hi, Mom." Harlen kissed her mother's soft rosy cheek. "You look good."

"Always the flatterer." Her mother ushered her inside, then held her by the shoulders. Harlen knew what was happening. She tried not to squirm. "You seem…bothered." And there it was.

"I'm fine, Mom."

Her mother nodded. "We'll talk later." The doorbell rang and she smiled. "Go find your father before he burns the house down."

Harlen laughed and threw her coat on one of the dozen hooks her father had installed on the front hall coat rack. "Dad? I'm here to help." She gave him a side hug, careful not to jar the huge spoon he was stirring with.

"Harlen. It's good to see you, girl." People said she had his smile. Right then, she could almost see it. "Did your mother send you?"

She laughed. "What makes you say that?" This was her home. It would always be her home and she was grateful for her family. Despite all the teasing, they loved each other.

"If it wouldn't be such an inconvenience, I'd torch a potholder so she could have a real reason to talk about me in the kitchen."

"Dad!"

He chuckled before glancing at her as if to gauge something. "Your uncle's coming." He turned to the pot again.

Harlen's back stiffened. Freeman was the one member of the family that Harlen disliked. She understood there wasn't anything concrete to base her distrust on, though she couldn't deny it either. While her mind searched for the first time she had the feeling, her father finished stirring and stood in front of her with a couple of beers. He held one out to her.

"I get it. He gives you the creepy crawlers." Her father raised his bottle and drank.

"Creepy crawlers?" Harlen mimicked her father's actions.

"Yep. That's what you said when you were…" Her father looked up, tipping his head to one side. "About ten, I guess."

So, the feeling wasn't new. Maybe it was because of her uncle's misogynistic mindset, though it very well could have been some comment or action that gave Harlen that impression. Maybe she didn't have the term back then, but creepy crawlers sounded about right. "I'm not going to change my mind, Dad."

"I never said you should." He clapped her shoulder. "Let's go cop a squat. The gang will be here soon and I'm not sitting on a folding chair again."

Watching him walk, Harlen was struck by reality. He dropped into his recliner with a groan. He was getting old. His shirt, while newish and pressed, hung loose on his shoulders. The hand he wrapped around the bottle was heavily veined. She thought about the rest of the family. Her grandparents were somehow managing to be active in their nineties. Life was moving on for everyone she knew, except for hers. Her sister's voice trickled into her thoughts. Her father rose to go greet her and the brood of relatives that followed. Yet Harlen was stuck.

Here she was, waiting for her partner to be physically gone so she could end her obligation and move on. What did that say about her? Maybe it was fortuitous how her date with Annie went. What kind of a partner could she be when in the back of her mind, she wondered if there was some divine intervention keeping Chloe's body alive. Her mother's voice startled her.

"Harlen? Are you alright, dear?"

How long had she been lost in the fog of Chloe this time? "Daydreaming is all." She hoped she gave her mom a reassuring smile before greeting the group. "Hey, Jane, where's what's-his-name?"

"Ha-ha. Aron had to work, thanks for asking." Jane hugged her tight and whispered, "I want details."

Harlen extricated herself from her sister's grasp. "Not here," she mouthed.

"Fine." She tossed Harlen her coat and smiled dearly. "It's so good to see you, too." Jane turned to the others making their way inside.

All she had to do was smile, laugh, and try not to spend the entire evening wondering if she'd ever hear from Annie again.

Jane looked at her in disbelief. "Is that how you are on dates?"

Harlen ruffled her hair. She needed a cut. "How the heck do I know? I haven't dated in more than six years." God. She was pathetic.

"You just told me you abandoned your date at dinner and ended the night with a kiss on her cheek!"

"No, no. Even I'm not that much of a moron. I had no clue what I was doing. One minute we're talking, the next, Annie…" For a minute, Harlen lost herself in the memory of her panic. "She tipped her head like Chloe does—did—and I freaked."

Jane pursed her lips. They were sitting on the small porch of her home wearing hoodies and drinking coffee. The night air had turned from balmy to chilly though neither wanted to be inside. "You're still caught up in that mess?"

Harlen didn't talk about the never-ending saga surrounding her undying love for someone technically dead. Even the thought soured her stomach. "Her parents have forbidden me to visit the hospital."

"Thank goodness someone's being rational." Jane hadn't been a huge fan of her and Chloe's relationship. Looking back, it's possible she was wrong about having judged her so harshly. Jane loved her. Chloe hurt her. Case closed.

"They aren't being rational about Chloe." The words came out harshly. She was so tired of everyone telling her to move on and let go. In her eyes, a promise was a promise, no matter what. It was no one's fault that she hadn't gotten to the "I do" part before Chloe put on the brakes. None of her family knew her intention to propose and it meant nothing now. The missed opportunity had cut her so deep, Harlen could sometimes feel the life draining from her.

"So you say." Jane leaned as close as she could and met Harlen's gaze. "Chloe will never know if you walk away." When Harlen remained silent, she went on. "Stop being afraid to pick up the pieces."

Of course she was afraid. Who wouldn't be? Hadn't she proven she was in no state of mind to think about another relationship? She drained the lukewarm coffee from her mug before standing. "It's late and I'm cold." She waited while Jane once again pinned her in place.

"It's not over, Har," Jane said, then took the mug from her. "I know you still hurt." Empathy filled her eyes. "I also know it will become less. You just have to decide to let it be okay." She kissed Harlen's cheek. "Get some rest. I'll see you tomorrow."

All she could do was nod. In so many ways, Jane was more like a twin. She knew things about Harlen that no one else did. Like their mother, Jane had a sense about detecting inner turmoil in Harlen. She'd escaped her mother's inquisition at dinner. It was just a matter of time before her mother wouldn't let her avoid the conversation any longer. Until then, she owed Annie an apology. Could she get away with sending flowers a second time? Maybe something else, or a text apologizing for acting like a dork. Every time she thought of a viable way to escape Annie's scrutiny in person, the desire to see her again, to see her smile and hear her laugh, gave Harlen another opportunity to counter the argument. Taking the coward's way out wasn't going to work with Annie. Harlen pressed the start button. She glanced in the mirror and shook her head at the grin reflected back.

❖

A shifting weight on her chest woke Annie out of a sound sleep. She knew this because she was having the most delightful fantasy of Harlen showing up at her door with so many bouquets, Annie couldn't see anything but the top of her head.

"You're a real buzzkill, Maise." Annie snaked her hand from under the covers and stroked her spoiled, utterly loveable cat. She didn't need Harlen in her life. She wanted her. "Is Her Highness's dish empty?"

Maisie chortled and pushed into Annie's hand as she ruffled her fur.

"What if I don't want to get up?"

Maisie's eyes grew large as she peeked into the blanket tunnel Annie had left.

"Oh no. We are *not* doing nighttime snuggles." She sighed. Maisie was a taskmaster. When she was set on having Annie's attention, or wanting playtime, or whatever else cats wanted, her fur baby was determined to get her way. She would do every annoying thing she could to get Annie to do her bidding, and nine times out of ten, it worked. "Let's go." Maisie darted off the bed and Annie threw back the covers, cursing at the cold bedroom. Fall was fast approaching and she had to remember to set her thermostat to come on at six thirty on the weekend and five thirty when she worked. That and her coffee being brewed by the time she hit the kitchen were two things Annie was more than a little obsessed over and a lot grateful for.

After pulling on sweats and her worn but faithful slippers, Annie shuffled her way toward the smell of coffee with Maisie at her feet. She poured and yawned, then fixed her coffee. Before she took a sip, she glanced at the kitty dishes.

"Liar," she said. The chortle that followed and the innocent tip of Maisie's head made Annie laugh. Maisie's ears went back. "You are such a little shit." Annie patted her fur and the loud purr vibrated against her leg. The anxiety that used to torment her every day, all day, had become less over time. When she rescued the skittish kitten that couldn't have been more than eight or nine weeks old, little did she know how much of a therapy cat the ball of fluff would be. Maisie helped her keep her anxiety in a manageable range.

"We've been through stuff, Maise." Annie remembered their last move to where they lived now, and wished Maisie was better at traveling in the car. Not that she went many places that she could take her companion with her, but still, it would be nice if Maisie would curl up and nap while she drove rather than scream the entire time she was in the car.

Annie sat at the table and scrolled through her messages. Not hearing from Harlen came as no surprise. Maybe her lack of emotion played a part in what had transpired between them, but Annie refused to be caught up in things she might not be able to control. What spoke louder to her was her reluctance to talk to Char. As out there as her BF could sometimes be, Char had a sense of reality that Annie could not relate to, or perhaps, would not give space to. She needed that right now because nothing made sense. So why was she hesitating?

Without a clear direction, Annie took to the living room and dropped into her favorite armchair. There was only one chair. Nonetheless, the ownership was hers. Maisie would argue the point. Annie glanced at the hassock beneath her feet, and they locked eyes when her familiar jumped up, sat, and wrapped her incredibly fluffy tail around her feet.

The trait was an adaptation of the breed who had originally hunted in cold weather in Maine. The fur between their toes served a similar purpose. Maisie alternately enjoyed and was annoyed by the adornment. Annie chuckled at the memory of the time she played with a daddy long-leg and freaked when it got caught in her fur, shaking her foot and jumping around. Annie had finally stopped laughing long enough to rescue her by way of a tissue, telling Maisie it was, "All gone."

That was not the reason for the stare down they were engaged in at the moment. "It's awfully early to want my undivided attention."

Maisie trilled.

Grateful she had used dark roast, Annie sipped while not breaking eye contact. The idea that Maisie wanted more than attention crossed her mind. "I'm not ready to play with your fish."

Chortle.

"You're quite capable of playing on your own. Go get a spikey." She gestured to one of the three spikey balls in view. Three of too many to keep track of, but it saved Annie from having to crawl around on the floor with a flashlight and a yardstick more than once a week to replenish the supply. A victory in her book to be sure.

Maisie stood with what she could only describe as an impatience.

Then it hit her. "You think I should call Char." She didn't need to end the statement with a question mark. They both knew the answer. "I know. Here's the thing." She leaned closer and scratched with her unoccupied hand. "I'm not convinced there's an answer for the predicament."

Maisie, in true fashion, extended a paw when she stopped, touching her hand so lightly any annoyance disappeared.

"At least one pussy loves me." Laughter escaped and Maisie sauntered off, annoyed at the volume of her voice. Annie continued to delay the call she desperately needed to make. Fuck. "Fine."

On the way to replenish her mug, Annie replayed the evening in question. Did she do something out of the ordinary for typical types, meaning Harlen, to comprehend? Had she made her feel ill at ease? Everything Annie did or said had the potential for others to misinterpret, but she wasn't the one who had been the pursuer here. Harlen had chased her. A shiver of acknowledgement shot up her spine. She hustled to the table for her phone and prepared for the marathon that was sure to ensue.

Chapter Twelve

I was wondering when you'd call." Charlie made a grunting sound relaying her displeasure at being made to wait.

"The situation called for reflection." That much was true. She didn't want to assume or speculate on Harlen's behavior. Not just at the restaurant, either. Like…what was up with the cheek kiss? She wasn't an elderly relative that Harlen had been forced to see home after a family gathering. They were on a date for Christ's sake. If they weren't going to lip-lock a handshake would have been sufficient. She laughed.

"What?"

"Nothing."

"Bullshit," Char blurted. "I can't help if you won't share what's going on in that maudlin mind of yours."

"Hey!" Annie gasped.

"At least I have your attention. Time to share."

Annie sucked in air, then let out a couple of deep breaths. There was no easy way to begin. "I haven't heard from Harlen."

"Did you reach out?"

"No."

"Dump her."

"Char, not helping."

"Okay, okay. Let's do the pro/con list." Clattering in the background meant Char was getting provisions for their talk.

"That's a good idea." Annie grabbed her note pad and a pen.

"Let's avoid the obvious that she's a hot catch. Name something you like about her."

"She's punctual."

Char crunched. "That's a biggie for you."

Annie nodded. "She's thoughtful." The flowers had been an unexpected delight.

"Another plus. Go on." Annie's recall was spot-on. "She loved on Maisie."

"Oh, I bet that got her brownie points. What did Maisie do?" Char slurped from a can.

"She was all in for the scratches and pets. I take that as a good sign." Annie chewed her lip.

"Maisie would take those from a serial killer as long as she was getting attention."

Annie's motherly instinct rose. "She would not!"

"Then you're kidding yourself." Char banged a cupboard door before the telltale sound of her dropping onto the pleather bean bag tucked in a corner of her living room. A certain indication she was going nowhere fast.

"You're right. Maisie loves love." So did Annie. The way to her heart wasn't as difficult as people might think, though the one sticking point for all her relationships was being understood. If Harlen didn't understand the reasons behind Annie's actions, there was little hope for them. The sobering thought made her sad.

"Not so different from people," Char's tone had softened, and she appreciated their friendship more than she could fathom. "Did you talk on the car ride to the restaurant?"

Recalling the short drive, Annie had difficulty remembering if they'd talked at all. She was usually chatty in most situations, but anxiety over the impending date and realizing she was actually with Harlen made her clam up.

"Not really. I don't remember much about the ride."

"You? Annie, you have a mind like a steel trap. You remember shit I wish you would forget."

She chuckled, then became sullen. "The whole thing was weird."

"Weird how? Like stalkerish weird? Creepy weird?" Char wanted details and Annie was perplexed that she didn't have a lot of them. Caught between sexual attraction, nervous tension, and reality, Annie had retreated into herself to avoid disappointment. She'd been so unlike her usual confident self, she was terrified of putting Harlen off.

"Like Harlen was going through the motions. Or maybe she wanted to be somewhere else." She threw her hands in the air. "I don't fucking know, Char. That's why I called."

"Breathe. You're going to hyperventilate if you don't, and you know what happens then."

Char was right. Annie would be barfing if she didn't get herself on stable footing. Thinking about Harlen made that difficult. She'd tuck that tidbit away for another time. "Got it." Annie took the calming kind of breaths her therapist insisted she make second nature and used the technique whenever she felt off-kilter. In the middle of the exercise, Maisie rubbed against her leg, and the vibration of her purr slowed Annie's pulse. "I'm good."

"Alright. The ride was a bust. Did she open the door for you?"

"It wasn't a bust."

"We both know it was."

"No. She didn't open the door." She'd half expected Harlen's hand to land on the small of her back as they headed inside and admitted she'd ached for her touch. "The staff knew her."

"So she brought you to a familiar spot where she knew the food and service." Char made a derisive noise.

"What are you tsking about?"

"Nothing. What happened next?"

Annie left out the part where the silence continued for a stretch. "She ordered wine and an appetizer."

"Is that what you wanted?"

Annie shrugged before remembering Harlen checking first. "She asked and I agreed."

"You've gotten soft in your desperation for a lay." Leave it to Charlie not to mince words.

"Are we going there?"

"Sorry. Gee, you're awfully sensitive." Charlie's words reverberated in her head.

Being put off and taking offense to Char's critiques never bothered her before. What was different this time? "Now I'm sorry."

"Don't be. That's what best friends do. We taunt and tease until the other person gives up or gives in." She could hear the smile in Char's voice, but the last sentence made Annie see what was different.

"I wanted Harlen to fuck me."

Char gasped. "Whoa, Nelly. You hadn't even had the obligatory dinner date and you wanted to have sex with her?"

Annie rested her chin in her palm. "Seems so."

"You must have been a little disappointed when she didn't."

As unjustified as it was, she couldn't shake the fact she had expectations that weren't met, and that was on her. "It wasn't fair to Harlen either way." She couldn't talk about the implications her emotions were pointing to. How could she be so invested in someone she hardly knew? "I've got to go." Annie jumped up, sending the chair back.

"What? Oh, no you don't. You can't leave me hanging without the full picture." Char was outraged. It would pass. They'd been through these kinds of scenarios before.

"I am and you'll love me anyway."

"Annie…" Char's tone morphed from annoyance to understanding in a heartbeat. "You know I do."

"I love you, too. Promise we'll finish this soon." Annie set the phone on the table before heading for her bedroom. She needed to be prepared in the off chance that Harlen was willing to see her. The only way to resolve a misunderstanding was face-to-face and Annie had always been good at logistics. Maisie jumped on the bed, watching her pull clothes from her dresser.

"This has to work, baby girl."

She wasn't as desperate as Char made her out to be. Annie could take care of her sexual urges by herself if need be. In Harlen's case, she wanted a mind-meld. They had to be on the same wavelength if things weren't going to be strange between them. The only way Annie could get there was to talk about the awkward date and how they were going to move forward, if at all. If they couldn't come to an agreement, Annie wouldn't be happy. It was the first time in a very long time she was relying on someone else to get her there.

CHAPTER THIRTEEN

I hate this shit." Harlen mumbled under her breath. Over the last few days, work had become an intrusion in her already fucked up life. The last thing she wanted to do was spend more hours on a project she had no desire to be involved in. She needed to talk to someone other than her siblings. Harlen walked from her cubicle to the elevator. Luckily for her, the person she needed most worked in a law firm eight stories above her.

The shiny surface of the elevator doors reflected an almost identical likeness of her. All except the tightness of her jaw and the way she held her shoulders. The small placard next to the number twenty stated "Woodard, Forrest, and Witherby," the firm her mother was a partner in. Her specialty was family law, but she knew enough to make recommendations regarding other types of legal predicaments. Harlen didn't need legal advice. What she needed was information on how to extract herself from the family business without turning the entire twelfth floor against her.

She rode the elevator alone, a rare occurrence. The numbers over the doors lit up one at a time as she rose higher and higher. A few years ago, when the Forrest business moved into its current suite, Harlen asked her mother why law firms were always on the upper floors.

"Prestige, my dear. Corporations believe that the lower on the totem pole a company is, the lower they are in a building."

When pressed for more, she went on. "It's a symbol of stature when a company rises to the top, so to speak." She would forever be confused why anyone fixated on appearances.

A pleasant chime announced her arrival and the doors quietly opened. The décor left a bit to be desired. The orange was more of a distraction, especially these days. Maybe she'd suggest changing the color to something less garish and a lot calmer. The entire country needed to be led with understanding and inclusive caring for all citizens.

"Hi, Harlen." Faith, the receptionist, greeted her with a smile. "Here to see Lenore?"

She shoved her hands in her pants. Now that she was there, second thoughts crept in. Surely she could handle her discontent in an adult manner by herself. "If she's busy, I can come back."

"You'll do no such thing." Lenore McGhee, Attorney at Law, stood a few feet behind her. Her salt-and-pepper hair was mostly salt at this point, and cut in a semi-short, untamed style that made her look ten years younger. The cobalt blue short-sleeve sweater brought out her eye color, a trait they inherited from her maternal side. The relaxed-fit black slacks and woven mesh black-and-white, low-heeled shoes added the right amount of contrast to her wardrobe. Harlen always admired her mother's taste in clothes. Her appearance showed a refined style without being stuffy. Harlen disliked stuffy lawyers. However, her face clearly revealed how glad she was to see her.

"Thanks, Faith." Harlen covered the distance in a few steps before wrapping her arms around her mother's familiar frame. She felt a little thinner than a few weeks ago. Everything felt different lately. "Hi, Mom."

"Harlen." She held her by the shoulders with an intense gaze. She shouldn't have come. They never had the discussion her mother mentioned at the recent family dinner and there'd be no escaping it now. Her mother moved her hands downward until they held Harlen's. "We'll talk."

Uh-oh. She shook off the omen. Why was she dreading the conversation that was about to happen? Wasn't this why she'd sought her mother's sage advice? To talk about the things that weighed heavily on her mind? Harlen held her hand while she was led to where Faith sat watching the exchange.

"Would you please order us lunch?" Her mother's head tipped. "Something indulgent from that place that makes their own bread. And some drinks would be good."

"Yes, Mrs. McGhee." Faith grinned.

Her mother had fought with her receptionist, insisting she call her by her first name. Faith had refused to do so, especially with a named partner. The best Faith could offer was using her first name unless her mother was in another person's company. Then it had to be Mrs. McGhee.

"Now," her mother began as she hooked her arm through Harlen's. "Tell me what's got you so worked up that you rode the elevator in search of your mother."

"Mom…" Harlen protested. She felt like a child. Maybe that was because she was acting like one. Her mother pointed and she lowered into one of the thickly padded leather chairs circling a small conference table.

"You're not too old to need your mother are you?"

A loving family wasn't a luxury everyone enjoyed. Harlen was luckier than most. In fact, there were one or two members she could do without. That was definitely a topic for another time. "Never."

Her mother took the adjacent seat and crossed her legs, looking like the relaxed lawyer she always presented outside the privacy of her own home. Most of the time anyway. Harlen had heard stories about her fiery objections and well-orchestrated cross examinations. "I hope that never changes."

She swallowed hard. They shared a moment of silence. Harlen wondered if they were both paying respect to the relationship they had. Mother and daughter. She'd never been jealous of Jane and

Peter being closer to Dad. The middle child was often thought of as the forgotten one, but Harlen knew better.

"We've got some time before lunch arrives. Tell me what's upset you."

Where should she begin? If she started with how her first date with Annie had bombed, her mother would be sympathetic and maybe a little biased in her reflection on the other issue. Work was the safer subject. "I don't like what I'm doing."

Her mother's finely shaped brows knit. "In what context?"

Harlen blew out her breath. *Be clearer*. The admonishment was meant to help speed along the process. At this rate, they'd still be here at dinner time with her mom pulling bits and pieces of the story from her. "Work." She wanted to pace. "I've never been thrilled about being in acquisitions."

"You're good at it."

Ha. "Only because I have to be. I take pride in my work, but I don't like it." Harlen was on a roll and she wasn't about to stop. "I got the short straw when we brought more people on." She'd been clear from the start, the real estate business wasn't her dream profession. It was temporary until she decided how she wanted to set up her interior design business. "It's been more than seven years, Mom." Where had the time gone?

Seven long years of wasting time and energy doing what she despised. She wasn't a salesperson. Harlen learned from her grandmother how to work acquisitions and make the most from each purchase. At the same time, Harlen and Chloe moved in together. Two years later, her grandparents stepped away from the day-to-day management of the business, leaving those decisions to the family. She told herself the job was temporary, and she focused her energy on their new, exciting relationship. She thought she'd have time to set up her own business and move on, yet here she was without having gotten any closer to her dream. Emotion choked her airflow. Harlen couldn't think about Chloe and her ongoing battle with wanting to do the right thing when her newest dream was washing her hands and walking away from her obligation to both her partner and her family's business. Those obligations hung over her like a hangman's noose.

"There's nothing wrong with wanting a change. Lord knows you've had a lot on your plate." Lenore's tone held empathy regarding Harlen's feelings for Chloe rather than sympathy for her self-imposed situation. She had raised her children to be independent thinkers and doers. "So, what do you want to do about your job?"

Harlen hadn't told Dan about her struggle with work aside from it being mentally exhausting. The anguish Harlen experienced by not having an outlet for her artistic side drained what little life she had left. "I don't want to die like this."

"Are you sick?" Her mother's face blanched.

"No. I'm sorry. I'm fine, Mom." She placed her hand on her mother's shoulder, refusing to notice the flesh and bone beneath her fingers, but it urged her on to not waste another day. "I'm not happy if I'm not designing. My loyalty to my family…"

"And Chloe."

Harlen almost smiled. She should have known better than to think she'd get away without that tidbit. Her mother's insight slowed her rambling. She didn't need to get everything out in a minute. A knock on the door startled her. Harlen sat back while her mother went to answer it. This was her opportunity to think about what she was really trying to say without worrying about being careful how she got there. Her mother knew her better than she knew herself. She'd forgive her.

"Come in, Faith. I think it's safe to say we'd eat just about anything."

"Thank you, Mrs. McGhee. The restaurant was packed. Calling ahead helped." Faith began to spread the food.

"You don't need to do that." Her mother and Faith exchanged a look. "I didn't mean to sound ungrateful. Harlen and I were at a critical mass in the mother/daughter department. Food may improve the negotiations."

Faith smiled with relief. She nodded and quietly left. Harlen got busy unbagging the food. There was a ton. Way more than two people could eat.

"Are we having company?" Harlen wanted to sound upbeat, but if she didn't get this out soon, she'd lose her nerve again.

Her mother chuckled. "I've always asked for plus-one." She opened a carton and inhaled. A bright orange soup with pepitas sprinkled on top caught her eye. "This is their special soup and why I wanted to order from the deli." She held up a coffee mug with a spoon in it. Harlen had no idea when that happened. She really needed to get her shit together.

"You were promoting your loyalties when we were interrupted." Her mother slid the mug over before holding her in place with her gaze. Her mother possessed many admirable qualities. Not wasting anyone's time was one. She'd come to appreciate it.

"Yes. I'm proposing the company let me withdraw to part-time status at twenty-five or thirty hours a week, tops, to start." Unable to gauge her mother's reaction, she dipped her spoon into the soup. Flavors burst in her mouth. The sweetness of a hearty squash along with fresh herbs and the crunch of nuts made her moan. "You weren't kidding. This is delicious."

"I know."

The awkward silence that followed left her confidence waning. Harlen put down the soup, knowing it would get cold. But she also knew she had to finish. "During the transition period, I'll stage open houses and contract for renovations." If Harlen was a person who sweated under pressure, she'd be drenched. "In a year's time, I move to full-time on the design side of the business." She'd let herself daydream to the extreme, seeing her business flourish by providing her services to home buyers looking to renovate their newly purchased home to fit their needs. Harlen's entire body tingled. For the first time in her life, the prospect of finding happiness in her work life was obtainable. If only she could count on her heart to reach for the obtainable, though the lack of contact made it pretty clear that Annie wasn't about to get involved with a woman who was chasing a ghost.

"It's a great plan. You should present it at the next board meeting."

The oxygen was gone. As much as she hoped for her mother's support, bringing her idea to the board was a big deal. "You think it's that good?"

"I think it's great." Her mother patted her hand. She shoved a white-paper-wrapped package in her direction. "That's roast beef. Also a winner. Doesn't go well with the iced latte I'm about to snatch." The playful attitude wasn't new outside the office, and she considered if this was how her mother moved in the world all the time. Certain. Straightforward. Forgiving. Kind. She could go on and on.

"Thank you for being my mother." Her mother sat up, all movement ceased. "Harlen…" Her eyes were so full of emotion, Harlen recognized her own battles in them. It couldn't have been easy for her mother to wage the daily battles it took to survive, yet women did it every day of their lives.

"I haven't told you nearly enough." She took a napkin and dabbed at the tear that gathered and fell from her mother's eye. This was what it felt like to love someone so unconditionally they don't realize it. With a strength Harlen had often witnessed without being able to name, her mother gathered herself.

"I love you," her mother said. Harlen did see it then. "Don't tell the others, you've always been my favorite." Her smile lit up the room. "The job situation will be resolved." She opened the wrapping and moaned. "Chicken salad." She glanced her way. "I love you but not enough to share this."

Harlen laughed. "I wouldn't think of asking."

Her mom picked up the huge half, bulging with pieces of chicken and what looked like avocado, and took a bite. When her eyes rolled, Harlen could only stare.

"What? Navigating family stuff burns calories."

"Is that the secret behind managing the chaos of family dinners?" There hadn't been one time she could remember when the family gathered and didn't end up discussing some drama or other. Good times. Her mother wiped her mouth and stuck a straw in the latte. Harlen's nose wrinkled. She wasn't sure it would go any better with chicken salad, but her mom looked happy.

"Food brings family together." She waved her hand between them. "We got through this without raising voices." Her mom cupped her cheek. "If only your brother would learn to not get so excited. We're all listening, for God's sake." She shook her head and returned to the sandwich.

Suddenly hungry, Harlen took a big bite. It was all she could do not to moan, too. The beef was melt-in-your-mouth tender. The horseradish sauce was hot enough to get her attention without overpowering, and the marble rye stood up to the hefty contents. In the middle of her swallow, her mom pulled her back to the present.

"Where are you with the Chloe situation?"

"Nowhere." The hesitation gave her time to decide what to share. "Her parents have forbidden me to see her anymore."

Her mother studied her. "That won't stop you."

Harlen looked at the partially eaten sandwich before dropping it on the paper, her appetite gone. "No, it won't."

"They could get a restraining order." Her mother had over thirty years practicing the law.

She sat back. Her iced tea was nearly gone, and so was her patience. "They might." The perfect opportunity to give her the whole picture was now. "I went on a date last week." Was it just last week? To Harlen, it felt like she hadn't seen Annie in forever. Annie hadn't reached out and she couldn't blame her. By most standards, the date was a disaster.

"Oh." Her mother's voice revealed her excitement. "Did you have a good time?"

Harlen laughed bitterly. "I'm not sure how to answer that." The reassuring squeeze on her forearm served as encouragement. "It started out fine. Reservations at the Paris Tower. Annie was excited and so was I." None of the disastrous night was Annie's fault and she was determined that her mother understood. "Then she tipped her head like Chloe, and…" Her breath stilled as she relived the moment. *It's just a memory. Annie isn't Chloe and she never will be.* This time her heart plummeted. Had she deliberately sabotaged the date that held promise because she wanted the woman across from her to *be* Chloe? Harlen stood abruptly.

"I have to go, Mom."

"You haven't finished." The height difference between them was minimal, making it hard for Harlen to avoid her mother's searching gaze for clues to what was going on.

"I know. I need to fix this with Annie." She kissed her mother's cheek. "I promise to tell you the rest." After a few harrowing minutes when she thought her mother would demand more, she nodded.

"You'll call if you need anything?" Her mother's love helped anchor her to the present. She used to think Chloe was her anchor, but that hadn't been true for a while. Harlen's devotion was an anchor holding her down, keeping her from any chance at happiness.

"Promise."

That was a promise Harlen could keep. Some promises were meant to be broken. At the very least, her time stamp on her promise to Chloe was running out. First things first. She needed to talk with Annie, knowing it might already be too late.

Chapter Fourteen

Harlen sat in her car in silence. A gentle breeze swayed the leaves on the trees surrounding the parking area, showing the first signs of their changing color. True fall weather would arrive in the next few weeks. Her favorite time of year was when the daytime heat abated and evenings turned cool. This was when Harlen would go for a walk on her lunch hour and pick up street food along the way. The routine was as much a break from the frustration that coursed through her by the job she was currently locked into as it was to clear her mind while amid the sights and sounds of everyday life.

The talk with her mother had given her the grounding she needed. Her work situation would improve, pending her presentation to the board. Of course, first she had to request attending the next meeting to do so, which should be top on her list. However, the notion that Annie might slip away if she delayed the conversation they should have had following the fumbled kiss churned her stomach.

What was she doing sitting there when she had work to do? Just thinking about returning to her desk made her anxious. She could do some of her work from home. That would provide an opportunity to gather her thoughts on how to present her ideas to the board. Harlen admitted she was stalling for time.

Her phone screen was dark, akin to her mood of late. She hadn't given enough thought to what the next step of her relationship with Annie should be, if at all. One thing was certain, Harlen didn't want to hurt Annie any more than she likely had already. She couldn't bear making a hasty decision she would later regret. Lost in thoughts of considering what to do, she jumped when her phone announced an incoming call with a trumpet blast. The time to change the ringtone had come.

When she looked at the screen, shock and fear took turns bouncing around inside her head as Annie's name appeared. Why was she calling after more than a week of silence? Telling herself she needed to reach out to Annie was not the same as being ready for the conversation that until a minute ago was still to be determined. A second ring came, then the third. If she didn't pick up before it got to the fifth ring, the call would go to voicemail.

"Hello," she said, breathing as though she'd just run a race.

"Glad to hear you're alive, Harlen," Annie said in a clear, calm voice.

No excuses. "We should talk."

"Great minds think divergently." Annie chuckled. "So talk."

Fuck. This woman infuriated and excited her on both fronts. "Not over the phone."

"Do you want a replay of our last dinner?"

Harlen groaned, then laughed. "Not exactly. Can you meet me for a drink later?" The lack of response reinforced her original thought that talking to Annie without a game plan was a bad idea.

"No."

Her insides roiled unpleasantly. She'd blown it with Annie. "Okay." There wasn't much left to say. "I understand." She rubbed her face, not wanting to end what had barely begun between them. Harlen wasn't surprised. Her last relationship had fallen into despair, too.

"I don't think you do. I want you to come to my place to talk. That way if you feel the need to leave, I'll already be home."

The corners of her mouth twitched. Annie's way of dealing with situations and being up front about what she wanted was refreshing. Harlen had to admit it was one of the reasons she found her so attractive. "Got it. What would work for you?" Putting the ball in Annie's court was her best option.

"Tonight at seven. I'll make something to eat. Are you allergic to anything?"

"You don't have to—"

"Harlen, you asked what would work. Making dinner works for me."

When Annie made up her mind she didn't leave any room for negotiation. "Fine. Can I at least bring wine, or whatever?"

"I know how to pick out wine."

She could almost hear the gears of Annie's mind turning on the other end.

"Bring dessert. I'm not in the mood for measuring."

There was no holding in the laughter that erupted. "You are without a doubt the most interesting woman I've ever met, Annie."

"I know. Don't be late."

Harlen once again stared at the screen. This time it showed a wallpaper of her favorite family picture from their Labor Day gathering a couple of years ago. Maybe it was time to put a different picture up. She needed to stop daydreaming and get moving. A quick stop at the Epicurean Delights bakery would take care of her contribution. After that she'd draft a memo to the board members requesting time at the next meeting. Putting together the presentation would have to wait. The chance to right the wrong with Annie was within reach and she'd do whatever she had to do to keep the spark alive.

"We're having company, Maise," Annie said as she moved around the kitchen. Her mother was a decent cook though she was stuck in the seventies, when seasoning meant salt and pepper were the tried-and-true choices. Annie was more adventurous, having watched way too many cooking shows and taking classes to expand her knowledge and techniques. When she was in her early twenties and dealing with her newly diagnosed thought process, cooking had given her a break from the stress of not understanding why her thoughts ran in conflict with most of the population.

"Harlen might be the one." Far from being someone to get her hopes up, Annie also was open to entertaining the idea of having a partner. Whether on a full- or part-time basis didn't matter. If Harlen was willing to engage, she would pursue the attraction.

"She likes you. That's a huge plus in my book of pros and cons."

Maisie chortled as she rubbed along Annie's calf.

She hadn't actually gotten to writing down the points of Harlen's character and the reasons she had for following her gut for more than sex. "She's handsome and has a dry sense of humor." Annie ticked off the obvious qualities. "The restaurant she chose tells me she wanted to make a good first impression." Annie stirred the pot of spaghetti sauce that she started the minute she got home. Luckily, she had meatballs and sausage in the freezer. Once the sauce was simmering and the meat defrosted, she tossed them in to infuse a flavor exchange. A glance at the clock affirmed she had forty-five minutes before Harlen arrived.

"Ceasar salad is next." She pulled ingredients from the refrigerator. While she worked, she imagined how Harlen's lips and the way her mouth moved made her wet. How would they feel on her skin? Would she enjoy licking Annie's clit, or was Harlen one of the thirty percent of lesbians who were turned off by the mere thought of doing so?

"That," she said, pointing the knife at Maisie knowing there was no chance Maisie would jump on the counter, "would be a deal breaker." Annie could put up with a lot of things, not participating in oral sex wasn't one of them. Maisie trilled and snapped her fluffy boa of a tail before it settled around her feet. "I know. Right?

That percentage is way out of whack. How many pillow princesses were there? I mean, if you're not willing to taste me, I sure as fuck am not going down on you, either. I intend to have my cake and eat it, too!"

With obvious indifference, Maisie turned tail and sauntered off to somewhere she didn't have to listen to Annie's ruminations.

"Huh. We'll see who's in charge when there's nothing in your dish."

They both knew it wasn't true. Annie would never try to prove a point by withholding food or water, but it sounded reasonable on TV. Annie washed her hands before moving the bowl to the table where two candles would burn, acting as a barrier to the fantasy of inviting Harlen to her bed.

"I should write a book." She paused long enough to consider it. "Maybe."

Annie turned the burner beneath the pot of water on low. Being on time didn't mean the same thing to everyone, and she didn't want it to appear as though she was in any hurry to get their talk done and her time with Harlen over as soon as possible. One last glance around and she took off the apron she wore to keep her clothes clean. The movement reminded her of the aprons her grandmother always wore whenever she was in the kitchen. The style depended on the type of food. Annie chose one with a bib since tomato sauce had a tendency to bubble and splatter no matter how careful she was when she stirred.

The doorbell rang and she froze. *Take a breath.* Yes. She could do that. In, hold, out. On feet she hardly felt hit the floor, Annie reached for the door handle.

"Hi. Again." She smiled. It was good to see Harlen.

"Hi." Harlen held up a bakery box tied with string. "I hope I'm not late."

"You're right on time." Annie waved her in. "I like a woman who can tell time."

Harlen shook her head, a wide smile appearing as she walked into the living room.

"What are you smiling about?" Why did she care what Harlen thought? Because she did.

"You have a wonderful sense of humor, Annie." Harlen handed her the box and her face warmed.

"Thanks. I'm glad you appreciate my humor. Not everyone does." When she took the package, their fingers brushed, and a new image appeared with Harlen as a key player.

"That's a shame," Harlen said before finally letting go. "I find you delightful."

"Thanks for the treat." Annie raised the box as she moved it to the counter. The slickness between her thighs made her wish she were wearing her moisture-proof underwear, but she'd neglected to consider she might need them.

"It smells wonderful." Harlen visibly inhaled. "What are we having?" Harlen followed her to the stove, her eyes were focused and laser sharp, paying attention to everything Annie said and did. Annie's body came to full alert.

"Spaghetti with meatballs and sausage. Can't go wrong with Italian." Shit. She hadn't thought of having bread. "And there's Ceasar salad." The scent of Harlen's skin was too close, she needed space she couldn't ask for. This sweet torture was an experience she had longed for, apart from whenever they made it to being naked in her bed. Hopefully. Definitely.

"Mmm…I can't wait to have some." Harlen's breath tickled her ear.

"Can you pour the wine? It's been breathing for a while." Unlike her. Passing out was not an option. The urge to stim didn't come and Annie tried to connect the dots that refused to line up.

"Glad to help."

Harlen's absence was noted, however it gave her the break to be able to think. Now, where was she? Pasta. Right. She turned the heat up to max and opened the box of cavatelli. The idea of fettuccine had crossed her mind. While the pasta shape was her favorite it was unwieldy and would cover them both in sauce. Her synapses fired off, creating a scene where she used licking the splatter from Harlen's skin an excuse to map her body. Goodness.

"What else can I do?" Harlen's crystal blue eyes sparkled. With what, she didn't know. She definitely couldn't let her get close.

"Pasta bowls, upper right." Annie pointed. "And salad bowls."

Harlen opened the cupboard. Annie returned to stirring the pasta.

"Are these okay, Annie?"

Something in Harlen's voice sent a shiver down her spine, landing squarely in the middle of her crotch. Great. She glanced without looking. "Fine."

Harlen brought them to the table and returned with their glasses. "No sense letting it sit there alone." She held the wine out. For a second, Annie wasn't sure she wanted to feel Harlen's skin brush hers.

"Thank you." When Harlen handed the drink off without any physical contact, her disappointment soared. "How was the rest of your day?"

"It was okay. I went to the bakery." She tipped her head toward the box.

"What did you decide on?" Annie resisted the temptation of sweets some of the time, but rarely when it was bakery fresh food.

"Don't you want to be surprised?" The mischievous twinkle in Harlen's eyes reminded her of her childhood when other children would tease her on purpose to see if she'd freak out.

"Being surprised never made me feel good."

Harlen's smile disappeared. "Six delectable pastries. Each one different."

In her need to be honest, it appeared she had unintentionally soured the moment. "That came out wrong, but thank you for telling me." Annie focused on the pasta before fishing a piece out. She blew across the slotted spoon, then gave it a chew. It was on the edge of al dente. If she let it cook any longer it would quickly turn to mush. She drained the pasta, moved it into a serving dish and added a pad of butter and a little sauce to keep it from sticking together.

"Can I take that to the table for you?" Harlen looked like a puppy who peed on the carpet and wanted to regain their owner's affection.

Annie placed the glass cover on the dish. "You can now." With Harlen out of her space, she took a couple of seconds to remember the order of events was playing out as planned. Things were fine. She rolled her eyes. Everyone knew when a person said things were "fine" they never were. Not where it counted. She closed her eyes and a mental snapshot of her list appeared. Get through dinner. Right. She carried a second dish containing the meat and sauce to the table. Harlen had lit the candles, and any misgivings she had about Harlen's intentions faded.

"It smells wonderful, Annie. Thank you for inviting me over." Harlen held up her glass. "To us."

What did that mean? Was there something going on that Annie wasn't aware of? Granted she wasn't herself when it came to Harlen, but she had faith that she hadn't missed any glaring signs of the mood between them having changed, except for one comment that was glanced over by them both. Harlen looked at her with beseeching eyes, as though she hoped they were on the same page.

"To us." She waved at the table contents. "Help yourself. I don't believe in serving," she said.

"Why not?" Harlen asked as she scooped a generous amount of pasta.

"If I give you a small portion, does that mean I don't want you to have more? If I serve a big portion that's too much for you to eat, do I still expect you to eat it so it's not wasted?" Annie shrugged. "If you take what you want, I'm not involved in the decision."

Harlen's fork paused on the way to her mouth. "I've never thought of it like that." She chewed, then moaned.

"I'm not surprised."

"You shouldn't be. You're a really good cook."

Annie shook her head. "Not about the food, about the way you think. You can't process like I can because you're neurotypical." With as many times as she'd explained the concept, people in general rarely got it without a few examples. Some needed ongoing lessons to grasp the global concept of thinking differently.

Harlen's face became serious. "Then there's no hope for me to understand?" She visibly swallowed and Annie had empathy for her.

"You can understand if it's important to you." She watched the myriad of emotions cross Harlen's features. Had she said too much? Annie was going to short-circuit if she had to analyze everything she said. How in the world did people deal with the nonstop bombardment of meaningless stress and worry?

Harlen moved her hand across the table before stopping. "At dinner last week..." She paused as if considering what or how to say what would come next. "I was a jerk. You deserved a nice evening and you didn't get one. I'm sorry."

Annie took in the words, knowing they had to be moved around into an order she could interpret. Short clips of the date flashed as she moved parts of sentences around, splicing them in a comprehensible line. Finally, she saw them in her head. "What happened, Harlen? What did I do that made you so upset you had to leave the restaurant?"

"Oh, God. You saw me go outside?"

"Yes. When you came back what you told me didn't make sense."

"I know."

"Then when you kissed my cheek..." She had barely felt the brush of her lips, yet her body craved more. It still did. "What happened there?"

"I—"

"Wait." She picked up the bottle of wine and filled her glass with a generous amount before holding it out to Harlen, who shook her head. "Suit yourself." Annie took a drink. The wine got better the longer it breathed, and she reminded herself that with any luck, the philosophy would hold true for her and Harlen. "Continue."

"Fuck if I know, Annie." Harlen sat back. All the bluster and bravado she'd displayed a minute ago was gone. "I *wanted* to kiss you. Then I was too embarrassed to follow through. I felt terrible."

"You sure have a funny way of showing it." Annie settled into saying what she was thinking. "Do you want me to heat up your food because we're not wasting it?" When she smiled at Harlen being there with her talking rather than posturing, she was glad she called her.

Harlen chuckled. "I wouldn't think of doing that." Harlen broke off a hunk of a meatball. As she chewed, her eyes closed. Annie watched, wondering if she looked like that when she came. But when Harlen moaned again, Annie reached for her wine while wet heat trickled into her panties.

"Annie, this is the best ball I've ever had," Harlen said with such earnest enthusiasm Annie burst out laughing.

"Now there's something you don't hear every day." Annie crunched salad. Harlen nearly choked. All kidding aside while knowing it was too soon, Annie could imagine how genuine Harlen's compliments sounded. She could also easily conjure a life with Harlen, spending interesting evenings recounting their day and catching up on family dirt. Or maybe it was only her family that got caught up in the gossip tree. Surely if Harlen had a large enough family to run a business like Forrest Enterprises, there'd be plenty of "Did you hear?" at the dinner table. When she refocused on the here and now, and Harlen, she gathered her wits. "Do I need to do the Heimlich maneuver?"

After some water, Harlen waved her off. "No," she croaked. Another drink and clearing of her throat helped. "I'm fine." She smiled. "You're dangerous."

Annie was rarely at a loss for words. Harlen had a way of disarming her. If she wasn't experiencing it, Annie would not have thought it possible. If anyone was dangerous, it was Harlen, and

Annie had every intention of finding out how much danger she was already in.

❖

"How long have you had her?" Harlen stroked Maisie's soft fur, making her purr loudly.

Annie was curled up in the corner of the couch with a cup of coffee. "She was eight weeks old when I rescued her from her humans."

"Wow. No wonder she's so attached to her mommie." She smiled. The bond between them was as obvious as a mother with their child. Harlen enjoyed a similar bond with her own mother.

"Yes, well…it's not all perfect symmetry. The little shit does everything she can to get my attention." Annie smiled fondly when she patted the arm of the couch and Maisie landed there to garner Annie's scratches and soft coos.

"You two have an unrivaled affection for each other."

"That's because she doesn't make excuses. She knows when I need her quiet company and gives me unconditional love." Annie's gaze met hers. "She gives me what I need."

Something in Annie's tone made her think there was a hidden message. Dinner had been a mix of seriousness and laughter, but she hadn't told Annie the real reason she'd escaped her company, if only for a brief time.

"I left the table because you did something that reminded me of my former partner." Acid gathered in her stomach. She pushed down the queasiness. Annie would want details.

"I take it that's a bad thing?" Annie continued to scratch and pet Maisie who looked like she had no intention of going anywhere.

Was it a bad thing? At one time, Harlen had found Chloe's characteristics endearing. "Not bad. Wistful, I guess." She longed for the days when Chloe was happy with their life together. Harlen believed they would be together for the long haul. When the rug was pulled out from under her by Chloe's declaration of no longer being in love with Harlen and the ending was in sight, Harlen went into reparation mode. She could fix what was wrong in the relationship. It was just a bump on the couple's road.

Annie set her cup on the coffee table before addressing Maisie. "Go take a nap. Mommie has to have an adult conversation with someone who uses words." Maisie lifted a paw and softly patted Annie's arm. The touch was careful and loving. Harlen understood why Annie was so attached and vice versa. "Go ahead, little girl. We'll do loves later." With a chortle, Maisie jumped down and disappeared.

"Explain what made you sad."

Replaying the reasons in her head made it sound as though Annie couldn't possibly fill Chloe's shoes. Harlen came to the conclusion she didn't want her to. Annie was not Chloe. The one-time love of her life was gone. People could have more than one, right? Harlen could find love again, all she had to do was give it room.

"Chloe, my former partner, used to tip her head a certain way that brought back all the things I love—loved—about her. I didn't want to have those feelings intruding on our date." She fingered her hair, a nervous habit from childhood when she didn't understand being gay was why she was different from most of her schoolmates. "I panicked."

Annie was quiet for a long time in that way she did when processing. "Do you still love her?"

Being honest was the only option with Annie. Harlen had no doubt she would see through the veil of any lie. "It's complicated. She's been in a coma for two years."

"That must be a difficult situation." Annie began to fidget, a mannerism that Harlen had never seen her exhibit. "Are you ready for dessert?" Without waiting for her to answer, Annie disappeared. Harlen followed.

"I'm ready if you are." She set their empty mugs on the counter and made eye contact. Did she mean for there to be a double entendre? A Freudian slip of the tongue so to speak?

Laughter threatened to bubble out and Harlen pushed it down. Certain Annie had caught the faux pas, she did the only thing she could think of. "More coffee?" she asked louder than necessary.

"Okay." Again, Annie lacked her earlier enthusiasm. Instead, she appeared ill at ease, wanting to hurry things along. "You bring those and I'll meet you at the table."

The mood had cooled. The joking and jovial responses Annie had shared a few minutes ago were gone and Harlen struggled to pinpoint the moment it changed. Either her brain wasn't functioning or some other unexplained phenomena had occurred. For the time being, she decided to leave the question alone. After all, her track record with Annie had already been lackluster.

Chapter Fifteen

"It's just a coincidence, Maise." Annie cleaned up the few items that needed tending to in the kitchen, spinning like a top as she worked. "How could my luck be that bad?"

Maisie chortled and looked up at her expectantly.

"What were the odds of Harlen's Chloe being *that* Chloe." She hadn't dared to ask what Harlen's former partner's last name was. Instead she could fixate on the possibility that Harlen was in love with another woman. One who had been dormant for so long? "Two years." She found her activity journal, the place where she documented all the things she might need to reference someday, including dates and times of major events. Each year was tabbed, as was each month. Maisie sat on the corner of the desk watching her flip pages. Her paw moved toward one of the year tabs that ran along the top.

"No, Maisie. Mommie's book."

Maisie looked at her, then the tempting blue tabs, before withdrawing. The intensity of her studying the pages as Annie flipped meant she was far from done wanting to touch it, chew it, or see if it would move…with help.

"The accident was in October." The yellow tabs running along the side marked the months. She flipped a few more pages looking for the entry before stopping.

A freak, two-day stretch of freezing temperatures that included light rain on the second day made black ice form on windblown sections of the road. Annie was driving home from work, her focus on the sparse traffic and the dark road ahead of her. She was going at a snail's pace, staying well below the thirty-mile-an-hour speed limit. Unfortunately, the wildlife hadn't gotten the memo about how treacherous conditions were. When a rabbit darted across her path, Annie's first reaction was to brake. The car began to skid, and she held tight to the steering wheel before remembering the class she went to years ago. Steer into a skid. But when she took evasive action, her car began spinning in the opposite direction. There weren't a lot of cars on the road, but one was heading straight for her. Somehow she managed to avoid the other car and landed facing the right way up against an embankment a few feet off the road.

The other vehicle wasn't as lucky. Red lights flared in the distance for a moment before Annie watched in horror as the car left the road, became airborne, then rolled several times before landing on its side against a stand of trees. She pressed the emergency assistance service button on the overhead pad. Whoever was in the other vehicle needed help.

It wasn't until she stood shivering in the wet cold talking with a responding officer that she learned the other driver, Chloe Williams, hadn't been wearing a seat belt. The next day, Annie had gone to the hospital in search of her.

"Oh, God." Annie looked at Maisie in disbelief. "Harlen was there."

That's why she vaguely recognized her. Harlen had been in Chloe's ICU room. The figure in the bed was surrounded by monitoring machines, and a large bandage covered one side of her face and head. Annie was stopped from going in by the sign on the door that read Family Members Only. Asking the nurse at the desk hadn't garnered any information except that the outcome wasn't good. She left without knowing any more, though she looked in the obituaries for a week. Incorrectly, she assumed that meant the woman had recovered.

She put the pieces of the puzzle together. Harlen and Chloe had been partners. Chloe was still at the hospital. She never woke up and she never left. Had Harlen been at her bedside all this time? Did she still visit her every day? Talk about complicated.

Maybe she was assuming too much. Harlen had asked her on a date, and accepted Annie's invitation to her home. Surely that meant Harlen's feelings for Chloe had waned, didn't it? Annie closed the journal, tapping the cover once.

"Did she ask me out because she knows I had a part in the accident?" She ruffled Maisie's fur, making her lean into the touch.

Because there had been no physical contact between the two vehicles, the police didn't cite her name on the official report. She'd checked. When she turned in the damage estimate to her insurance, she told them the truth. She'd been listed as "a witness" who called for help. Harlen couldn't know it was her.

"Good," she said out loud. At least there wasn't a nefarious reason for Harlen asking her out. Annie should have been relieved, but she was far from it. They hadn't discussed whether there would be more dates. They hadn't talked about much of anything of substance once Harlen revealed her lingering feelings for Chloe.

"That's a tough nut to crack." She chuckled. Her grandmother had gifted her with dozens of euphemisms. Using them brought memories of her cherished grandmother to the forefront.

Too wound up to sleep, Annie went to her desk. Armed with her sketch pad and far too many pencils, she began to sketch wherever her mind took her. Without focusing on the actual subject, she crafted lines, shades, and contours erasing here and there to suit her needs and keep her attention firmly on the page. Two hours later, she sat back and looked at the entire picture in front of her. Annie wasn't surprised by Harlen's bright blue eyes looking back at her. They held both conflict and desire, reflecting Annie's own inner turmoil.

"I guess we're both going to have to battle our demons." Annie wanted to feel Harlen's lips on hers, experience the ecstasy of skin on skin, and be enraptured in the heat of touch more than she had ever wanted another person. With tonight's revelation, she wasn't sure that would ever happen. Annie was convinced that if Harlen found out she was the one whose car crossed Chloe's path that icy night and fundamentally ended her life and their relationship, Harlen wouldn't want anything to do with her.

When she dragged herself to bed hours later, Annie had one goal in mind. To pursue a deeper connection with Harlen after revealing she was responsible for putting the person she loved into a coma. The only question left was how could she do both without ruining her chances of succeeding?

❖

"Good afternoon, Ms. McGhee. We're looking forward to your presentation. Please." Andrew Barns, the chairman of the board for Forrest Enterprises, smiled warmly and gestured to the podium.

Harlen knew most of them by name, though there were several new members. For the last week, she'd focused on preparing the presentation she was about to give. It highlighted the advantages of having an in-house interior designer for Forrest properties. As it was, they spent an enormous amount of money on staging properties that were on the market, not to mention the ancillary moving crews that often overcharged with "travel fees" and similar expenses that inflated the bottom-line cost.

"Good afternoon." She smiled and nodded at the members on each side of the long table. Everyone who worked at the business was aware their nickname was the Firing Squad. The connotations went from simply voting against a proposal to the removal of underperforming staff, based on not only financial considerations, but also how Forrest was viewed by the public, who were always seen as potential customers.

"In front of each of you is a statistical report with the breakdown of expenditures per year related to the staging and ultimate showing of properties for sale or lease." Harlen took a breath as she used a neon green laser to point out where those figures were located. "Here you will see that an unstaged home sat on the market for an average of more than three times as long as staged homes. This suggests that buyers may find it hard to picture their belongings in an empty shell, therefore they hesitate to commit." Harlen didn't like being in the spotlight. "Ask for what you want, Harlen." Her mother's soft voice reminded her of the importance of what she was saying.

"Consequently, when one of our residential properties sits on the market for more than ninety days, we expend between eight and twenty thousand dollars in loan payments and related fees every thirty days the property goes unsold." Groans emerged from the board as they took in the numbers and soon led to escalated voices among them until the chair called them to order.

"You may continue, Ms. McGhee." Andrew nodded, smiling.

"Harlen, please." She took a breath and looked at her audience once more. "I'm proposing the creation of a new position, director of design. The person would be responsible for acquiring a warehouse of furniture and household accessories, as well as oversee the staging of all Forrest open houses." There were several minutes before one of the members looked up.

"Charles Wellington. This position would be best suited for someone with an interior design degree."

"It would, sir. As well as some hands-on experience within the real estate industry."

"Mindy Pike. Do you have someone in mind?"

Harlen smiled. "Yes. I would immediately apply for the position, if the board approves of creating it." This was where she had to make her case. "Not only would I work as the company's stager, I would also offer my design services to buyers looking to renovate their newly purchased homes. In return, Forrest would receive a twenty-percent finders' fee of the total renovation cost."

"Dan Forsythe. If all goes according to your plan, you'd vacate your current position in acquisitions?"

"At some point in the future, sir. To start, I would work part-time in acquisitions and part-time staging. As soon as a replacement is hired, I'd begin to shift to billable hours of no more than forty hours per week, less if sales fall." Harlen clicked the slide advancer. "As you can see, even if I bill for a full week's pay, Forrest will save a minimum of approximately seventy-thousand dollars in the first year."

"Aside from being a sound idea, what's your reason for wanting this change?" Dan asked.

Harlen put down the pointer and left the security of the podium. "I'm not in love with acquisitions." Mild chuckles emanated from the board. "I have a degree in interior design and color theory. It's time I use them. Design is my passion, and it's where I'll give my very best to make each and every client happy with not only Forrest Enterprises, but with my designs."

"Kathy Jennings. It sounds like a bit of a reach for the company."

She'd prepared for this argument. "Not at all. When Forrest acquires properties to sell, or renovate, then put on the market, tens of thousands of dollars are spent preparing, advertising, and hiring people outside of the company to do what I can do from inside the company." Many in front of her were sitting up, intently listening. "Forrest started out as a small, independent company, but it hasn't stayed that way over the last forty years. It's grown with market demands. Buyers don't want to have to imagine what a home looks like with furniture. They want to *see* it. If you want them to buy a home, it has to *feel* like home." She picked up the advancer and moved to the next slide depicting various shots of one of the three homes she'd staged when their usual crew wasn't available. "Home buyers aren't interested in investing in a structure. They want warmth." Click. A slide of a welcoming sage green living room with white trim, a fireplace, and comfortable furnishings appeared. "They want character." Click. A staircase with storage beneath and a well-lit coat closet at the tallest end came on. "They want a home they can enjoy and grow in." Click. A family room painted sea blue with a big screen TV surrounded by storage shelves and bookcases, a large sectional leather sofa with complementing throws, and a thick navy-blue carpet was next. "And they want a company who will listen to them." Click. A picture of Harlen with a same-sex couple sitting at a small table. They were obviously discussing the designs that were laid out, excitement showing in their expressions. Click. The slide depicted a couple in a breakfast nook having a meal by candlelight. "They want a place to enjoy life."

Harlen took her seat at the table. "What that all amounts to…" she said and pressed the button one last time. The slide showed Forrest Enterprises employees at this year's summer picnic. "Is a company people can trust regarding one of the most important and costly decisions of their life." She let out a long breath and glanced around the table. "Any questions?"

"Only one," Andrew said. "When can you start?"

Chapter Sixteen

"I could have driven," Harlen said to Dan as she snapped her seat belt into place. For an instant she wondered how many times Chloe had not followed the law.

"No, you couldn't. We're on our way to celebrate your new position." Dan's grin displayed her small, white teeth in the dark car like a neon sign.

"I haven't started yet." The excitement she felt when the chair asked about her start date hadn't dissipated. She was on cloud nine. Her mother had been the first to congratulate her with a huge hug and telling her she could do anything she put her mind to and effort in. The struggle with going to work every day had become a chore rather than a joy. Come next Monday, she would begin the transition of handing off a portion of her acquisitions contacts and pending contracts to one of the senior agents until a full-time employee was hired.

"Come on. We both know you've landed the position you've wanted since you started at your family's company." Dan squeezed her shoulder as they sat at a light. "I'm really happy for you, Har."

"Thanks." The time it had taken for her to prepare for this day had been shoved to the back burner for close to a year while she dealt with the knowledge that each passing day made it more likely that Chloe would never wake up again. Of course, the neurologist said miracles did happen, but not nearly as often as television would have her believe. Chloe's parents refused to listen to Harlen. Refused to accept Chloe's ghostly appearance as visible proof she was gone. She couldn't blame them when she had touted the same belief until…until meeting Annie. There'd been no interest in any women except for a night of their company, and even that bit of comfort had only happened more than a year into Chloe's coma. "So where are we going?" Dan had been her first call after talking with her mother.

"I thought you liked surprises?" Dan flashed a mischievous grin.

She'd asked Annie a similar question. Was that when the mood had gone from flirty and fun to somber?

"Earth to Harlen."

Harlen shook the cobwebs away. "Please don't tell me we're going to a strip club." Harlen appreciated the women who danced for a living, but she preferred a private show to a public display.

"I know you better than that."

True. Dan knew things about her that no one else did. Over the years when dark moments threatened to bring her world crashing down, Dan had pulled her from the brink of despair. She still wasn't in the best of places regarding Chloe, though she was beginning to think her parents had done her a favor by banishing her from the hospital. Not having the constant reminder of how hopeless the future was came as a relief. It didn't mean that she didn't want to see her ever again, but she wasn't in any hurry. Her gut told her the next time she saw Chloe would be the last.

Dan was intuitive enough to sense Harlen had a lot going on inside and remained quiet. Mixed emotions about the second date with Annie left her feeling ambiguous. This time it was Annie whose mood had suddenly cooled. What had caused the change remained a mystery. Replaying the evening had not revealed any blaring wrongdoing on her part. Harlen considered whether she should leave well enough alone.

"Here we are." Dan's enthusiasm was endearing.

She glanced out the window at a single-story building that might have been a grocery store at one time. "What's here?" she asked. Dan was already waiting outside the car. Harlen smiled and shook her head, content to let Dan do what she did best. Help Harlen let go for a night and keep the demons at bay.

Dan wrapped her arm around Harlen's shoulder as they headed inside. "Let the celebration begin."

❖

"How's your cocktail?" Char asked as she swirled a purple concoction in a highball glass.

"It's good. Spicy." Annie sipped the drink appropriately named Hot Tamale. Made with tequila, pear seltzer, and a slice of jalapeno with a spicy sugar rim, the drink suited her mood. She needed something to displace the constant image of Harlen telling her about the accident that she couldn't help feeling partially responsible for.

Char bumped her shoulder. "Like you." She chuckled and Annie joined in.

Annie needed this. With more than a week's passing, she still lamented the very real possibility that she would have to end things with Harlen before they got too deep. She didn't waste time crying or being upset over an unavoidable fate that affected everyone in some way. That didn't make it any easier. By effectively turning the table after dinner, Annie had likely left Harlen to think she was fickle, or perhaps unable to make up her mind like a lot of women. Oh well, Harlen hadn't called or texted her, so there was no sense feeling anything or wishing it had worked out differently.

"This band is really good." Char jumped up. "Let's dance."

She locked eyes with Char. "On one condition."

Char put her hands on her hips. "What?"

"Do not, and I repeat, do not try to spin me like a top. I nearly barfed last time." For some ungodly reason, the last time they went dancing, Char had put her through a series of spins, dips, and twirls that sent her careening into the half wall that surrounded two sides of the dance floor.

"Promise." Char held up interlocked pinkies while trying her best to look chagrined.

Annie stood. "Yeah, yeah. I've heard that before."

Char dropped her arms to her sides. "And you definitely will again. Come on." When they reached the black-and-white checked tiles that marked the dance floor, the music changed to a semi-slow number.

"How do you expect me to dance to this?" Fast music was a rhythm she was comfortable with all on her own.

"Like this." Char held her arms open.

"Char, no." The whine sounded like she felt. Childish. Char stamped her foot. Two children having a tantrum. She laughed, then moved into her waiting arms.

"I'm leading this time," Char said.

"Good idea." Annie had insisted she lead the last time they slow-danced only to repeatedly step on Char's toes until she held up her hand and hobbled back to her seat. Annie's apology was sincere, but Char refused to dance for the rest of the night.

Annie settled into a strange mix of steps that Char led her in as she babbled on about some hot woman she saw in the bank. Her mind wandered to the endless stream of everything Harlen. How would her hand feel on Annie's hip? Would Harlen's breath be hot against her sensitive skin? Her eyes fluttered shut. Harlen's mouth was moving closer until there was the barest of space separating their lips and—Annie stumbled. Char pulled her tighter, keeping her upright, and stopped.

"You good?" Char asked, the corner of her mouth twitching.

"Did I step on you?" Panic set in. Char was going to ban her from the dance floor.

"You did." Char chuckled before pointing to the construction boots she wore. "After the last time, I invested in steel-toed boots."

All she could do was flick her gaze from the boots to Char's smiling face. She pulled her in for a crushing hug. "This is why you are my best friend. I love you." Annie planted a wet one on her cheek, knowing it freaked Char out. She let go, glancing over Char's shoulder toward the bar. *It couldn't be.* The more she stared the more she tried to come up with excuses why the woman with her back to Annie couldn't possibly be Harlen.

"Oh, my God."

"Hey." Char moved, blocking her view. "You don't look so good."

Annie's mouth was full of sand. "It's…" she croaked. "Harlen." Definitely, positively Harlen, and she wasn't alone.

Char steered her to their table and shoved one of the water glasses in her direction. "Christ, you're pale. Bend over and put you head between your knees." She tried to push Annie into position.

Annie slapped her hand away. "Stop it before she looks this way." Harlen stood sideways with a bottle of beer while the other woman tapped it with hers. Each of them took a drink before Harlen's companion leaned close. It might have been an innocuous comment being shared. The alternative had Annie imagining unkind things about Harlen, like how dare she move on without giving Annie another thought.

"Shit." Char's face scrunched. "I'm not sure I'd get that excited over her."

From where they sat, they couldn't see Harlan's face. "Not her. The woman she's talking to." In the next moment, Harlen looked over the room and Annie's heart felt like a war drum beating hard and fast, signaling the siege was on.

"Take this." Char shoved a paper bag into her hand. She never knew from where Char could produce the oddest assortment of items.

"I don't need this." Annie held the bag out. Char's lips pressed together and she snatched the offensive bag from her.

"Fine, but we are *not* leaving." She grabbed her phone. "I'm going for fresh drinks."

Annie latched on to Char's wrist. "I'll go." Her gaze homed in on Harlen like a missile to a target. Harlen was responsible for the awkward first date, but the second one was squarely on her.

"Are you sure you want to do that?" Char asked, empathy in her eyes.

"Yes." She hadn't been thinking clearly for a week as she battled swinging emotions that centered around Harlen and the unanticipated circumstances that brought them together. It was time she let Harlen know they weren't done.

Chapter Seventeen

"Excuse me."

Harlen turned. *Annie*. "Hi." She wanted to kiss her, but Harlen wasn't about to make their relationship any stranger than it already was. How they managed to keep having chance meetings must have had some serendipitous meaning, not that it mattered. Except if Dan pulled off another spectacularly unwanted surprise. Not that she wasn't glad to see Annie, but if she was here because Dan arranged it, she'd be pissed. She'd deal with her later. Excitement coursed through every fiber even if she wasn't sure what to do about the feeling.

"Can we talk?" Annie said. Her face gave no hint of the topic.

"Uh…" She glanced at Dan, who shrugged, then reached around her and stuck out her hand.

"Hi, I'm Dan," she said.

"Annie Dawson."

Dan nodded. "If you'll excuse me, I need the restroom." She put her hand on Harlen's shoulder and whispered. "Don't fuck up."

Without Dan as a buffer, Harlen was left to maneuver the conversation on her own. "What do want to talk about?"

"We've sabotaged our first two dates." Annie's eye color deepened from mid-tone to a dark brown with flecks of green. "I want to try for a third."

Harlen mouth twitched. "Do you think we're doing it on purpose?" It was all she could do not to grin. Annie's left brow rose.

"You know that's not what I meant."

Harlen straightened, regretting the cavalier remark. "You're right." The beer in her hand gave her a minute to get her shit together as she took a drink. "Would you like something?" She tipped her bottle in Annie's direction.

"No, thanks." Annie closed the narrow distance. "I want another date with you where neither of us get twitchy, and if we manage that, we have sex."

She could hardly misconstrue the statement for anything but the truth. Annie had spelled out her expectation for date number three in no uncertain terms. "Do you think that's a good idea?" The logical thought traveled from her brain to her mouth, but her heart was in fibrillation.

Annie tipped her head side to side and shrugged. "Damned if I know."

Harlen laughed out loud. When Annie joined her, she came to the same conclusion that Annie might have made. No matter what had happened, they were drawn to each other. "Then I see no reason not to."

"Good." Annie got the bartender's attention. "The purple drink with vodka and a hot tamale, easy on the ice, heavy on the alcohol." She placed her bank card on the reflective surface of the bar.

"Let me." She reached for her pocket, but Annie's fingers closed on her wrist.

"No. This isn't a date. I pay my own way."

The bottomless depth of Annie's eyes threatened to obscure everything else. Annie, in a beautiful black lace blouse with a hint of a deep shade of red beneath, and Harlen barely able to breathe she wanted to taste her sweet-looking mouth so badly. Dan approached from behind Annie, raising her eyebrows to find out if she should disappear again. Harlen nodded enough to let her know all was well and Dan took her seat. Annie leaned to make eye contact.

"Nice to meet you, Dan." Annie picked up her drinks. "I'll text you," Annie said, her eyes holding Harlen's for too brief a moment. She was slack-jawed and wondering if things would be different the next time, but Harlen had to agree it was time they addressed the question about having sex.

"I take it that went well?" Dan asked as she turned to face her.

Harlen smiled. "As well as it can when Annie and I are together." She couldn't wait to hear from her, certain it would be soon.

❖

"How did it go?" Char asked conspiratorially.

Annie shrugged. "I won't know until after I text her."

Char took a sip and made a scrunched face like she always did when the drink of the night was whiskey sours. "Huh, this one's actually not too sour." She took another sip.

"That's because I told the bartender what I wanted."

"Is that what you're going to do with Harlen? Tell her what you want?" Char's smirk told her she was teasing. Kind of.

"My hope is the 'dry spell' is over," she said with air quotes, making Char chuckle.

"I'm all for that. You're getting cranky."

"I'm not cranky."

Char's hand went to her hip. "Seriously?"

Annie sighed. Sometimes Char knew her too well. She also knew Annie would go home and replay every sentence to find nuances or innuendos she'd missed in the moment. "Fine, but it's not a conscious thing."

"Oh, I know. You're only snappy when your jets are running and you can't get off."

She slapped her arm and they grinned at the same time. "Let's just say when my toys no longer get the job done, we both suffer."

"I'll drink to that." Char took a healthy gulp and stood. "Dance with me. Maybe it will help take the edge off until you and the handsome tamale get your groove on."

It certainly couldn't hurt. Her sexual frustration was through the roof. Grinding on the dance floor would only be a temporary solution, but Annie hoped to be grinding in bed with Harlen in the not-too-distant future.

Chapter Eighteen

"We're so proud of you." Her mother beamed.

"Let's not make a big deal, Mom," Harlen said as she joined the rest of her family at the dinner table. A typical Sunday surrounded by her parents, siblings, and grandparents.

"What's going on?" Peter, her older brother, asked.

Harlen leaned into him. "It's nothing." She kept her voice low.

Her mother placed her silverware on her plate. "Harlen has board approval for a new position."

This was why she almost didn't come, knowing her mom would be bursting at the seams to share the news. Truth be told, Harlen was excited to get started. She'd already put together binders of various designs to show prospective clients. They sat in a tote bag with her paint samples, fabric swatches, and other tools to help her capture what a client would consider the perfect renovation.

"What position is that?" Her grandfather's handle on the day-to-day operations of the company had slipped a bit in the last year, though he was still sharp in many areas.

She couldn't ignore the inquisitive looks she got and sighed. Her food would be cold if she didn't explain what her parents and Jane already knew. "I've never liked being in acquisitions. What I enjoy is designing, and with all the staging the company pays for, I suggested we invest in our own staging and design department to save money and make more on the sales we're already invested in."

Grandpa let the news sink in. "Sound idea." He cut off a piece of beef. "Who we hiring?"

From the look on her face, Harlen's mother was chomping at the bit to be the informant. She gave in, gesturing for her to take the lead.

"Harlen will be the designer."

Those who didn't already know were obviously surprised by the news, and she prepared to be peppered with questions. Before anyone started, she took the reins. "I'll stay in acquisitions part-time while I build a warehouse of staging furniture and accessories. I'm also going to offer renovation design services for clients who want to update or change the houses they buy from Forrest." Mom and Dad had already heard her sales pitch, but everyone showed interest in what she had to say, so Harlen continued. "Once things are in place, I'll leave acquisitions and move into design full-time."

Peter, who likely wanted to know if he'd be involved in covering her position, spoke up. "Who will step in for you?"

Harlen shrugged as she chewed. Grandma came to her rescue.

"We're going to hire from within, or advertise if no current employee wants the position." Gram had a firm handle on the inner working for Forrest Enterprises.

Jane touched her hand. "Congrats, big sister. I know you've wanted this for a while." The rest of the family soon chimed in with their own words of encouragement.

With the focus on her news over, the conversation moved to general gossip and topics like upcoming vacations, the approaching holidays, and a plethora of items that elicited moans and laughter in equal measure. Harlen enjoyed their close-knit lives and the love they shared. When the banter settled and their plates were empty, everyone pitched in with the cleanup. One of her tasks was fixing the coffee pot, a necessary accompaniment to dessert. Her mom wiped the counter next to where she worked.

"I knew everyone would be happy for you." She squeezed Harlen's arm.

"You should have given me a chance to tell them, Mom." Her mother's enthusiasm wasn't unwanted, and Harlen had gotten used to her inability to keep a secret for long. A characteristic that ran in the family, though Jane was the usual culprit for breaking news, good or bad.

"I know, dear. I was too excited to wait any longer." She attempted to look chagrined, but her mouth twitched as she fought against smiling.

Harlen kissed her cheek. "It's okay. I survived." The bond they shared was easy to see, and no one in the family questioned Mom showing a bit of favoritism toward her.

"How far along are you in stocking a warehouse?" her mother asked while she placed cups, sugar, and cream on a tray. Harlen added napkins, spoons, and forks. They fell into their easy pattern in the kitchen, and she wondered if her mother ever wished she'd chosen a career in the culinary world rather than law. Neither were easy.

"I toured one of the smaller stager's warehouses." Rows of easily accessible furniture lined the walls and large shelves stocked with every manner of household goods, sans appliances. Each collection had its own labeled section. The owner had done the painstaking task of taking inventory as she built her stock. "I've secured a space that was acceptable to the board." She leaned against the counter while the coffee brewed. "I'm going to ask Dad to put together a shared-use contract."

Mom took the top off the cake keeper and began cutting a dozen slices. The way she was able to make every slice the same size still baffled and amazed Harlen. "What will that cover?"

"My goal is to eventually stock enough items to not only stage homes for sale, but to provide mock-up spaces tailored to a client's renovation ideas. It doesn't make sense for me to try to fill a second warehouse for the design business when many of the same items would be used for both staging and renovations.

While Forrest will pay for the warehouse rental and the bulk of the furnishings, I'm going to cover the cost of amassing accessories, like dishware, linens, throw pillows, etc."

Harlen had come up with the idea of sharing when it became clear how much of an investment would be required. The initial cost would run into a few hundred thousand dollars. More than she had saved to get her own business up and running. She'd do the preliminary staging of rooms for a reno based on what her client wanted. Once they saw how a space looked in reality versus their original ideas, there were bound to be changes. She'd gather their input and create virtual models before a project began so that everyone was on the same page to avoid late changes. Mid-renovation modifications were costly. When the beep sounded, Harlen pulled the filled carafe and added it to the tray. Her mother watched her intently, a curious look on her face.

"What?" Harlen glanced at the tray. Had she forgotten something?

"I've never seen you this excited talking about work before." Her mom hugged her tightly. "You deserve being happy. It's been far too long."

"Thanks, Mom." The depth of mother-daughter love between them brought tears to her eyes, and she fought for control. "I don't regret being part of the Forrest crew, only my part in it."

"You should have said so a long time ago. No one would have blamed you for wanting a different career." Her mother lifted the cake plate and Harlen followed her into the dining room.

Maybe her mother was right. The starting salary provided a solid financial base for her and Chloe when they moved in together. Time got away from her while their relationship blossomed and she believed they would be together forever. Then Chloe dropped the bomb about her not being happy, and Harlen abandoned all thoughts of changing jobs in order to focus on fixing their relationship. Then came the accident, leaving her to carry on by going through the motions. Basically, the last five years she'd been reaching for the brass ring only to fall off the horse.

Things were finally looking up. The bleak situation with Chloe needed closure, at least on her end. She had to shake off the vestige of responsibility that lingered. Annie offered a fresh and different way of looking at life that she wanted to explore. Whether their previous issues were a sign the relationship might not work after all remained to be seen.

❖

"Since we've been so successful at the tried-and-true dating thing, let's do something different." Annie didn't want to seem pushy, but she wasn't going to fall into a pattern that clearly wasn't working for either of them.

"What do you have in mind?" Harlen asked. Her voice wasn't strained like it had been, and Annie wondered what had changed in the two weeks since she spoke to her at the lounge.

She glanced out the window. Fall had arrived in all its glory. Sweater weather was her jam and she hoped it was Harlen's, too. "A drive to the mountains and a picnic lunch for starters." The local butcher shop offered made-to-order picnic baskets at a reasonable price.

"That's a cool idea. What else do you have planned?"

"I don't like to plan sex as a rule, but in this case rules are meant to be broken." She and Char had argued over the wisdom of telling Harlen she wanted to have sex with her. Char went on and on about putting undue pressure on Harlen and how it wasn't a great way to start a relationship. Annie argued a third date was already past the "start stage" and she wasn't about to get any more deeply involved if they weren't sexually compatible. Sooner or later, it would be the reason for a breakup because Annie considered difficulties in the bedroom to be a deal breaker.

Harlen chuckled. "I see. So I should come packing?"

Annie checked her phone. The screen name was Harlen McGhee. This was a much more playful person than she remembered. "Yes. And bring along a change of clothes and a toothbrush."

"Never leave home without them."

"Are you really Harlen of Forrest Enterprises?" What had transpired to change her demeanor from tentative and sometimes sullen to the upbeat woman she was talking with?

"Yeah, one and the same." Harlen was quiet. "I know things haven't gone well between us in the past, but I'd like to see that change."

"So would I." Annie chewed her lip. She wasn't the same person she was a bit ago either. Back then, she would have told Harlen about being in the other car on the night of Chloe's accident. If she hadn't slid on the ice Chloe probably wouldn't have had to take evasive action. But she had to remember the act of avoiding Annie's car wasn't what killed her. Not wearing a seat belt had been her demise. Still, Harlen might not see it that way.

"I'm glad to hear that. What time should I pick you up?"

"Would eleven work for you?" A leisurely drive to a picnic area she'd found via Google that promised "Pristine views surrounded by fall foliage" was her idea of a perfect date. The start of one anyway. Hopefully this time, her fantasies would be taken out for a spin, too. If Harlen drove and wasn't enjoying their time together, Harlen would have the option of leaving whenever she wanted.

"Sure. What can I bring in addition to a toothbrush?"

Annie chuckled. "I can't think of anything, but I'll let you know if that changes." Three days. That's how long she had to make sure she was ready for overnight company. "Harlen, I'm really looking forward to spending time with you."

"So am I, Annie." Harlen's voice was low and soft. "Have a good work week. I'll see you on Saturday."

The rapid beating of her heart began to slow. Harlen affected her both mentally and physically. She stared at her monitor blankly. Work was secondary, giving space to her growing infatuation. She wanted to tell Harlen she recognized her from the hospital. Not coming clean didn't sit well with her moral compass. How could she explain the whole scenario in a way that wouldn't feel like a huge betrayal on her part?

Annie made a to-do list. Order a picnic basket. Prepare for sharing her bed and bath with another person. Come up with a plausible explanation for having deceived Harlen for weeks. Easy. Not. She'd rather handle a work crisis than be the cause of a crisis with Harlen, one that might doom their budding romance for good.

Chapter Nineteen

The butter-soft jeans, dark green T-shirt, and flannel plaid shirt Harlen wore helped bolster the feeling of contentment that surrounded her. This was a nice change from the formal date she'd made a mess of. While she had no idea where they were going, she wasn't worried. If she knew Annie at all, their jaunt into nature was mapped out and a place for their picnic already in mind.

Pinprick sensations ran through her, accompanying the anticipation of sleeping with Annie. Not just sleeping though. Annie wanted sex, and she wasn't the only one. Harlen flashed back to the last time she had sex with a woman for pleasure rather than need. Even the last time she and Chloe had sex together was because she was grasping on to the hope of rekindling the kind of emotions that had driven them together in the first place. Having those kind of sensations again with Annie had taken Harlen by surprise.

Whether the resolution of finally letting go of Chloe and the unreasonable expectations she imposed on herself happened before or after didn't matter. She had a duty to be good to herself. Like asking for the job she wanted to do rather than the one that was given to her, she had to be open to experiencing attraction and desire again.

Harlen pulled into the driveway and turned off the car. She had a one-on-one about remembering to have fun. So what if she wasn't the one to bring up the idea of sex, it wasn't like she hadn't been thinking sexually about Annie. *Let's stay in the moment for a change.* She heard the bell ring inside and the live wire that was her pulse, jumped.

"Are you okay?" Annie asked as a way of greeting.

"Hi. I'm fine." Harlen was at a loss. Annie studied her, head tilted.

"Glad to hear it." Annie stepped back then she stepped forward again, as if they were dancing. "I have to grab one more thing before we go."

Harlen stood in place. The awkwardness of the moment that never came stunned her. She glanced around for Maisie.

"Lose something?"

"Uh…I was wondering if Maisie was coming with us." Harlen should have slapped herself for the unbelievable excuse, but she could already feel the flush rising up her chest.

"That would be a hard no, thanks for asking. The little shit's more demanding than I am, and it's parental-duty break day. Besides, she screams like she's going to the gallows whenever she's in a car."

She couldn't help chuckling. "That would be a strange way to start a date."

"Right? Here." Annie held out an insulated wine sleeve and a modern-day version of a picnic basket.

"This it?" she asked, surprised at how heavy the basket was.

"Lord, no. I'm all for romance in its place, but there's nothing provocative about sitting on the damp ground this time of year." Annie opened a door that revealed the coat closet and pulled out a hoodie. "Maisie," she called. "Come get a pet from Harlen. Do you have a hoodie? I have extra."

"I have one, thanks." Again, nerves were getting the best of her, evidenced by a lack of vocabulary. Maisie rounded the corner, blinking, and in no hurry to join the humans.

"Get over here or we're leaving without loves."

Maisie chortled and trotted over to Annie who lavished her with neck scratches and words too soft for Harlen to hear.

"Go see Harlen."

Squatting, she extended her hand. "Hi, Maisie." Maisie brushed it, purring loudly. Harlen scratched the top of her head. When she stopped and Maisie moved away, she thought they were done. Instead, she went belly up and continued to make soft noises.

"Maise, seriously. We need to go." Annie didn't look as annoyed as she was pretending to sound. Their gazes met. "Please give her a belly rub or I'll never hear the end of it."

Unsure if the encounter would end badly based on what she knew about cats, Harlen rubbed her hand over the cat's exposed belly tentatively. Maisie wriggled in apparent delight before flipping onto her feet. Harlen picked up the basket and wine.

"Well, you've done it now. One more person added to Maisie's sucker list." Annie put on a slingback, gathered a large tote from the entry, then shoved her phone in the outer pocket. "Daylight's burning." She opened the door and waved for her to go.

On the way to the car, Harlen replayed the last five minutes, trying her best to remember the details of the funny banter she and Annie had shared. Having fun had been nonexistent except for family outings and other people's celebrations. Since she'd given in to her mother's encouragement regarding work and it had turned out so well, Harlen vowed to make positive changes in her personal life, too.

"Where are we going?" She glanced at Annie, smiling.

"Get on the Northway and head north." Annie clipped in her seat belt, took a water bottle from the tote, and stowed it in the cupholder. Harlen hesitated. "Relax. I'm not kidnapping you." Annie smiled and she looked Harlen over like she wanted to devour her. "Hope you don't mind driving. It's about an hour away."

Harlen's mind and body were all in. If Annie could send shock waves through her with a look, she could only imagine what other delights she was capable of producing in her. "North," she said as she slid her sunglasses on. "I can do that."

Annie placed her hand on her thigh, and she almost gunned the gas. "I knew you could."

❖

"This place is awe-inspiring." Harlen took Annie's offer of binoculars and tracked where she pointed. She watched a couple of deer take a well-worn path up the mountainside until they were lost in the forest pines.

"I thought so, too. I found it a few years ago when I was in my nature phase." Annie unloaded the cushions, placing them across from each other on the benches. "White or red?" Containers of all shapes and sizes appeared on the plastic tablecloth. Harlen believed Annie could have been a magician in another life.

"You pick." She scanned the edge of the small stream that ran below where they were looking for more signs of wildlife. She turned as Annie moved closer with two glasses of red.

"Cooler weather calls for red." Annie's gaze held hers. Electricity crackled in the air between them.

Harlen took the offering and raised her glass. There was so much that wasn't known in her future. So many dreams, wants, and wishes that had been ignored while all she could do was put one foot in front of the other. "To splendid views that include a beautiful woman."

Annie toasted her with a smile, looking over the rim. Her long lashes momentarily obscured her eyes. "I'll drink to that."

They stood side by side gazing at the vista. Harlen thought about how much Chloe would have enjoyed standing in the sunshine. How when she'd snuck into the hospital during the shift change, the staff were sympathetic to her situation and didn't stop her. How she'd wished for the hundredth time that Chloe would wake up with all her faculties, or peacefully slip away. In her heart, she knew Chloe wasn't coming back to her even if a miracle happened and she awoke. As if on cue, Annie touched her arm, rousing her from her sadness.

"We should eat." Annie went to the table, giving her time to gather her thoughts back to the here and now. Annie was real, alive and awake in ways Chloe would never be.

"What delights have you brought to share, Annie Dawson?"

"A little of a lot. A local butcher offers a number of different baskets, and they don't make a fuss if you want to swap an item out for another, which I appreciate. Who the hell eats pickled sardines?" Annie began to remove the lids and she helped.

"What did you swap for sardines?" Harlen wasn't a huge fan of the salty, hairy little fish either.

"Caviar," Annie said in that no-nonsense manner that Harlen found so refreshing. Why couldn't more people be open and honest? Why couldn't she see her way to telling Annie the truth about her lingering commitment to another woman? How had she gotten herself into this predicament?

"Wow. That's a hell of a swap, Annie."

Annie shrugged. "Extravagance is good for the soul." She dropped some food items on the gold-rimmed plastic plate in front of her and included a petite spoon of tiny fish eggs. "Have you had caviar before?"

She'd been to her share of fancy receptions and fancy restaurants, but she'd never indulged. "No. Is there something I should know before I do?" Harlen matched Annie's helping. She didn't know much about exotic foods, but she knew caviar was expensive.

"This isn't Beluga, which we can't get in the States without connections. This is Kaluga. Almost as good as the best, but with a slightly less salt content and easier on a first-timer's palate. I like it on crostini." She held up her bread, then took a bite.

Harlen wasn't sure she was going to like it. She fixed hers with a bit less caviar.

"Don't anticipate you won't like it. There's a lot of things you might believe you don't like until you try them." Annie winked and Harlen was glad she was sitting. The simple gesture sent a thrilling rush through her limbs. She tried to swallow, but her mouth was dry. Not wanting to choke and spew fish eggs, she opened one of the bottles of water and drank deeply.

"I'm ready now." Harlen hoped her smile was as warm and inviting as Annie's. She picked up the slice of toasted bread and held it in front of her.

"Go ahead. It's not going to bite back, Harlen." Annie took a sizeable bite.

Harlen closed her eyes as she bit down. Despite Annie's sage advice, she was prepared to spit it out if it came to that. The bread had a nice crunch and a buttery, savory flavor that she enjoyed. What was, indeed, surprising was the little pops the eggs made while she chewed, emitting a slightly salty and fresh flavor unlike anything she could compare it to. The moan that followed was also unexpected.

"Oh, my. That's delicious, Annie."

"Mmm-hmm. Right? Who'd have thought fish eggs could be so good?" Annie dropped another dollop on another slice and added a thin piece of parmesan cheese. She washed it down with wine, then cracked the seal on a bottle of Perrier water. Annie studied her again. "There's something different about you." Annie rested her chin in her upturned palms. "What is it?"

"I've taken a new position. Maybe that's it." Harlen was still pulling a lot of the pieces together. The human resources person wanted her to create a written job description and associated tasks since there was no other position like it in the company.

"Seriously? You left Forrest?" Annie sat back.

"I'm still at Forrest. I haven't been in love with what I was doing for a while, so I pitched my ideas to the board, and they agreed to give the position a one-year trial." She'd crunched the numbers again, making sure she hadn't falsely represented any of the information. Selling herself under false pretense would not make a good impression.

"I'm not sure I knew what you did before. What are you doing now?" Annie picked up a wedge of sandwich.

Harlen wiped her mouth. "I'm still in acquisitions for a the time being while I transition into the interior design director slot full-time." When the stress of doing a job she disliked could no longer be ignored, Harlen had found her voice. Could she do the same when it came to Annie and the undeniable feelings she wanted to explore?

"Like I said, a woman of many talents. Tell me more."

Annie seemed content to listen as she went on to describe her vision for not only the company, but also for the personal business she hoped to eventually get off the ground. The picture that formed in her head had some blank spots and the questions were many, but she was tired of spending more time on the "what-ifs" in her life rather than the "I can do anythings," she was ready to make happen.

"What about your fundraising? How is that going?" Harlen had been paying attention when she wasn't fixated on Annie's squeezable ass, or how kissable her lips looked, especially when Annie ran her tongue over them.

"It's going well, thanks to contributors like Forrest jumping on board." Annie's eyes glassed over. "Now my attention is on the winter gala I'm going to pitch next week."

"The organization hasn't done that in the past?" Harlen looked at the partially eaten containers. Did she have room for a few more bites? She emptied the wine between their glasses.

"I'm the first person hired to head the fundraising division." She pointed to the tiny bit of caviar and Harlen handed her the container. "They didn't obtain their nonprofit status until the beginning of this year. I was told to start small with my expectations, but that's not my style. Go big or go home. There's no in between for me."

Harlen reflected on what the equivalent of that philosophy might mean in their relationship. "So it's all or nothing for you?"

Annie's face became contemplative. "My entire personal life is a gray area if you ask the general population. How could I have meaningful connections if I wasn't capable of accepting that not everything in life fits neatly into a box?" Annie rested her chin in her hand. "I'm quite flexible outside of work."

She laughed out loud. Annie's remarks once more took her by surprise. "I have no doubt you are." Harlen sipped her wine. Life with Annie would be anything but complacent, of that she was certain. She could almost picture the two of them spending time doing what they loved, like picnicking at one of the many vistas available in the state. All she had to do to get there was walk away from the shell of a human that resembled Chloe.

Chapter Twenty

Annie carried the basket of leftovers to the kitchen. "Would you like coffee?" she asked, calling to Harlen who had stopped to give Maisie love. Harlen joined her, a wide smile on her face.

"I've never met a cat like yours."

The realization Harlen meant it as a compliment wasn't hard to figure out. "She's quirky, like me." Annie shoved food into the refrigerator and stacked non-perishables on the counter. She lifted the carafe and pointed.

"Sorry. Yes, coffee sounds good." Harlen rubbed her arms. "That wind came out of nowhere."

She'd been preoccupied by thoughts of how flexible she could be in the bedroom when a frigid wind had whipped through the hillside, ending the serenity of their outing. "The temperature must have dropped at least ten degrees. I've got a chill."

"Can I warm you?" Harlen asked. Her nearness was a surprise. Annie turned to find her standing very close and her reflexes took over, creating more space between them. Harlen's face dropped. "I'm so sorry. I didn't—"

Annie shook her head. "It's fine. You have to ask if it's okay to invade my personal space if I don't expect it. Some people like me have to establish control of a situation before they can enjoy it." These were the times she wished she was neurotypical, even if wishing to be so were rare occurrences.

"That must be hard at times." Harlen's gaze moved to her mouth and her compassion melted Annie's heart. "What would be the best way to prepare you for intimacy?"

Annie heart began to drum. "You can say something like, 'Do you mind if I come closer?' or 'Can I touch you?'" Annie rarely had to explain the spatial requirements that most other people didn't think about. If she went with a woman with the clear expectation of having sex, closeness was expected. But they weren't in bed. Harlen hadn't even properly kissed her. Yet. She mentally crossed her fingers. The smoke screen they'd hidden behind was gone. Harlen's gaze was soft, kind yet focused.

"May I come closer, Annie?" Harlen's voice was a caress she longed for.

Oh, fuck. "Yes."

Harlen stood a foot away. "Will I need to ask every time we're being intimate?"

Annie's eyes fluttered in rhythm with her heartbeat. "Only until intimacy is established." She needed air. *Breathe, for God's sake.*

"Would a kiss establish intimacy?"

"Yes." She swallowed so hard she might have strained something. Did she say it out loud? Maybe she should say it again just to be sure, but she never got there because Harlen's lips covered hers firmly, but undemanding of more. Annie wanted and needed more. She responded by pressing back, slightly parting her lips to welcome Harlen in. Harlen groaned as she slipped inside and the fireworks Annie had doubted were anything more than urban legend exploded on her inner eyelids. Her knees wobbled. Harlen's lips moved away as her arm wrapped around Annie's waist.

"I've got you." Harlen returned to her needy mouth by kissing her cheek, her chin, her trembling lower lip.

Again, Annie wanted more. This time, she was the one to slip her tongue into the wet warmth of Harlen's mouth. She gently stroked her in counterpoint, wanting to memorize each point of contact. Every groan for more, and every moan of pleasure. The unique flavor of Harlen would be recalled later, along with the strength of her arms and the firmness of her body. Annie wanted to create a memory movie that she could replay whenever she wanted. She knew all too well how a perfect moment might not be repeated. Annie moved her hands over Harlen's shoulders and down her chest wanting more, wanting Harlen naked.

"Annie, we need to stop." Harlen touched her face, cupped her cheek.

"Why?"

Harlen softly smiled. "Because when we have sex for the first time, I don't think it should be rushed."

"Are we rushing?" Panic began to set in. "Date number three isn't rushing."

"True, but I want us to take our time tonight." Harlen kissed her without lingering. "We can rip our clothes off the next time."

Her whole body trembled. She'd been with enough women to know that wham bam, thank you, ma'am was not what she wanted, not with Harlen. Given they were already in the moment in all the ways that mattered, going slow was going to be a hard sell. Despite all of her fantasizing about frantic, hot sex, she considered slow might be better even when her body wanted no part in putting on the brakes.

"I can't argue with your reasoning."

"That's good." Harlen pulled her fingers through her unruly hair. "Because if you had said otherwise, things could get dicey fast."

Annie poured coffee into mugs. "Rain check on the kitchen counter sex then?" she asked, enjoying the playful interactions between them.

"Absolutely!" Harlen said as she added a little sugar and cream to hers.

"Do you want dessert now?"

Harlen raised her brow. "I thought we'd have dessert in the bedroom. We can have something sweet later."

This wasn't the first time during the day that Annie took note of how much more relaxed Harlen was. Not only in her way of speaking, but also in the ease with how she moved her body. Maybe the change in her job title had something to do with it, but Annie hoped it was more that their date was going exceptionally well. The awkwardness of their prior times together was missing. Whether their compatibility continued in the bedroom remained to be seen, but Annie had hope. The one emotion she'd never put stock in before.

❖

Harlen stood next to the bed, facing Annie. For all the innuendos swapped between them and the unmistakable desire she'd seen in Annie's eyes, perhaps nothing was as it appeared.

"Do you still want me to touch you, Annie?" Harlen held her fingertips an inch from Annie's neck.

"More than I thought possible." Annie's gaze remained steady. "You can start here." Annie took her hand and moved it to the top button.

Harlen reminded herself to go slow. Annie wasn't fragile by any means, but it was their first time.

"Like this?" She flicked the first button open. Annie's eyes sparkled as she nodded. "You'll have to use your words, baby. As much as I'd like to, I can't read your mind."

"Yes, like that." Annie kept her eyes on Harlen's.

"And this?" Flick two, then three. Annie made a little sound. She reached inside and cupped her breast, liking how Annie's hard nipple poked the material of her bra. Unable to resist, she pinched the point and Annie swore. Maybe she'd gone too far. "Should I stop?"

"If you do I'll slap you, and not in the fun, kinky kind of way." Annie's flushed face and half-lidded eyes spoke volumes.

"Does that mean you want me to hurry?" Harlen undid another button before trailing her fingertips lightly over Annie's exposed skin.

"Harlen," Annie said as she placed her hand on her shoulder. "This is the only place I like to give up control, but if you drag your feet, I'm going to take it back."

"No worries," Harlen said. The question of how to proceed answered, she grabbed the material of Annie's shirt and yanked, sending the two remaining buttons flying across the room before she pulled it all the way off. "Problem solved." She backed Annie to the bed. "Lie down."

Annie scrambled backward until she was in the middle. "Like this?" she asked. Her voice sounded anything but innocent.

"Uh-huh." Harlen began removing her clothes until all she wore was a sports bra and boxers, then she climbed beside her. "I like this." She traced the edge of deep purple lace where Annie's flesh was visible. Her skin erupted in gooseflesh as she panted. Without access to the clasp, Harlen tugged the material out of the way until both breasts were in full view. They were large with rosy centers and small nipples, the kind she loved to suck and bite. "I'm going to enjoy playing with your body."

"I'm okay with that." Annie's fingertips traced her jawline, her lips, and her cheekbones.

"You have a soft touch."

"I'm memorizing your body."

Harlen wondered if that was possible.

"Keep going."

Moving lower, Harlen placed her lips around Annie's nipple and sucked. "Do you like nipple play?"

"I do now."

Harlen smiled before running her tongue around the pebbled flesh, while palming the other. Annie groaned, fingers in Harlen's hair and pulling her in for a searing kiss. She kept squeezing and kneading Annie's pale flesh.

"You have an amazing mouth." Harlen's clothes were too tight.

"I know." Annie sat up. "These clothes have to go," she said as she tossed her bra in the air.

"It is freeing," Harlen proclaimed as she tossed her own. Annie reached for her panties. "Wait. Can I take them off?"

Annie lay back on her elbows. "I'm going to watch."

Harlen loved the banter they so easily fell into. The silk and lace looked good on Annie. She'd admire them later, kissing along her leg as she guided the fabric. Harlen met Annie's eyes.

"Don't stop."

She didn't.

"Now yours." Annie scooted against the headboard, hunger displayed on her face.

Harlen didn't make a show, though her boxers were gone and she was over Annie in an instant, her body pressed upward, ensuring contact. She'd wanted Annie from the start. How had the longing grown into this all-consuming desire in such a short time? What would happen after they had sex?

"What are you thinking about?"

"How much I want to touch you." Harlen swallowed back the white lie. She'd fucked up enough already.

"That's a great idea. I have an idea, too." Annie traced her lips. Harlen couldn't tell if she was going to like Annie's idea.

"What?"

"Show, don't tell."

It took her a minute to get it. Harlen captured Annie's mouth and pressed inside, moving her fingers to play at Annie's nipple, before going lower. Annie pushed her away.

"Air," Annie said, gasping before laughing. "How can you breathe?"

"I'm a swimmer." She hadn't been in months. There was no excuse since she wasn't going to the hospital. Being in the pool gave her nonstop brain a break.

"That explains your body." Annie lightly scored along her sides before moving on to her ass. "An exceptional ass, too. How lucky can a woman be?" For a split second, Harlen thought Annie might be joking until she squeezed both cheeks. "The padding will be good when I ride you."

"Are you trying to distract me?" she asked, brushing her fingertips through fine curly hair and into the slickness. Annie's chest arched. The hunger hit her hard. Her penance of being alone was done. Harlen wanted to feel alive again. She wanted someone to care about her for a change. Annie might be her savior. She needed to have faith in what they had together.

❖

Annie might have whimpered. She couldn't be sure. Harlen's fingers were moving in and out slowly, each time a little deeper. She didn't want to come this soon. They'd only just begun, right?

"God, you feel amazing," Harlen said, her lips exploring Annie's tummy. At some point, Harlen had straddled one leg, her hot slick center coating her thigh. "I've fantasized about watching you come." Her thumb rubbed her clit, her fingered buried inside.

"Was that all? Me coming?" Even during sex conversations, Annie wasn't going to hold back. Her orgasm would take over soon.

"No, baby." Harlen bent for a kiss. A hard, mashing of mouths while knuckles deep. "I won't stop until you beg me to."

Like a tidal wave, it struck unannounced, coating Harlen's hand and dripping from her center. Harlen slowed to the contractions, meeting them in time. On and on until the spark flared inside her, and Harlen knew as she stretched her throbbing pussy to give her more. She'd come so hard. "I don't know if I can come again." Her gasps beginning to recede.

"Yes, yes, you can. I've got you." Harlen rubbed her clit.

"Fuck." Annie cried out, grabbing at the sheets, hoping it was enough to ground her. She swore she rose off the bed like someone possessed when she climaxed. Harlen's mumbles were lost in her screams. Seconds, minutes, hours? "What the actual fuck," she moaned, once she got her voice back.

Harlen chuckled and helped her up to drink. Her face turned serious. "You didn't want fireworks?" To her credit, she maintained the innocent demeanor longer than Annie would have been able to before she burst out laughing. "So, it was good."

Annie slapped her. "Yes. It was spectacular."

Harlen fist pumped.

She slapped her again. "You did not just pull a macho move."

"Of course not. It was a gigolo move." Harlen tried not to smile around the bottle, dribbling a little.

"I'll have to think what my signature move will be after I return the favor."

"Oh, really? And what are you going to do to earn a move?"

Annie pushed Harlen to her back and adjusted pillows. "I'm going to do what I do best." She slid lower, tucking pillows under Harlen's knees. "I'm going to use my mouth." Priceless was the word that came to mind as Annie focused on Harlen's semi-shaved center. Pearls of moisture hung to the hairs and she liked that she was responsible. The night was going well. Her only worry was if there'd be another once she told Harlen about knowing where she recognized her from.

Chapter Twenty-one

"How do you want me to touch you?" Harlen asked.

A hundred fantasies featuring Harlen in the starring role flashed before Annie. Each held a vision of how they would play out. Harlen was giving her an opportunity to have one of them come true.

"Touch me everywhere. Like you're touching me in so many places I can't think." Telling Harlen what she wanted was much harder than she thought it would be. Harlen's fingers stroked her inner thigh, her thumb brushing the sensitive folds.

"Is there anything you don't want me to do?" Harlen kissed the outside of her breast, her ribs, her tummy. Her hands roamed over her body, exploring every inch.

"Not that I can…" She trailed off when Harlen gathered moisture from her opening, painted her nipple with it, then licked it off. "Oh, God."

Harlen smiled down at her as she moved over her and lowered to her forearms. "I've been called a lot of things, Ms. Duncan. God wasn't one of them." She nipped at her lower lip.

"Are you having fun?" Annie squirmed beneath her, chasing whatever pressure she could find for relief. Harlen appeared content to deny her need at the moment.

"I am." Harlen nipped the skin at her throat, sending new ripples of excitement through her and causing her frustration to spike. "Are you?"

"No. Yes." She couldn't think coherently. Harlen *was* everywhere. How was that even possible?

"Which is it?" Harlen straddled her thighs and squeezed her breasts in a firm and delightful way.

"Both. Your touches aren't where I need them." Annie wiggled some more. Harlen pinned her hands next to her ears.

"Can you stay like that?" Harlen's fingers tightened on her wrists.

"It might kill me." *But as long as you get to my clit in the next thirty seconds...*

Harlen smiled. "Just think how every time you move, I stop."

This really was torture, in the best possible way. "I'll try to remember that."

Harlen let go and kissed her possessively. After each kiss, Annie thought it would be the last one before she moved to a different part of her body, only to have to wait again and again. She touched Harlen's muscled back. Harlen rose on her elbows.

"Please?"

Harlen's eyes flared like hot embers. "Don't touch me until I'm done."

"Harlen, please. I can't take it anymore." She was close to begging with more than a simple please, but Harlen didn't need to know that. Giving up control only went so far in Annie's book.

"Sure you can. You have complete control in deciding to move or hold still and let me do whatever I want to you." Harlen licked her lips.

How would those lips feel on Annie's hot, slick, needy pussy? Would she last more than a few minutes, or would having contact of any kind send her soaring into climax territory? Annie took each light touch on her body, each stroke of Harlen's tongue in all the wrong places until she stopped trying to control the pace. Harlen moved lower. Soon, the anticipation was too much for her to bear. She palmed Harlen's breast, knowing she'd pay for it.

"I'm sorry. I had to feel you."

"Not good enough, Annie."

"I want to cum, God damn it." The look on Harlen's face was hard to discern.

"How?"

She didn't answer because her brain was no longer functioning.

Harlen held her chin. "How do you want me to make you cum?"

Annie short-circuited. "I don't care. Fuck me, lick me. Just… please do it." Annie would have flipped Harlen over and ridden her thigh like her favorite dildo if she wasn't afraid Harlen would stop again. Maybe for good the next time. She groaned when Harlen entered her.

"Is this what you want, baby? You want me to finger fuck you?" She added a second.

"Yes, yes." Annie wanted to feel how wet Harlen was, but she was too far away, her arms too short. She couldn't risk another delay.

"You're so velvety and wet, baby. So tight around me." She stroked in and out a few times, the knuckle on her thumb tapping Morse code on her clit. "Do you want more?"

Annie groaned. Her orgasm continued to build, but it was taking its sweet time. Time Annie had no intention of suffering through. Warmth surrounded her throbbing clit. Harlen was between her legs, watching her. She began to lick between thrusts, gently at first. As she grew harder, Harlen sucked in counterpoint to the thrusts that were so deep inside, stroking her walls, she couldn't breathe. Harlen stopped. She looked along her belly.

"It's going to feel so good when you cum, baby."

Harlen entered and turned her hand. Her mouth latched on to her clit and she began to suck and lick. Annie's body tensed. Heat rose along her torso until it reached her face, and her heart pounded like a tom-tom drum. The vibration was so strong, Annie felt it everywhere. She held Harlen's head to her center. The explosion ripped incohesive words from her mouth. She might have been screaming, but the pounding of her clit and the rhythmic clutching of her walls around Harlen's fingers were all that mattered. Her orgasm went on and on.

"Holy fuck." Annie gasped, her fingers still entwined in Harlen's hair. "Damn." She chuckled weakly.

"Mmm." Harlen hummed against her inner thigh. "I couldn't agree more." Her lips moved to the top of her slit to kiss the spot. The intimacy of the moment wasn't lost on her and she filed it for later examination. "I'm going to pull out." With slow care, Harlen removed her fingers, and a wave of weak contractions followed.

Annie sighed at the loss.

"I know, baby. We should have gotten water." Harlen stood and stepped into her boxers. "And maybe dessert?" Harlen's stomach rumbled.

She laughed. "I guess I need to move." Annie rolled to the edge and put her feet on the floor. When she stood, the room spun, and her arms stuck out, trying to find balance.

"Whoa, hang on." Harlen's hands rested on her hips, hers on Harlen's shoulders.

We should go dancing. Now who's in their head too much? She laughed. "That was one hell of a head rush."

Harlen ducked her head until their eyes met. "You good?"

"Yup." Annie glanced around on the floor

"Here." She handed Annie her underwear and bra. "I'm afraid your shirt needs repair."

Annie took the items. "Worth every penny." She stepped into the crumpled underwear. "I'm not wearing these." Annie tossed the wrinkled slacks into a hamper by her closet door. She found a pair of lounge pants and pulled them on. "They'll swim on you, but I've got more of these."

Harlen rummaged in a bright blue duffle. "Thanks, I'm good." She yanked out a pair of sweats and retrieved her flannel shirt from the bedpost.

"Where did you get that from?"

"I went to the car when you went to the bathroom and stashed it in the hall closet." Harlen had a moment of guilt for the sneaky action.

"Why didn't you bring it in when we got back?" Annie pulled a sweatshirt over her bird's nest hair.

"Assumptions can be wrong." Harlen had been a fool to think Chloe would love her forever even though she'd assumed otherwise. Things happened in life that sucked. People got over them and moved on. Harlen hoped she was moving on, too.

Annie came to her. "Hey," she said softly, waiting until Harlen looked up. "I'm not the one who hurt you. You weren't wrong to assume with me."

The shuddery breath she took spoke volumes. "Thank you. I'm working on learning the difference."

Annie took her hand. "Come on. There's coffee and a delightful cheesecake to be had."

They took a couple of steps before Harlen stopped. "I like knowing where I stand with you."

"Like I said, I'm not like most people you know." Annie tugged her along.

There was more to be shared, but this wasn't the time for a heart to heart. The only decision she needed to make was how long she'd keep from telling Annie about her commitment to Chloe.

Harlen stared at the spreadsheets, lists, and various other documents laid out across the folding table she'd brought from home for her sparse office. The company management, aka her grandparents, insisted that the "design director" had to have a walled office to meet with clients. Over the last week, she'd begun the daunting task of separating her acquisitions work from her design work.

A few of her younger cousins were doing internships while they worked on their college degrees, others decided to wait before they committed to college to earn a degree they wouldn't use or need. Grandpa was okay with either way of thinking, but her grandmother insisted everyone needed to pick a passion *and* get a degree because "You never know what the future holds." Harlen was living proof of that ideology.

"I think you're going to need a secretary." Her mother leaned against the doorway, a potted plant in her hands.

"Hi, Mom. What brings you down to the bottom dwellers?" It was an inside joke. Harlen liked working somewhat closer to the ground floor. The high-rise was located in a walkable part of the city, and the foot traffic, while nothing like New York City, was steady. It had a nicer view than watching birds crash into the plate glass windows, a common occurrence above her floor.

"Every office needs greenery." She set her gift on the corner of Harlen's desk, turning it until she nodded her approval. "What are you doing here?" She pointed at the sea of papers.

"Thanks for the plant." Harlen kissed her cheek. "I'm making a mess." Anxiety coursed through her. Maybe she'd bitten off more than she could chew. Starting from scratch was proving to be much harder than she originally thought. Her mom's arm circled her waist.

"That doesn't sound like the determined woman I spoke with a couple of weeks ago. Tell me what you're hung up on."

Harlen explained how she was buying staging items with the generous start-up budget she'd been given. "As pieces come in, I need to check for damage, log them into the inventory system, and give each item at least one tag for location purposes."

Her mother picked up the one-page spreadsheet. "Explain how that works."

"Let's say I buy a side chair and I tag it as LR for living room. But it could also be used in a den, bedroom, etc. If I'm designing or redesigning a bedroom and that chair would be perfect, I won't know its multiple uses if I only mark it for the living room."

"Ah, that makes sense. So where are you stuck?"

Harlen ran her fingers through her hair. "I need to know where to find the pieces once they're coded. If I only have one of a particular chair, how do I locate it in the warehouse?" She'd been looking for a solution for the last hour.

"Color-coding might work." Mom put the spreadsheet in its original place. "The chair's primary use is in the living room, so it makes sense to store it with other living room pieces."

"Go on." Harlen's mind began to work again.

"Let's say you code the living room column blue and those items are stored in the blue section of the warehouse. You can still check off the chair for use in other rooms, but you'd find it in the blue section, or primary use area, of the warehouse."

Harlen studied the purchased items lists and spreadsheet. Her mother's suggestion could work. It would take time to code what she already had, but she could use the same method for her reference pictures, coding them in a similar way. She kissed her mother resoundingly on the cheek.

"Oh my. What was that for?" Her mother blushed a delightful shade of pink.

"You're a genius. This will solve the problem, Mom." She tapped the table, excited to start color coding her inventory. An X next to an item would indicate its primary use and location, and a check mark in other columns would indicate it was appropriate for those rooms, too.

"You got your genes from someone, dear." Her mother patted her arm. "Don't forget to tag the items with the color code, too. Unless you plan on doing all the grunt work yourself, staff will need to know where to return items." Her mom smiled and headed for the door. "Water your plant once a week."

"Love you, Mom."

"Love you too, dear."

She gathered up the papers. With a reasonable solution found, she needed to catch up on categorizing everything in the warehouse. Her mother had been instrumental in her pursuit of her bachelor's degree and fine arts focus. Until now, her college years had almost felt like a waste of time.

"At least something is going my way." She mouthed the thought out loud. Harlen smiled as the last date with Annie crossed her mind. "Okay, two things."

When she left Annie's the morning after their picnic, there hadn't been any indication that what they shared was a one and done event. Sex with Annie was not only hot, but fun. Who knew sex was even better when she was relaxed enough to do something silly or crack a joke? Since then, they had texted or spoken every day except for one. Annie said she was struggling with an ethical issue that needed resolution but didn't expand, and Harlen hadn't asked. Harlen had her own dilemma to resolve. Annie might be the impetus, but how she reached a resolution was all on her.

"I'm stuck."

"On what?" Jane stood in the doorway. Family week was every week at work.

"Hi." The last thing she needed was having another discussion about Chloe with Jane. "It's nothing."

"Liar," Jane said affectionately.

"Things with Annie are good." She didn't quite know how to tell Jane what she'd been doing.

Jane stepped closer, her brows knit. "And you're feeling stuck already?"

Harlen pointed to the leather chair facing her. She hated having conversations when she had to look up, making her feel like what she had to say was insignificant. "Stuck as in what to tell her about Chloe."

Jane rolled her eyes. "Big sis, we've had this conversation. You tell her she was your partner before an accident left her in a vegetative state, and you're ready to move on."

Harlen sat still, the weight of her ongoing predicament pushing her deeper into the chair. She couldn't lie to Jane and she didn't want to lie to Annie.

"Shit. You still haven't let go. That's where you're stuck." Jane's tone went from a normal level to peak annoyance in record time. "What the fuck, Har."

She got up and closed the door. Just because she didn't have any clients scheduled didn't mean the rest of the office had to know her business. When she dropped into her chair, Jane pinned her there with a laser gaze. Mount Vesuvius was going to blow.

"Stop seeing Annie."

"No." Harlen intended on standing her ground.

"You're treating her like her feelings don't matter if you're still not willing to walk away from a corpse." Jane had a reputation for being blunt, something she had in common with Annie. She'd always admired the trait, except when she was on the receiving end.

"That's harsh." Even as she pushed back, Harlen knew Jane was right.

"Too bad. It's the truth." Jane scooted to the edge of her seat. "You say you like Annie and that you want to see where the relationship goes, but I don't believe you. How can it go anywhere when you're still involved with Chloe?" Jane was adamant and tenacious when it came to family.

Harlen winced. Jane jumped up and began to pace.

"You're still visiting her bedside, aren't you?"

She nodded. "Before work, when I know her parents aren't around." The last time she visited Chloe had been a close call. Her mother was dropping off a Christmas cactus, hoping it was in bloom when Chloe woke up. A nurse's aide had hustled Harlen out of the room before she got caught.

"What are you thinking?" Jane asked, demanding an answer.

Harlen's temper flared. It was her turn to stand. "I don't know!" Why was she arguing when she knew she was the reason the situation was a fiasco. "Everyone keeps telling me to walk away, but no one thinks about how they'd act if the situation was reversed." Emotions ran high in the Forrest clan because passions ran deep. From the start, she'd been passionate about her relationship with Chloe. It didn't matter that Chloe had called it quits before the accident. Though she'd postured about leaving, Chloe hadn't walked away. She was right there, in the hospital. Maybe if she woke up, she'd regret saying she was done, and if Harlen gave up and moved on… A sob escaped. Jane held her. Nothing could shake the loving bond they shared.

"You know as well as I do Chloe isn't coming back to you, Har." She held her by the shoulders, forcing her to meet Jane's gaze. "Chloe isn't coming back to anyone because she's already gone. For that, I really am sorry." She thumbed away tears Harlen hadn't noticed. "If you have any emotional ties to Annie, she deserves to hear what's going on in that thick skull of yours." She pressed her finger to the middle of Harlen's forehead. "Don't build her up to let her down. That's not fair to either of you."

Harlen hated when Jane was right. She was always right. It was kind of spooky. "I'll tell her, I promise."

Jane hugged her and left. She had some work to do on herself before she could explain to Annie why she hadn't told her the truth. That she still loved Chloe and was driven to keep her promise. Annie was a reasonable person. She'd understand that Harlen enjoyed her company and sex between them had been great, but her loyalty remained with Chloe. Not sexual, of course, but just as solid a commitment. Annie wouldn't have an issue with giving her some time to cut herself loose.

"Ha." Who was she kidding? If the situation was reversed, Harlen couldn't guarantee she'd be as generous.

Harlen put her head on her desk, refraining from banging the surface until she knocked some sense into herself. She wasn't ready to let either woman go. What did that say about her as a person? How could she be in love with two people at—

She bolted upright. "No. No. No."

There was no way she could be in love with Annie. She barely knew her. One sexual encounter did not equal love. Did it? Harlen pulled her phone off the bookshelf next to her desk. She scrolled through her favorites and pressed the call icon.

"Hey, stranger. Do you miss me?" Dan asked in her "Knew it would happen" tone.

"I need your help." No matter what situation Harlen found herself in, she could always count on Dan to make her see things from a different perspective. She needed that now more than ever. Between the sneaking in to see Chloe and hiding her situation from Annie, Harlen was sending out an SOS signal.

"Where?"

Relief forced the air from her lungs. "Bring a bottle to the house. I'll order food."

"See you at six."

Communicating with her best friend was so much easier than communicating with the person she was sleeping with. Until then, Harlen had work to do. Fingers-crossed she could concentrate without screwing up one more thing.

Chapter Twenty-two

"Remember that girl in tenth grade who had a crush on you, and you got all scared because her boobs were big and you thought you might smother?" Dan refilled the shot glasses, then handed off a set to her.

"Good times." Harlen held them up.

"To not being afraid of boobs."

"Hear, hear." She downed the whiskey and followed with a shot of pickle juice. Picklebacks had been her and Dan's go-to drink when one of them was in a quandary and needed intervention.

Dan shivered after hers. "No matter how many of these I drink, that pickle juice gets me every time."

"So, it's the juice, not the alcohol?"

"Yep." Dan grabbed a handful of salted nuts and tossed a couple in her mouth. "Just so I have the story correct, you and Annie had a great date followed by a fantastic time in bed, and now you're thinking of calling it off because…?"

"When you say it, the whole thing sounds ridiculous."

"Not true, my friend." Dan tossed the last of her nuts and poured another round. "*You* sound ridiculous."

"Another already?"

"Stop whining. This situation calls for the heavy hitters." Dan tossed back the amber fireball followed by the cloudy neon green chaser, then shivered. "Shit."

Harlen laughed. She'd left the beverage choice to Dan and didn't feel the least bit sorry for her. She might have been in a dirty martini frame of mind if the decision had been hers. Like Dan said, tonight was not a night for the timid.

"You're still going to the hospital," Dan said, stating rather than asking.

She knew it was useless to make excuses for her behavior. "Once a week."

Dan faced her. "To make yourself feel better?" When she didn't answer, Dan shook her head. "To what end, Har? You don't have a future with Chloe."

Dan didn't have to tell her what she already knew, but apparently she needed to hear it from multiple sources. "That's why I need you. I keep thinking there has to be a way to keep my promise *and* move on." She laughed sarcastically. "You'd think after all this time I'd have learned it's hopeless."

Dan rested her hand on Harlen's thigh and squeezed. "Having hope the first six months was understandable. You're well past that point. You've given her every day since that night, and you never stopped loving her and you probably never will." She squeezed again. "It's time to remember that Chloe will never recover. She'll never walk this earth again, nor will she ever have to know how it feels to not be loved by you. You gave her the best you had." Dan moved closer. "Chloe showed you what kind of love you were capable of giving. Don't let that message slip away, Har." Dan snatched the tattered book from her coffee table. "There's a reason you keep reading this, too." She studied Harlen, her eyes searching.

She'd read *Carly's Sound* by Ali Vali for the first time in college. When she closed the cover, Harlen couldn't wait to start reading the book again. People asked about the story because she carried it everywhere for a year before ordering a second copy. If she lost the book in the middle of a read…well, she didn't want to think about it. The book's lost love had many similarities to Chloe. Not all, of course, but enough. It was more than that though.

Poppy, the main character, showed her what real love meant. For the second time that day, Harlen started to sob in big, breath-stealing gulps. Dan pulled her in for the kind of hug she reserved giving only to Harlen. The kind of ride or die friend she was lucky enough to find.

"It's so hard." She struggled to breathe, let alone speak.

"Yeah. I get that." Dan let her go. She was surprised by the tears on Dan's cheeks. "You're still being an asshole when it comes to Annie."

"Oh, I'm sure you'll keep reminding me." Harlen reached for the bottle before meeting Dan's gaze, silently asking if they should keep drinking.

"I don't see why not. If we're going to keep to tradition, I'm going to have to be loaded enough to sleep in your shitty guest bed."

"Hey." Harlen chuckled. The bed needed to be replaced at least a few years ago. "You're special. You can have the couch."

"Down the hatch." Dan managed to suppress the ensuing shiver. Mostly. Once she recovered, she picked up the remote. "Do you know what you're going to do?"

Harlen sat back, content to let the buzz in her head lull her. "Not a clue."

"Glad we worked that out," Dan said. "Sci-fi or crime drama?"

"Fiction. I've had enough of reality for one night." As the opening credits ran, Harlen thought about Annie. She'd never settle for Harlen's explanation if she didn't tell her soon, before she was invested any further. Did being in love leave any room for excuses?

❖

Annie studied the printout of SFN's current corporate sponsors and individual supporters. When she added in the staff, there were over a hundred names, half of whom might bring a guest. She would have liked it higher, but it was a good number for her first gala. The best part was how well-prepared she was when she presented the idea to Allison. As the president of the organization, Allison had the distinct privilege of having the only veto to use at her discretion. Of course, Annie was pretty sure her coworkers hadn't made a slide presentation and a mock-up flyer to help with the publicity that would be required.

The only thing left was obtaining a firmer estimate on expenses and the possible monetary gain from such an event. Annie knew that elaborate and elegant didn't mean the same thing. She would put together a cost-conscious list without fireworks or other extravagant displays.

As she laid out the columns for the revised estimation, Annie grumbled under her breath. A lot of autistic people enjoyed dealing with concrete facts. Numbers fell into that realm, but she'd never found an appreciation for spreadsheets or how they worked. She was afflicted by transposing numbers. The same thing sometimes happened when she typed out memos and letters. Initially, when she typed a sentence or paragraph, she put them in the order they were imagined. A second or third read-through revealed hard to understand phrases, often due to their reversed order.

When Annie woke the morning Harlen had stayed over, she sat at the kitchen table staring at her laptop, her brows knit in frustration.

"Good morning."

"Morning," Annie said distractedly.

Harlen got coffee and joined her. "What are you working on?"

Annie growled. "I'm staring at the screen because what I wrote isn't working." She explained what she was trying to convey and how she put words or phrases in an unconventional order, making it hard to read.

Harlen suggested a trick she'd learned in college. "Write without any punctuation, one line at a time. When you read what you wrote a few times out loud, you'll naturally stop where there should be a comma or kind of a break. The next read-through will give you an opportunity to change the order of words to make the meaning clearer. Those changes may affect punctuation but help the structure." Harlen smiled and kissed her cheek before heading to the shower.

The battle over numbers was different and those rules wouldn't be of help. Maybe she could see if there was any trick for spreadsheets. Harlen had a busy week with her new position. They hadn't seen each other since they had sex, but that was okay. Annie wasn't in any hurry to reach the point of discussing the "next step" of their relationship. She chewed her lip. Every day that passed was a lost opportunity to come clean with Harlen about the accident that led to Chloe being in a coma. The police report stated that black ice had been the culprit, but Annie couldn't help thinking if she hadn't stayed late at work that night, she wouldn't have been on the road when Chloe was. There wasn't an easy way to tell Harlen. Annie wasn't going to *not* tell her, but they'd had such a good time before, during, and after sex, which was saying something, she didn't want to burst the expanding bubble.

"It's not fair," she said.

"Aww…what's not fair, Annie?" Michael sauntered through her open door with a steaming cup of an espresso concoction revealed by the strong scent. A small plate held a cheese Danish.

"You need to stop pampering me, Michael." She couldn't decide which to have first.

"The coffee looks hotter than it is, but the Danish will cool quicker."

"You heated it?"

"Of course. You like your cheese Danish warmed."

"How do you know all these things?" she asked before biting a small corner of the gooey sweet goodness, followed by a tentative sip. As promised, the coffee was the perfect drinking temperature.

"It's my job to know things." He smiled in a way that pulled her from the melancholy that had threatened to flip her mood.

"How's your schedule look for today?" She nibbled on more of the pastry, wanting to savor the treat.

"It's quiet." He tapped his knuckles on her wooden desk, then straightened a pile of magazines on the corner.

"Do you have time to do a bit of research?" She hated asking anyone to help her do her job, but in some cases it was necessary.

"Heck yeah. My days revolve around answering the phone, scheduling meetings, and knowing what the staff like. Research will be a fun change." Michael produced his phone, tapped it twice, then looked up, excitement written all over his face. "What do you need?"

Ten minutes later, Michael practically ran out of her office, anxious to start researching the cost for formal invitations. Annie considered sending out an electronic invitation for the gala, however, she was a firm believer in paper ones. People liked the significance of receiving a "hand delivered" invitation as a show of respect. The recipient was of importance to the sender. Annie had read somewhere that the tradition stemmed from England and the United Kingdom, where anything less than a written invitation was a societal slap in the face.

To tell the truth though, Annie was excited for an occasion to dress up. There was another reason, too. By the time the winter ball came around, she hoped there'd be no doubt who she would invite to escort her. Harlen would be turning heads. The image appeared on its own as she stared into space, lost in another fantasy.

Harlen could easily pull off a black tux. A ruffled shirt would offset her harder lines. Maybe a hint of color with a pocket square. Annie wouldn't try to match her. That wasn't her thing. People commented on her quirky style with good reason. It was one of the character traits Annie loved about herself. Maybe Harlen would go with a gray tux and a royal blue shirt to bring out her eye color. Maybe Harlen wasn't the tux type at all. Her fantasy refused to believe that was the case.

Annie would need to go shopping. She hated shopping. Styles for today's full-shaped woman hadn't gotten much better over the years. For a woman like Annie, who had just entered her fifties but felt and dressed like she was in her thirties, there was even less to choose from. If she had known selections wouldn't improve, she might have put a concerted effort into the size fourteen to twenty-eight clothing industry. Other than work clothes, Annie hadn't ventured into evening wear for a formal occasion.

"Annie?" Michael stood at her open door, a look of wonder on his face. "Can I clarify something since I think autocorrect struck again."

Annie's heart thudded in her chest. She'd been so wrapped up in fantasyland, hearing Michael startled her. "Sure." She was only half listening, though she managed to answer the two questions he had. A few minutes later, and with her door closed, she began the daunting task of filling the spreadsheet with the information she'd gathered so far. All she had to do was figure out the column headings, put in the auto sum code that she somehow always did wrong on the first try, and keep her fingers crossed. Maybe she should have given this part to Michael and done the research herself.

Chapter Twenty-three

Harlen grabbed a beer and dropped to the couch. She hadn't been this tired from work in years. It didn't help that she'd been pulling double duty to train the part-time person taking on acquisitions while she stocked the warehouse. The combination meant she was working twelve-hour days. Still, it was better than full-time in a job she hated.

With her feet on the coffee table, she picked up the stack of mail that had accumulated. She pulled out the three magazines she always made time to read and tossed them beside her feet. A mass of postcards from various businesses made up a good portion of the remaining mail. Harlen fingered through the rest, stopping at a padded manilla envelope. She didn't recognize the return address. The contents, a folded piece of paper and an SD card, elevated her curiosity. She unfolded the paper, expecting a promotional advertisement.

Dear Harlen,

I hope you are well. I'm a coworker of Chloe's and recently came across a video of a holiday party from a few years ago. The staff who knew Chloe watched it and were moved beyond tears, but we also laughed and smiled at Chloe's obvious joy.

We hope you find comfort by the reminder of what a vibrant person Chloe was.

Take care, Jackie

Her heart pounded in her chest. Harlen wasn't the only one who had a hard time believing Chloe was gone. This was an of out of the blue event that came when she needed it.

She had plenty of photos of Chloe and the two of them together. The video of Chloe was priceless. She held the SD card and stared at the miniscule handwritten title, Holiday Office Party.

Shortly after graduation, Harlen went to work at the family business while she figured out what to do with her degree. Chloe had been so happy to land an intern job with the local newspaper that she'd rambled on for days after getting the call. They moved in together following a steamy summer of sex.

Harlen retrieved her laptop. Her fingers shook as she slipped the tiny disc into place. As much as she wanted to catch a glimpse of Chloe alive, she dreaded stirring up the pain that would undoubtedly follow. After several failed attempts at keying up the right driver, she made herself take a minute to gather her thoughts. This could be the connection she'd longed for since the morning she watched Chloe leave for work and never come home.

She tried not to anticipate what she might see and clicked the arrow. There weren't any graphic introductions or a title emblazoned across the screen. Christmas music played in the background and the entire room displayed tacky holiday decorations. People moved in and out of the space without narration. The pan was a bit shaky, but not bad. The person taking it had the wherewithal to keep their fingers out of the way. Harlen guessed the cubicles in the center of the open floor space housed the staff. A couple of tables laden with food and beverages had been pushed up against one wall. The photographer tried to snag a cookie, but was stopped by a slap on their hand.

"Don't you dare." A female voice threatened. Harlen sat up and clicked to pause. *It couldn't be.* Harlen had hoped for a glimpse. Perhaps hear her infectious laughter a time or two. Hearing Chloe's voice was a gift. This was all she'd have of Chloe alive and well a few months before she wasn't.

After she listened again, Harlen knew it was Chloe. What she hadn't been prepared for was the close-up of a radiant-looking Chloe, so different from the pale wisp of the woman she was now, and whose hair had begun to thin. Her eyes were full of joy, and the mischievous glint was hard to miss. Harlen could only recall the veil-thin lids and the blue-green veins that ran through them.

"Merry Christmas, Betty." Chloe reached for something, then presented it to Betty. "I'm really not a Grinch, you know." Chloe held three different cookies on a holiday napkin.

"You're sweet. I'll tuck them for later. I'm trying to get the beginning, middle, and end of the party." Betty swung the camera away. "Thanks for getting us in the spirit."

Harlen hit pause. That was Chloe alright. She loved everything about the celebratory season between Halloween and New Year's. She decorated for each annual event without it being gaudy, unlike the office, but she didn't judge if others celebrated or not.

"Just because *I* love this time of year doesn't mean everyone has to, Harlen. It's a choice." That was Chloe, clarifying why she wasn't upset when people treated the season as any other.

The trip to the kitchen for another beer was as necessary as the detour to the bathroom. This time she brought tissues. There was bound to be another sighting of Chloe. The next image on the screen was out of focus. Words of "Here, like this," and "No, no. This way," followed as the view tipped up and down at a dizzying rate. For a second, she thought she'd have to stop watching, but someone had their wits about them and righted the picture. Harlen was grateful.

The screen changed to a conference room, the table crammed with people eating, drinking, and laughing. The music had changed from traditional to contemporary, and heads were bopping. The primary colors of everything were red and green, with some silver and gold thrown in here and there. Harlen missed not seeing the house decorated, a tradition she hadn't had the heart to continue without Chloe. Another pan and a pause on Chloe leaning against a wall, holding a plate of food in one hand, a fork in the other, waving it like a baton as she talked with a vaguely familiar woman. Harlen had accompanied Chloe to a retirement dinner a few years ago. Maybe they'd spoken.

"How'd you end up with the honors, Mike?" Chloe wrinkled her nose. Harlen wasn't sure if it was because of something she ate, or something she saw that caused the reaction.

"Betty is a bit into the spiked punch." That explained the jumbled section.

"She isn't driving." It wasn't a question. More like a direct statement. No one messed with Chloe when she was serious.

"Uber."

"Okay, then. Punch away."

There were a few shots of Chloe in the background. They were a little grainy, but she had no trouble picking her out. She knew Chloe better than she knew herself. Every detail, every mole and scar and freckle. Each mood, every desire, wish, and want. The woman in the video was the woman she remembered so well her heart ached.

Only a few minutes were left on the video. She'd made it this far. The camera panned slowly before stopping at the decimated remnants of food. A similar shot of the conference rooms showed piles of paper plates and overflowing garbage. Down the hallway, people talked in low voices. It was obviously well past the party stage. Chloe came into the frame with some others who'd pulled chairs from cubicles into the walkway to talk or listen.

"You still filming?" Chloe blew across a hot beverage in the work mug Harlen had bought her when she started the job. It depicted a newspaper with a headline, "World's Greatest Shopper." Chloe had been excited. "It's perfect."

"Almost done," Mike said, "Any parting words?" He didn't know how fateful his question had been.

"Yeah. Hold on." Chloe held her mug and stared into the contents. The frame froze and for the first time in a very long time, Harlen admitted her sadness. When she started the video again Chloe smiled at the camera. "I believe holidays are meant to be celebrated. Like in life, you have to find what brings you happiness. Whatever makes your heart light, wish for that. Always. Merry Christmas." She held up her mug and drank as the solemn toast resounded and the video ended.

Harlen sat unmoving. There was a lot to process. She was surprised she hadn't cried. Maybe she'd done enough crying about Chloe, or the changes that happened when Chloe said it was over, and about the unresolved issues that remained. It was well past midnight when Harlen woke, slumped over, her arm pins and needled from being caught under her weight.

Rubbing her face, Harlen wondered if she'd be able to sleep once she got between the sheets. She was exhausted. Bed sounded like the perfect solution. She pulled the covers around her. The brisk air from the window reminded her summer was gone for good. Things being gone seemed to be the motto lately. But deciphering what had to happen next would have to wait. The sandman had arrived and it was one feeling she wasn't about to fight.

"Come on. It will be fun." Char chomped on her salad.

Annie had called her for a lunch date. The office had become stifling, Harlen was ghosting her—sort of—and planning the gala was far more time-consuming than she could have imagined. "Why do you want to dress up like a freak?" Annie didn't mean it as in a weird freak. Char came up with the bright idea that she needed cheering up and what better way than to go to a Halloween costume party.

"You hurt my heart." Char feigned a mortal wound, then kept eating. Never get between Char and her meal. Never. "It'll be fun."

"Fun is a subjective definition." As much as she was protesting, there was a little part of her that wanted to do something silly. Lord knows, her mood could use a boost.

"You don't have to do a thing. I'll put together your costume." Char wiped her mouth and smiled.

"Gee, that's sweet of you. No." The last time she'd left her wardrobe choice for an event to Char had been a disaster. She looked like a bumble bee, all yellow-and-black stripes and accessories…for a nighttime retirement dinner. Char had gone goth, and she got fewer stares than Annie.

"I remember when you used to be fun."

"I was never fun." Annie dipped focaccia bread into her tomato basil soup and tasted pure heaven. The spice was just right in the thick, rich broth and the homemade bread slathered with butter made for the perfect bite. "I was undisciplined."

Char sat up. "Since when did you give up your bad-girl, badass persona?"

Annie didn't have to be a mind reader to catch the reference to her twenties when she was known as the woman who took what she wanted, no questions asked. "Since I turned thirty."

"Huh, that long ago?"

Annie threw her crumpled napkin at Char, making her laugh. Annie stuck her tongue out.

Char pointed her fork. "You better keep that lethal weapon in your mouth."

The number of times Annie blushed was a lot less than the number of women she'd slept with, but it was happening more often. She closed her mouth and covered her heated skin with a good scrubbing from a fresh napkin.

"Are you going to the party with me or not?" This was the first time she saw real doubt on Char's face. Annie needed to examine her friendship status. Just because she was fixated on Harlen and their questionable status didn't mean she could neglect the people who mattered to her.

"Since when have I ever said no to you?"

Char brightened. "Never."

Annie pushed her empty bowl to the side and unwrapped the oversized peanut butter cookie. She broke off half and slid the other to Char. "What are you thinking of wearing?"

"Well," Char began, her voice as excited as her big eyes and wide smile indicated. "I might go traditional with a vampire or witch, but that's not really my cup of tea."

Annie could only imagine what brew Char would come up with.

Char licked crumbs from her lips. "What are you going to go as?"

Annie wrinkled her nose. "Not a bumble bee, that's for sure." Agreeing to go with Char was a no-brainer. It would provide her something else to think about besides Harlen. Still, she wondered what type of costume Harlen would wear to a Halloween party. Maybe next year they could go together. Dreams helped Annie keep her hopes alive.

Chapter Twenty-four

Annie geared up for whatever the night had in store. The civic center was graciously hosting the costume party for free since it was also a fundraiser to support the center and the diverse community it served. While the focus was on the LGBTQIA+ residents, everyone who needed help would receive it through the many organizations that were participating.

"You could have told me it was a charity event."

"Right. Like you would have come in costume if I did." Char knew better. Annie didn't have anything against fundraisers, especially since she was planning one herself. If she'd worn work attire, she could have represented SFN as a respected organization, though she had to remember she wasn't working tonight. She was there to have fun.

"That's not the point. I didn't bring my checkbook." Thankfully, her costume would provide anonymity. Funny how she'd found her professional niche as a fundraiser.

"No worries. I made a large enough donation for both of us. You'll receive a thank you letter that you can keep for tax purposes or toss."

Annie pursed her lips below the half mask she wore. "Let's get a drink."

Char clapped her gloved hands. She'd gone with a Cruella de Vil costume, saying it was goth enough to keep to her roots, but flashy enough to nurture that side of her personality. "Is it an old-fashioned night?"

The mention of the long-standing cocktail made her tummy flip. The last time they indulged in an endless supply of the concoction, Annie had suffered a headache that lasted an entire day. "You do come up with the best ideas, but no. I'm in a bloody mary kind of mood."

Char nodded as they reached the bar. "It will go well with your theme," she said, referring to the fifties "June Cleaver" dress she wore, the kitten heels on her feet, and the petite handbag she carried that barely fit her phone and the lipstick she'd need to refresh. She would have liked to have added a hat with an oversized brim, but when she tested it with the mask on it just didn't work.

Annie scanned the crowd wondering if she knew anyone there. It wasn't like she'd recognize someone wearing the required mask for attending, as stated on the printed invitation Char showed her. Perhaps she wasn't the only one who didn't want to be recognized.

"Still no word from the hot tamale?" Char asked and handed her a drink minus the stem of celery. When she hesitated, Char pressed it into her hand. "I asked. It's a liability issue. People in masks have poor depth perception and poke themselves in the eye with the celery." She shrugged.

Annie ignored the question. "Thanks." She sipped and waited for the heat to hit. She wasn't disappointed.

"Don't ignore me."

With Char, she didn't have a choice. "She has a name. It's Harlen." There wasn't much that annoyed Annie to the point of irritation, but referring to someone by some cliché rather than their name irked her.

"Fine. Just so you know, Harlen is on my hit list."

For a second, Annie thought about how that might actually be a thing for Char. "Well, take her off. *I'm* not done with her." She was far from letting their situation go without resolution. Annie believed what they had was mutual. The chilly vibe from

Harlen the last few weeks not only made her sad, but also made her wonder if there was a valid reason for Harlen's disappearing act.

"Hey, let's go check out the hors d'oeuvres. I'm starving."

Annie followed her through the crowd, checking out the imaginative and interesting costumes.

"Oh, look." Char snagged a small plate, put several large shrimp on it along with cocktail sauce, then proceeded to balance it on top of her glass.

"You're tempting fate there," she said, pointing to the stack Char held.

"If you went to more parties you wouldn't think so. This is all the rage." Char smiled before biting into a shrimp, and Annie got a glimpse of the small napkin tucked in her palm.

Annie returned to checking out the crowd as she sipped her spicy drink. There were the traditional clowns, witches, vampires, goblins, and so on. Following those were the ones she liked to call "mid-century." They consisted of blue- and white-collar workers, musicians, famous actors, and the like. But her favorite was the cast of characters from popular movies and television shows. A few Star Wars die-hards, though Chewbacca was sorely missing the last decade. Adults indulging their childhood again by wearing Disney characters. The group rounded out with superheroes like Transformers and Avengers. She circled back to Char. "You really are talented. I should give you more credit."

"You should." Char wiped her mouth and placed the remnants on a tray. "I could teach you so many tricks, you'd be a star." Char giggled.

Annie had to admit she was starting to have fun. The last couple of weeks had been late work nights and limited interactions with Harlen. She'd misplaced two crucial notes that had taken three hours to locate. Whoever said sticky notes were the answer to everyone's prayers had never had one stick to the back of a folder and filed away. She was tired of feeling undone. It was nice to unwind. The alcohol was helping her stay in the moment.

Because if she let her mind wander it would, without question, return to Harlen.

"Finish that before it gets watered down." Char stood in front of her, waiting.

Annie handed her the tomato-sludge-coated glass. "What's the hurry?" Leave it to Char to jostle her from a pleasant buzz.

Char's eyes lit up. She'd opted for a half-mask that had larger eye openings, wanting to show off her eyelid makeup. "There's dancing!" She practically squealed.

"Not tonight."

"Don't be a Debbie Downer. It'll be fun." How Char managed to hold both glasses and pull her along like a lost child was beyond reasoning. When they arrived at the bar, she yanked her hand free.

"You always say that, but one of us ends up taking a header on the dance floor every time."

"Not true. The last time we both stayed upright." Char ordered their drinks, clearly flirting with the cute bartender.

Annie remembered the night, wishing it were yesterday rather than more than a month ago. She'd gladly give up the memory of sex for not having been ghosted. Not that she hadn't met people who never reached out to her, but they also hadn't been someone Annie wanted to reach out. The resulting feeling sucked. Char shoved a fresh drink in her hand. This one had three olives.

"I told him in lieu of celery, he had to up the fruit." Char's nose twitched, liked she'd made it happen through magic. Samantha was her favorite character from *Bewitched.*

"Thanks." She pinched the end of swizzle stick that barely broke the surface, stirred, and drank. There might have been some magic in the olive after all. "Let's find that band or whatever."

"Now you're talking."

Annie looped her arm through Char's, minding the swirling dress that trailed behind. She was done worrying about the what-ifs. Not everything associated with Harlen was good. Prior to meeting her, Annie hadn't suffered from emotional turmoil in ages. She'd been focused, organized, and knew how she needed to take care of herself for her mental health. Neither had she worried about what anyone thought. That's the one that was the hardest to understand. Since when was she willing to not be her authentic self because Harlen might not understand her?

Though that hadn't been the case at all. What Annie had to focus on was why Harlen didn't ask Annie if she had a question regarding their relationship, no matter what it was. That wasn't Harlen's typical behavior, unless it was all for show, but that didn't make sense either. Her chest tightened. She couldn't go down that rabbit hole. She didn't need Harlen in her world to continue to move through it. Annie already knew how to do that. What had her world turned upside down was *wanting* Harlen in her life.

"Let's go over there with our drinks." Char pointed to a high-top with several empty glasses and a small clutch. The DJ faded one song out while starting another. Instantly familiar, Annie knew her fate. "Now."

Annie let herself be led into the sea of humanity, right where she belonged. Harlen could go fuck herself for all she cared.

Music surrounded her and the vibration traveled through the soles of her feet, the only thing that was grounding her. Annie could be strong; she'd done it her whole life. Unfortunately, nothing matched how safe she'd felt in Harlen's arms, or how comfortable Harlen was being vulnerable with her. She didn't want to let go of the fantasy, but what if that was all it had been?

Chapter Twenty-five

"You suck at relationships."

Harlen stared at her reflection. There were dark circles under her eyes. Her last good night's sleep was shortly before she'd gotten the video of Chloe. She'd lost a few pounds and her shoulders sagged. Her appetite was nonexistent. Worst of all, she hadn't seen Annie in more than a month, and texting had dwindled to a "How are you?" once a week.

She hadn't meant for her melancholy to get out of hand. After making two copies of the video with every intention to give one to Chloe's parents, she'd chickened out. The Williamses were unrelenting parents, and the word hostile didn't begin to describe them, especially Chloe's mom. Once she confronted them, whether to give them something precious or not, it would be the last time she'd ever get into the hospital to see Chloe. They had connections beyond calling in a favor. Not that she feared for her life. That the Williams would not appreciate a scandal was fortuitous for her.

Harlen stood at the open closet door, then turned away. She pressed the speed number and flopped back onto the bed.

"Hey. What's up?" Peter asked. They weren't nearly as close as she was with her sister, which was the reason she called him. Jane would ask too many questions.

"Can you call the office and tell whoever needs to know that I'm not coming in?" Maybe she should paint the ceiling.

"I'm not your sitter." Peter also didn't have a lot of patience when it came to her.

"I know, but I don't feel well. Maybe you can keep it from Mom for me?"

Peter was silent for a long beat. "You want me to cover for you, like I did when you were a kid, Har?"

Jane had been Harlen's partner in crime. The two of them never missed an opportunity to blame Peter for whatever trouble one or the other got into. They would gang up on Peter, threatening him with some teenage secret he didn't think they knew about, but they always did.

"No, not like then."

"Why not? My sisters don't have any deep, dark secrets of mine in their war chest?" Peter sounded bitter and she couldn't blame him.

"It was a mistake to call. I'm sorry."

"A mistake? The great Harlen McGhee doesn't make mistakes. Ever. Isn't that right?"

Arrows embedded into her skin, the last one deep. On one level, Harlen knew she deserved her brother's wrath.

"I always stood up for you. Whether you deserved it or not. And I'd do it again because you're my sister and I love you, but not this time, Har. You've obviously fucked up the start of something special with Annie, and before you ask, Jane told me everything." Peter blew out a big huff. "Unlike you, she confides in *me*. You'll forgive me if I'm not sympathetic to your cause."

Harlen was out of steam. She didn't want to fight anyone for any reason. She almost hung up before her brother spoke.

"Get your ass to work and do something you're good at. I'll tell the staff you overslept." The line went dead.

Great. Now Peter was mad at her, too. Who else was on that list besides Annie? Harlen returned to the closet and picked out a pair of dark slacks, a sand color button-down, and a tweed jacket. While she dressed, she assessed the damages suffered for her no-action indifference to what would be reasonable, but difficult remedies.

Obsessing over the last known video of Chloe instead of accepting the memento as a beautiful gift, sent her on the edge of depression she was barely keeping at bay. Strike one.

She ignored repeated calls, texts, and visits from Dan, including when she'd showed up at one in the morning, ringing her bell and pounding on the door until she got up. They talked a couple of minutes before she promised to call in a couple of days. That was a week ago. Strike two.

Annie would be mad. She couldn't understand Harlen's silence because she didn't know about her continued devotion to Chloe. Annie would be hurt by the omission. Strike three.

Harlen sat on the bed to put on her socks and shoes. There was no going back. She had to be stronger than the draw of Chloe's image. So much for number one.

In the den, she rummaged around for her power cord, laptop, and invoices, then stuffed them in her bag. She pulled out her phone.

"Dan, it's me."

"Uh-huh."

Dan wasn't going to make this any easier, but that was okay. She deserved a cold shoulder…or two. "Asshole here. Can I see you later?"

"Yeah. My place. We're having beer and pizza, and the truth or don't bother showing."

"See you at six thirty." Number two, sort of handled.

Without searching her soul and really looking for the answers, number three, the most important one and the biggest of her fuck-ups, would have to wait until she talked with Dan. Harlen was in no frame of mind to be objective about anything of this magnitude. She tried several times to find a viable solution and kept coming back to the one that had haunted her. She'd failed to keep her promise to Chloe about stopping life support.

She had the beginning of an idea she hadn't thought of before. With her judgment being as clouded as it was, she didn't want to chance making things worse, if that was possible at this point. Who knew. She had become very familiar with the sad places in her house. The craft room downstairs was jammed with all of Chloe's belongings. She moved them there after six months without a change in her condition. She didn't want to see the glaring reminders that Chloe would never use them again. Harlen had eventually stowed her stuff away, along with the boxes that Chloe had packed. As soon as Chloe found a place convenient to work, she was moving out. Having Chloe's belongings visible hadn't helped Harlen let go. Chloe was everywhere, so she couldn't be gone.

❖

"You look like shit."

"Not now, Peter." Harlen rounded the corner of the cube farm seeking the refuge of her office.

"Well, when would Her Highness be free to discuss work? You remember? That thing you have to do to earn a paycheck?"

Harlen reined in her rising anger with what little control she had left. Why couldn't anyone understand what she was going through? "That's why I'm here."

"Good, because the budget for your design services just took a hit. You maxed out your business card, Harlen."

"It happens."

"You also forgot to submit invoices for payment to suppliers. They're all tacking on a ten percent late fee."

Had it been that many days since she'd paid attention to the stack of papers she'd carried back and forth to work? "I've got them right here." She emptied the contents of her messenger bag. The chaos in her head showed in the wrinkled, disheveled documents.

"Get your shit together, Har."

Harlen had enough of her brother's badgering. "You don't think I'm trying." Her voice was louder than she intended. What was done was done. "For two fucking years I've done my best to move on." She laughed sarcastically. "You all make it sound so easy to do by saying Chloe is dead. That she's never coming back." Her voice hitched, the fight suddenly gone, and she dropped into her chair. Finally, she met Peter's eyes. "Chloe was the love of my life. I've done everything I can to keep a promise that will never be possible because of piece of paper that was never fucking signed." Harlen didn't want to cry at work. "I can't do this anymore, Pete."

Her brother leaned close. "Everyone who knows you knows how much you love Chloe. That's never been in doubt, Har. We're worried about your mental health. You're so fixated on the sense of duty you insist you have to carry out, you can't see what's right in front of you, Har." Peter sat across from her. "Rumor has it, you have a reason to move on."

What could she say? The working part of her brain agreed. Annie was very different than Chloe and the change was refreshing, if their relationship ever got off the ground. Sure, Annie had a couple of mannerisms that reminded her of Chloe, but instead of being threatened by the likenesses, she could be embracing Annie for who *she* was, and who Harlen was with her. Peter stood.

"Make your peace about Chloe. Do whatever you need to do to move forward. You don't want to hear this, but I'm going to say it because you need to hear it until it hits home. You aren't the one who was careless by not wearing a seat belt. Don't think for one minute you're responsible for Chloe's reckless nature." He came around the desk and pulled her into a hug, a rare show of affection from him. "Do you want me to take care of this?" He pointed to the haphazard stack.

Harlen shook her head. "It's my mess."

Peter pursed his lips. "Just remember what's your mess and what isn't." He shut the door behind him, giving Harlen a minute to collect herself.

What Peter said made perfect sense in a perfect world, but that wasn't where she lived. Hers was flawed, just like her reason for maintaining the status quo was flawed. The plan she'd come up with was likely flawed too, but she had to see it through. Until that happened, a meaningful relationship with Annie would remain on the back burner. She didn't want to lose Annie in the melee. Harlen crossed her fingers. The plan had to work. If it failed, she had no idea what she'd do.

Chapter Twenty-six

Annie's entire life had been centered around the things she'd been told she'd never do, by people who considered themselves professionals in the neurological field. Every one of them was surprised when she finished high school, and again when she obtained her bachelor's degree in liberal arts, debunking theories that people on the spectrum shouldn't open themselves to the disappointments sure to come.

Then there were the couple of women in her adult life who had tried to understand her, but they didn't *appreciate* who she was. Judgment about certain social behaviors were ingrained into the cultural society. The excuses of "not knowing any better" or "she must have had a poor upbringing" left no room for individualism. The current generation, which she could never remember the moniker of, had pushed hard for the non-binary, queer, gender-neutral, non-identity climate. Not everyone was on board. History repeated itself.

There was a time when Annie was angry for having to be labeled as anything other than a human being, but she'd gotten over having expectations. At times, her way of expressing herself was a lot and she got that. She had a big personality and told it like it was, which could be off-putting. Harlen wasn't intimidated by her frankness. If anything, she was interested in Annie's way of looking at the world. How unafraid Annie was to ask for the reason behind a thought or action. Harlen wanted to know more about Annie, too. She wasn't afraid to ask Annie to explain things. Which made their current situation all the more puzzling and the reason she was waiting for Harlen.

Annie tightly gripped her purse as she sat in the building lobby where Forrest Enterprises resided. Her decision to make a move toward resolution hadn't been easy in light of Harlen's silence. The notion that Harlen had used her for sex wasn't what tipped the scale. She'd done the same thing more times than she cared to count. But Harlen's silence left her feeling like she wasn't good enough when Annie knew damned well she was more than enough, in spite of her involvement in Chloe's current situation. Annie had to tell Harlen the secret she didn't want to hold any longer.

She glanced at her phone. It was after six. Maybe Harlen was already gone. She should have called and asked to meet, but the fear of Harlen not answering after weeks of silence led her to take a chance on a face to face.

The elevator dinged and Annie sat motionless. Harlen and a handsome man who looked a lot like Harlen, talked as they walked in her direction. When she stood, Harlen slowed, a look of confusion on her face.

"Annie?" Harlen asked. "What are you doing here?"

"Hi." She glanced at the unknown man. "Can we talk?"

Harlen gazed from head to toe, taking her in. "I'll see you tomorrow, Pete."

"Sure." Pete held out his hand. "Peter McGhee. It's nice to meet you, Annie." His smile was a perfect match for Harlen's.

Annie shook his hand. "Annie Duncan." After a nod, Peter left.

"Would you like to go for coffee, or a drink?"

"No." Annie licked her lips. She needed to get on with it. Pleasantries might disrupt her resolve. She pointed to one of the many seating areas that was out of the way of foot traffic.

"I was there." The level of Annie's anxiety was hitting critical mass.

"What are you talking about?" Harlen asked.

"When Chloe had her accident. I was the witness who called nine-one-one."

Confusion returned to Harlen's face. "You saw Chloe?"

"Yes. No." Ugh. "The road was covered in black ice and I…I tried to stop." Annie saw the moment the blond woman realized Annie's car was headed for her because her eyes got really big. Then she jerked the wheel hard and her car skidded off the road. Annie watched in slow motion as the vehicle hit something and went airborne before crashing down, rolling several times before landing against a stand of trees.

"You were there?" Harlen asked, clearly trying to process the information.

"I'm so sorry." She moved her hand, wanting to comfort Harlen.

"I read the police report. There wasn't another car involved."

"My car didn't actually hit Chloe's. I tried to get out of the skid, but my wheels locked and…and my car headed for her car. When she realized we were going to crash, Chloe jerked the wheel. She must have slammed on her brakes too because I saw her brake lights as she careened off the side of the road." Her stomach did a flip.

Harlen palmed her face before leaning forward. "How long have you known about my connection to Chloe?" The blue of her eyes was so vivid.

"The night of our second date." Annie rushed on. "There was something familiar about you the day we met. I had no clue from where and was convinced it was just a random thought. Then when you told me the reason you were acting weird at the restaurant was because I'd done something that reminded you of Chloe, I put two and two together."

Harlen's coloring deepened. "And you didn't think it was important enough to tell me?"

"What was I going to say? Oh, by the way, your partner's in a coma because of me?"

"Fuck, Annie." Harlen stood and began pacing. "You should have told me." The accusation and anger in her voice surprised Annie. She stood.

"I'm telling you now."

The fact that Harlen was glaring at her like she was responsible for the pain reflected in her eyes, pushed her onward. Annie was far from done. If Harlen wanted to fight about the should-haves of their relationship, Annie was all in.

"And you should have told me you're still in love with Chloe." She wasn't about to be beat down by anyone, especially by the person she'd fallen hard for.

Harlen opened and closed her mouth several times. "Go home, Annie." Harlen turned away.

"Harlen, please. Don't keep disappearing. We have to talk about this." It wasn't in Annie's nature to beg, but she couldn't let things between them end. Not like this. Harlen was out the door before she could stop her. Annie sat. Her legs were weak and her breathing erratic. The worst-case scenario had happened. In the "any other day" mentality, she knew how to handle situations like this. Today's argument with Harlen wasn't just any day, and Harlen wasn't just anyone. Annie leaned back and looked up to the ceiling and stared at her wavy reflection in the marble.

"Excuse me," a young man said. "Are you alright?"

Annie almost laughed. "No, I'm not." She got up. "But I will be, thanks for asking." She headed out the same door as Harlen. The thought of attempting to chase her down crossed her mind. Pictures began to form and played in chronological order. The real Annie was back. No more second-guessing herself. Harlen had been the one to pursue her. She hadn't thought it important enough to tell Annie that she was nowhere near ready to get serious with anyone. Annie did casual dalliances under the stipulation that both parties agreed to keep it that way. Harlen had broken all the rules. If it was a fight Harlen wanted she had better be ready. Annie had learned at an early age how to be a fighter. She understood how Harlen felt, at least a bit. That didn't give her permission to drop

Annie like she didn't matter. This time was different because her heart didn't want to let go.

❖

The floor of the palliative care unit was quiet all the time. With the weight of Harlen's visit, the atmosphere was especially gloomy. Among the beeps and mechanical sounds, low voices could be heard drifting through the open doors. The staff showed respect to the patients and families of the terminally ill by maintaining a quiet decorum on the floor. The surroundings were hard enough to bear, and Harlen often wished someone would laugh and lighten the mood. It didn't matter that she had little to be happy about when it came to Chloe's condition. It also didn't mean life around her had to stop.

The video card that sat on the side table helped remind her she was there with a purpose. Her last hurrah so to speak. In preparation for the moment she saw the Williamses, she'd watched the video a few more times. By now she practically had it memorized, especially the sound of Chloe's voice and her telltale laughter.

Harlen thought about the scene with Annie from a few days ago, and the text she sent yesterday. Annie made it clear they weren't "done." Harlen didn't want them to be done either, but there were a few things that she had to take care of before she caused more damage to their relationship.

Annie's confession caught her off guard. The police report that she retrieved from the file that had grown over time didn't mention the Good Samaritan's name. According to the police there wasn't any need to clutter the report with unnecessary details. Annie, and therefore her car, wasn't involved in Chloe's accident. Black ice and road conditions were the culprit. The severity of Chloe's injuries was attributed to her not wearing a seat belt. The habit had been long-standing and one of the ongoing arguments between her and Chloe. Harlen would refuse to start the car until Chloe was buckled up. Chloe complained she hated being strapped down, and that the law was an "infringement on her freedom." So much for being free to fuck yourself up. Harlen pushed away the idea she should have tried harder to get Chloe to comply. She couldn't make anyone do anything they didn't want to do.

Harlen reflected back to the day she met Chloe. She was in her last year of college and had taken color theory to meet her curriculum requirements. On the first day of class, she and Chloe ended up sitting in the same row, one seat between them. Social distancing hadn't been ingrained in everyone's conscience yet, but personal space in lecture halls was a common courtesy at the time. She found out later that Chloe had signed up for the class as one of her electives toward her liberal arts degree.

Leaning closer, Harlen took Chloe's cool hand. The unnatural texture and stiffness only served to drive home no one lived inside the body on the bed. "I know you're not in there. Not really. I wanted to keep my promise, Clo. That carefree, 'I've got all the time in the world' attitude is to blame." She smiled. "It's one of the things I loved about you. I loved so many things about you and believed you were my forever person."

As she rubbed her thumb over the back of Chloe's hand, she let the last few months they were together before Chloe stated it was over between them play out. Harlen's work at the family company and the research needed to get her own design company up and running, while Chloe took on more assignments and freelance writing, meant they didn't spend much time together. When she examined the circumstances further, Harlen concluded that she and Chloe were already moving apart, she simply hadn't realized it back then. By the time Chloe said anything, it was too late. That, along with her inability to intervene and stop all medical treatment, were the basis for the guilt she carried for far too long. The video was her last-ditch effort to keep her promise. Familiar voices from the hallway reached her and she rose to her feet, ready to stand her ground.

"The Markensons are coming on Sunday," Margaret said before pulling up short when she saw Harlen. "What are you doing here?" She spat the words like she was trying to get rid of a foul taste. Jason put his hand on his wife's shoulder. He was the reasonable one of the couple.

"I'm here to see you both." Harlen's heart pounded.

"You needn't bother. We don't want to see *you*." Chloe's mom put a fresh plant on the table where Chloe would be able to see the partially open blooms. Harlen knew they'd remain unseen. Then she tossed the drooping bouquet from the previous week in the trash.

"I won't be long." She held onto the main reason for her visit. "Chloe's coworker mailed this to me." She handed the SD card to Chloe's dad.

"We aren't interested in seeing—"

"Let Harlen finish, Marge." Jason smiled kindly.

"It's a video from the holiday office party before Chloe's accident." Jason took it. "As far as I know, it's the last video of her when she was alive."

"How dare you." Margaret invaded Harlen's personal space, but she held firm. "Chloe can hear you. Get out."

Harlen shook her head. "As much as I prayed Chloe would come back to me—to you both—we know that's never going to happen."

Margaret tried to slap her, but Jason stopped the assault. "Let me go." She struggled in vain. Jason had managed to keep his athlete's body long after his college football days.

"Look at the video. That's how I want to remember Chloe. That's how I want to honor her life. I failed to keep my promise that if she were to have a terminal illness or an accident she couldn't recover from, I wouldn't make her linger. This"—she pointed to Chloe's still form—"isn't how Chloe would want to spend her last days on earth." She took a breath before going on as she moved to Chloe's side for the last time.

"I never doubted we belonged together, and I loved you the best I could." She kissed the back of Chloe's hand, then gently let Chloe's fingertips brush against her palm. It was a touch she remembered Chloe doing a thousand times. "I know I have to let you go. You deserve to rest in peace without machines keeping you prisoner." Harlen kissed Chloe's forehead, surprised it was warm against her lips. "I'll always love you, Chloe."

Harlen faced Margaret and Jason. "I hope after watching that, you will be able to let her go, too." She picked up her coat. She got as far as the door before hearing Margaret's venom-filled voice.

"Don't you dare show your face again."

Harlen paused. "I won't be back." Harlen was numb. She didn't remember the elevator ride, or walking to her car. Once inside, she glanced at the tall brick building she'd gotten to know so well, it almost felt like home. Harlen pressed the call button on the familiar name. Peter answered on the third ring.

"What is it this time?" Peter would get over his annoyance with her. They were family no matter what their disagreements were.

"I need a couple of days off. I'm going out of town."

"Who's going to do your work while you're on vacation?"

"I've said my last good-bye to Chloe and I need to be alone." She didn't want to have to explain what she was feeling to anyone. Mostly because she wasn't sure if she felt anything, knowing her emotions would eventually break through the haze that surrounded her. Peter was silent. Her eyes burned and she closed them, hoping the dark void would somehow bring comfort.

"Take as much time as you need." Peter's kindness was unexpected. It's not that he wasn't a good person. He and Harlen had a contentious relationship unless one of them was in trouble, emotionally or otherwise.

"Thanks."

"Let me know if you need brotherly advice."

"Pete?"

"Yeah?"

"Don't tell Mom. I'll do it when I get back." Having some time to herself would help Harlen decide how much she would say when asked the inevitable questions that her mother would want answers to. Until today, she hadn't thought about the pain her family was also dealing with since Harlen's world fell apart.

"Tell her what?" Pete said, playing the old game they used to play as kids before Peter believed she and Jane had it out for him. When either of them knew they'd done something against parental rules, the "Don't tell Mom" was always followed by blaming him. Adulthood had brought an agreed upon ignorance when there was a problem they needed to solve without involving their parents.

She chuckled. "I'll call you when I get back."

"You better."

On the ride home, thoughts of Annie wanted to occupy space. The fiery, unapologetic, sexy woman she was crazy about would have to wait. Her heart and head needed to get on the same page and that required all her processing attention. There would be a lot of sharing after she returned, but for the next few days Harlen would go stay by herself in the mountains. The wilds of nature had been her go-to place again and again whenever deep thinking was required.

At least she had the foresight to make a reservation when she made up her mind it would be the only way to dissolve the burden she carried by shifting the responsibility squarely to Chloe's parents, where it belonged. The last part was accepting she'd done the right thing—the only thing left to do—was to walk away. Harlen couldn't wait to see how well that went, and getting away would be paramount to making peace with herself.

Chapter Twenty-seven

"How many invitations have you sent out?" Michael asked. His help was critical to the success of the gala. He took on the task of opening invitation responses and recording them into the event spreadsheet Annie had created to keep track of various elements, such as expenses, invitations, and ancillary services. She still despised the tracking program, but she learned it had its value at times.

"Over a hundred, but I think that was a lofty list." Annie chewed her lip. "In order for the event to be considered a success, we need to raise more than a hundred and fifty thousand dollars in sponsorship." She'd done the research. Most nonprofit organizations considered a ten percent overhead for fundraising as optimal with thirty-five percent being the max. Annie had no intention of letting their expenses go above fifteen percent. Allison had been clear in her requirement of reviewing the bottom line. If all went in Annie's favor, Allison had also expressed interest in discussing other types of fundraising, and Annie was thrilled.

"I thought you'd be more upbeat." Michael fixed his gaze on Annie. "What are you down in the dumps about?"

Annie thought she managed to put on a mask of indifference. Apparently, she was wrong. "I'm okay. Personal stuff." There wasn't any way she was going to confide in a coworker. Michael was great, but she didn't know if he was part of the gossip mill that most offices had.

"Ah…having a love life is hard." Michael's telling grin made her laugh.

"Is there someone special in your life?" Annie wasn't prone to ask personal questions, but Michael had shown concern without asking for details. She liked that about him.

"Some ones." He corrected her. "I'm poly and currently have two partners, but I'm not against more." Michael winked.

"Do you find it difficult to spend time with both of them?" Annie couldn't imagine juggling several relationships at once. She could barely make one work. Lately, she couldn't even manage that, shouldering part of the blame for the standstill she and Harlen were at.

Michael slid the letter opener expertly under the corner flap and slipped it through with the precision of a surgeon. "Life gets in the way of life occasionally, but that's one of the tenets that attracted me. Everyone has to be open and honest about their partners while sharing feelings, wants, and needs. It's a lot easier to be understanding when we know the why, too." He tapped entries on his laptop. "It's not an easy path, but it's the right path for me. I also accept that being poly may not always be what I want."

Michael's words resonated in her head. What did she want at this point in her life? The gala was no excuse for her to ignore the uncertainty of tomorrow, in spite of today. There was a time when she would have settled for less than she dreamed of having. When she was a young, newly diagnosed autistic, being different gave her an out for not trying harder. Once she left her twenties behind, she took up the banner to prove she could achieve anything she wanted, even if it meant she'd have to work harder, or attain a goal in an unusual way.

Michael looked up from his screen. "Is there anyone special in your life, Annie?"

"Yes, but it's complicated."

Michael tipped his head side to side. "It's really not. Decide what, or who, you want and go for it. Even if you don't get it at least you'll have tried and be no worse off." Michael closed his laptop and stood. "We're all caught up with responses. I'll patch through any calls. Now that the advertising has circulated for a bit, I'm certain there will be inquiries from people who want to get involved."

"Thanks, Michael." Annie thought about what she could get him for taking on additional duties. Whether it was his job or not, Michael had been meticulous with details and didn't blink an eye when the responses started coming in.

Annie squinted at the time displayed on the lower right corner of her screen. She had a few hours left and a couple of feelers to follow up on, but sitting staring at her computer wouldn't accomplish anything. Try as she might, Annie couldn't shake the feeling something big was about to happen in her life. If she was going fight for Harlen, doing nothing would only add to her frustration. It was time she took Char's advice. Michael had said much the same thing, with both suggesting she take the reins instead of letting them dangle.

This time Annie was determined not to let Harlen walk away. Come hell or high water, as her father was fond of saying, the question of whether their quasi-relationship had any chance at all had to be settled.

Chapter Twenty-eight

Harlen woke to find a light coating of snow on the pine boughs that were almost close enough to brush against the cabin window. While her coffee brewed, she set about building a fire, picking out pieces of tinder and small logs from the copious supply both inside and out on the covered porch. Once the flame caught, she replaced the mesh metal screen. Harlen tried to stay in the moment by running her hand over the fieldstone that covered the fireplace. She was surprised the inanimate object was warm to the touch. The irony that warmth did not necessarily indicate whether something was alive wasn't lost to her. The memory of her lips brushing against Chloe's forehead came unabated. Instead of fighting the vision, she let it drift away.

The cabin wasn't as rustic as it might have initially appeared to a visitor, and she enjoyed the modern conveniences of heat, electricity, and running water. Her days of roughing it and sleeping on the ground were over, though the old-fashioned water pump lent an air of the long history of the Adirondacks. The lack of cell service inside the cabin hadn't deterred her. In fact, she looked forward to a few days of being unplugged. The wilderness vibe of the place was prominent wherever she looked. The modern windows were nine over nine paned, like she'd expect to see in the movies, minus the drafts. The wide floorboards hadn't been sanded smooth, but they were coated with a thick layer of protective sealant, making it shiny in some places and duller in others due to foot traffic. Braided rugs were strategically placed throughout the four-hundred-square-foot space.

The bed was extremely comfortable. Or it was simply that she'd actually been able to sleep after weeks of waking in the middle of the night. Lined plaid curtains hung at the sides of the large picture windows, giving her an expansive view of the forest that crowded the one-lane driveway. The builder had the foresight to put in a trip light. Whenever a car entered the long, winding driveway from either end, a light went on at the other, an ingenious way to keep a vehicle from having to back up.

The coffee beeped and she tossed on her jacket, fixed her mug, then stuffed her feet into the Merrells she'd been cognizant enough to wear. She'd gotten a text from Jane reminding her to pack warm clothes and weatherproof gear. Harlen had chuckled. Peter had shared the news with Jane. She'd been in no hurry to escape her home except for the possibility of Annie showing up at her door. Harlen wasn't capable of dealing with more than one emotional crisis at a time.

The crisp air hit her when she stepped out and she welcomed the shock of it. The steam of her breath clouded over the scene long enough for Harlen to imagine she was lost in the forest in front of her. Snow brought a fresh coating to the ground, like new paint on a wall, but muffled the forest sounds, adding to the quiet. If she listened closely, she swore she could hear the big flakes of snow that fell through the dense stillness. The peace the silence brought with it surrounded Harlen. Nothing could touch her or detract from her solitude. A feeling not to be confused with loneliness.

For too long, she'd been moving through her days without much in the way of reflection, relying on her pain to let her know she was still breathing. Meeting Annie had changed the way she processed her own emotions.

Harlen hadn't grieved losing Chloe because she refused to believe she was dead, and no longer a part of the living. A shuddery breath escaped as the cold began to seep in, chasing her inside. She put a large log on the fire after stirring the hot embers. Her intention was to have a stoked fire for the day. After refilling her mug and taking up a corner of the couch, angled perfectly for looking into the flames or out the window, Harlen stared at the beaten paperback that sat next to the new journal, an ink gel pen not far from both.

She'd read that journaling was an effective way to move past the issue. Like saying the words out loud but without the need for another person's presence. Harlen liked the idea of rereading what she'd written later to add annotations about alternatives, outcome, and other cues. The mere fact that she was willing to make a permanent record about her thoughts might represent how far she'd come from even a few months ago.

Emotions had been an enemy to defend against. She owed it to herself to allow them in, but to also remember to let them go out. Harlen turned to a blank page, dated it, and closed her eyes. Visions swam in front of her like a slide show and she grabbed on one of the happy scenes, letting it play out. She jotted the gist of the memory, then moved on. Three pages and another cup of coffee later, Harlen's stomach growled in protest of being ignored.

She stood and stretched her arms, laughing how close to the ceiling she reached. Anyone over six feet would have a hard time avoiding the overhead light fixture. She stood at the refrigerator. Eggs were always a good choice to start the day. Omelets were Chloe's favorite breakfast food, and they took turns making them, each adding their favorite ingredients. Chloe stuck to veggies and cheese. Harlen went with savory, using a variety of meats, along with fried potatoes and grilled vegetables. She beat the main ingredient with a little half and half since there wasn't any milk, and scrounged in the cabinet for garlic powder.

"I didn't eat many eggs until we moved in together."

An outsider might think it strange that she was talking out loud. To Harlen, it was her way of getting out what had been bottled up inside. There were many things she'd written down the first few weeks after the accident that she looked forward to sharing with Chloe when she woke. After a month and the reassurance by the medical staff that the only reason Chloe continued to breathe and her body functioned at all was the machines, Harlen stopped writing notes.

She chopped part of an onion, shaved slices of cheese the best she could, and sprinkled parsley on top before folding the concoction over and putting the lid on the pan. While it finished cooking, she put bread in the two-slot toaster. A glass of orange juice would serve as her fruit.

"It's all about the balance, Chloe."

Harlen brought her plate to the round wooden table and sat, staring at her food. She would never again share a meal with Chloe. Never hear her laughter as she talked to one of her many friends. Never see her eyes light up when Harlen managed to pick out the perfect gift. The food blurred and her tears fell silently, the same way she'd suffered the greatest loss she'd ever known.

When her tears dried and the breath she took no longer shook her body, Harlen nuked her food and ate. Starving herself wouldn't help to replenish the energy she spent crying. After cleaning up, Harlen stood with her hands on her hips looking out the window at the snow that had diminished to the tiny flakes that could last for ten minutes or ten hours. The one thing she hadn't thought to do was check the weather forecast. Not that she was worried. Her four-wheel drive vehicle was good in snow. She considered having a beer or a shot of whiskey before checking the time. Nine forty was too early by most people's standards. A walk in the woods sounded nice, but she was horrible at knowing what direction to go in, often turning herself around until she found a landmark. Even then, there remained the chance she might head in the opposite direction of where she wanted to go. Chloe had bought her a compass to keep in the car, "Just in case." She had no idea if it was still there and the idea of looking for it saddened her.

The journal, with its worn leather cover and leather thong sat waiting, as did her faithful book. No matter how many times she read it, the beauty of the love shared between the characters always made her cry and gave her hope. Needing to pass the time in a productive way, Harlen opened to the next blank page, closed her eyes, and focused inward. The pen was poised above the cream-colored paper, waiting for her words.

I said good-bye to you yesterday. I'm not sure what I expected. The tears I should have shed two years ago finally came. I loved you with every fiber of my being. For a time, I know you loved me that way, too.

In the midst of our time together, you discovered you wanted more for yourself. I'm not angry, though sometimes. It must have been hard to tell. You wanted your life to look differently, and I wanted mine to stay the fairy tale it was. Or maybe I didn't want a change if it meant not being with you. I never dreamt that a new way of seeing and thinking could exist, or that I could feel good about it. I'm smiling because I think the world is showing me how to think outside of the solid box I'd built around our life. My life.

I'm so very proud of you for recognizing your need to evolve. For not being afraid of reaching for the unknown, and being excited about your future. If only you'd worn that damned seat belt. If only you filled out the document. Ah, well. Water. Bridge. My life moved on without my taking notice, while you are stuck someplace in between.

I hope your parents are able to let you find what you were looking for and let go of what no longer serves you. You don't need a body to soar to new heights and scale unexplored mountains, or whatever else you had planned to do. You had a rogue streak in you. Another attribute that I loved about you. I could write a book. Who knows, maybe someday I will.

Harlen glanced at the familiar cover of *Carly's Sound.*

From now on, I'm not counting anything out. All bets are off, Chloe.

I've got a new position at work after being on the verge of walking away. Instead of leaving the family business, I'm doing staging and remodels. Eventually, I'll have my own design business. I can hear you saying, "It's about damn time." I couldn't agree more.

That's not all. There's a woman, Annie, who I think was born to show me how to step into the unknown and be spontaneous. I—we—have a thing that neither of us know what to call what we share. I want to step out with her, Chloe. I want to try dancing to an off-beat rhythm for a change. It's been a while since I've been excited about my life. This is a good thing and I know it will be good for me. You know better than anyone, change is hard for me.

You taught me a life well-lived has risks that include the unknown. As much as you loved me, you understood I wasn't ready to step out of the ordinary life we were living so we could enjoy an extraordinary one. I don't blame you for having to leave me behind, because that's what I have to do, too, Chloe. I have to leave you behind, in the past, where you belong.

I've loved you from the start and I will always love you.

Harlen read what she'd written. When she was done, she closed the cover on a chapter of her life. She didn't want to make what she had with Chloe seem trivial. The truth was they had a great time dating for a few months, and when graduation came and a guaranteed paycheck called to her, she asked Chloe to move in. Chloe agreed, but only if she paid for half of the expenses.

"What's fair is fair, relationship or not." A sexy wink followed. "Besides, I'll save a ton. My rent is double your mortgage." Chloe's parents had lucrative jobs and she was used to the finer things life offered those who could afford it. They insisted she draw on her inheritance while she could enjoy it. Little did they know how prophetic their words were.

Their relationship had run its course according to Chloe, and now she could finally admit Chloe was right. They weren't miserable per se, but the spark was barely there. Chloe moved in different circles while she traveled the world for her job. Harlen was content with the simpler life of her family and BF. They were all she needed aside from the love of her life.

Harlen wondered how many loves a person could have. If she believed the words in the book, there was room for more, all you had to do was make the space. Harlen had failed miserably in that department. The excuses had run dry, and her resolve had tumbled to its lowest point after she walked away from Annie the last time. It was becoming a habit she had to break.

There'd been minimal communication after arguing with Annie and it kept her tossing and turning at night. More than fretting over Chloe had stolen her sleep. The daylight hours were spent trying not to compare her love for one woman over the undeniable attraction to another. Did Annie struggle as much as she did with the tug-of-war they were in?

Her question was foolish. Why would Annie have waited in the lobby for God knows how long to talk to her? Annie knew what was important to her, and she knew what she wanted in life. Harlen gave her the utmost respect in both cases. If only she could have found her own resolve sooner. Perhaps, if surmising was her thing, Annie had been there to give her the kick in the ass she needed. Her best friend, her family, and just about everyone who knew her had cajoled, encouraged, and downright pleaded with her to accept Chloe would never be with her or anyone else. Ever. In a few short months, Annie had managed to change everything.

"Ha." Harlen raked her fingers through her hair, then glanced around, searching. "That drink sounds better and better." Her routine world had been flipped on its end after the run-in with Annie. Literally. The accident had been her fault. Annie's confession to being a witness to Chloe's was not.

Chloe lived life recklessly. The trait Harlen found cute in college turned into constant worry about what situation she would get into next. And that wasn't all. Chloe liked to be dared, and her friends egged her on. Harlen had found their lack of maturity in decision-making unseemly for a bunch of adults. When she tried to temper Chloe's wild streak, she laughed and told her to "lighten up." So much for looking out for the welfare of a partner.

Looking back, Harlen had a change of heart about a lot of the way Chloe lived every day to its fullest. She hoped her last day had been good. The anticipation of tears followed, but when her eyes stayed dry, Harlen felt another pound drop from her shoulders. Life was okay, and it was going to get better.

She considered venturing out to shovel the walkway and clean off her car. Instead, Harlen played with the fireplace and added another log. She dropped onto the center of the couch because it was the sweet spot, and opened *Carly's Sound* for the umpteenth time. The scent of pine filled the air, and like an old friend, Harlen looked forward to hearing the characters' story again.

Several hours later, Harlen woke to the book at her side and the fire burned low. The heat had likely kicked on, but lack of flickering flames left her wanting their cozy warmth. She found the page where she'd left off, and tucked her bookmark inside. You couldn't read anything as many times as she had without knowing the story.

The waning light meant darkness wasn't far away, but at least the snow had stopped. After the fire flared back to life under her ministrations, Harlen's stomach reminded her of the meal she'd missed. Lunch should have been a few hours ago. Steak sounded good right about now and she hoped the potato salad from the local grocer tasted as good as it looked. The small, well-stocked kitchen had a cast iron pan, the next best alternative to the grill that stood at the end of the porch. It wasn't that Harlen wasn't hardy. Under normal circumstances she'd jump at the chance to be outdoors, but the emotional comfort of being inside on a snowy evening with a nice fire kept her in.

The lone TV was hooked up to an antenna on the peak of the roof. The binder of renter information stated, "When the wind wasn't blowing too hard, several channels were available." While her steak seared, she clicked through the mostly static-filled stations until she found one she could hear and see. The familiar figure of *The Rifleman* filled the screen in grainy black-and-white. Harlen laughed, wondering if the next show would be *Gunsmoke*.

Somehow, she managed to cook her steak to the perfect temperature. The potato salad was a bit heavy on the onion, but a good accompaniment. The glass of wine she'd decided on over a beer brought out the flavors of her meal. While she ate, one show flowed into another and the last one proved the best with *The Andy Griffith Show*. Harlen propped her stocking feet on the coffee table that was the perfect height for lounging. Pa was someone she could relate to. He tried to do the right thing though it often meant sacrificing his feelings.

Is that what she'd done? Did it matter if she had? The past was written in stone and nothing could change it. She gazed at the darkness that wasn't pitch-black. The layer of snow reflected the moonlight, giving it a quasi-daylight vibe. Movement caught her eye and she went to the window. She hoped the windows were tempered glass and strong enough to withstand whatever creature lurked in the shadows.

There, near the tree line, a couple of deer pawed at the ground. Harlen took a drink. The deer raised their heads in concert and turned toward where she stood. It was a bit eerie having an animal pinpoint her location with so much accuracy, then she realized their very survival depended on their senses to react to a threat. Harlen wasn't a threat to the deer or any creature for that matter. Unless her life was threatened, she was content to bear witness to the beauty surrounding her.

Harlen knew breathing deep when she was stressed helped. She hadn't spent much time or effort making sure she took care of herself first. If she had, maybe she could have better handled past events that weighed her down. She watched as more deer followed the path made by the earlier visitors. When the last one disappeared behind a row of pine trees, Harlen refilled her glass, determined to finish the story she really didn't need to read.

By ten that evening, Harlen closed the book and smiled. Poppy had found love again. No one would ever take Carly's place and she didn't want anyone to try. Both of her loves were once-in-a-lifetime, bringing joy and harmony to the relationship. All because

Poppy had forged on, ignoring her fears, and found a different kind of fulfilment with a different love. Harlen could do that, too.

She thought about packing up to leave. A drive in the mountains at night, after a snowstorm, would not be the best of decisions. Harlen stoked the fire one last time, tidied up what she could, and got ready for bed. She'd let the rental office know she had to return home a day early, and didn't expect a refund. Money would never be as important as finding love. Tomorrow was Friday. Harlen planned to make the most of her time away from the office by thinking about what she was going to say to Annie, but that wasn't all. She also had to find a way to show Annie how sorry she was for her mixed messages and her less than understanding behavior. Her last thought was a prayer she wasn't too late to ask Annie for another chance. Lord knows she didn't deserve it, but that wasn't going to stop her. For once, she knew what she wanted, and she had every intention of going after her newfound love. She deserved happiness in more than her work life. Her only regret was not having the wherewithal to pursue it sooner.

Chapter Twenty-nine

"Cheers! We made it to Friday." Char clinked her glass with Annie's.

She took a tentative sip. The pucker level was just right. "I wasn't sure for a few days. Maybe planning the gala was a mistake." Between herself and Michael, they were astounded by the overwhelming affirmative responses of ninety-two percent. So far, one hundred and twenty-two people were attending. Wednesday's cut-off date couldn't come soon enough for Annie.

"Be serious. With all your planning, you don't have anything to worry about, girl." Char swayed to the piped-in music as she sipped the limoncello and Chambord martini.

Annie wished that was the case. Original estimates had been for eighty people. The increase by fifty percent meant she had to update her amounts for catering, thank you gifts, and supplies. Thank goodness the space wasn't an issue. It was a miracle that she had the foresight to find a venue that could accommodate two-hundred attendees.

"On paper it looks great." She agreed with Char's sentiment. Her plans were well thought out. "Making sure everything runs smoothly will be the bigger challenge."

The event was still several months away. There'd be time for last-minute changes, if need be. She also made sure the venue and most of the services she contracted included a clause about extreme weather. No one could predict what Mother Nature could throw at her. The clause stated if flights were canceled within eight hours of the event, the organization would receive a ninety percent refund on the down payment. The only monies she'd lose would be for the invitations and centerpiece flowers. She'd take that as a win.

"There's so many variables." Annie chewed her lip. A lack of self-confidence, the beast she had worked hard to put to rest, reared its debilitating head.

"You know, for a woman who said she wanted to party like it's nineteen ninety-nine, you're being a drag." Char, ever the consummate pointer-outer, stood with her hand on her hip. "Drink up."

Once again, she was right. They'd come here in celebration of surviving another work week, no easy task these days even under normal circumstances. Thanksgiving was a week away. After that, the chaos of Christmas, which she absolutely loved every minute of, would last until after New Year's. Then, a few weeks later, was the gala. What had she been thinking?

That part was easy to explain. Summer was a tough time to try to get large numbers of people together. From May through the fall, people were busy with camping, vacations, and endless gatherings like weddings and graduations. Annie banked on instincts. The idea centered around her hope that others would enjoy a stress-free night of adult socializing, eating good food, and dancing after the hustle and bustle of the holiday season. The only business part of the event would be a five-minute presentation of the services the society provided, what percent of their donation went directly to support neurodivergent clients, and appreciation for everyone's generosity.

Thank God she would not be the one to have to give the speech. Being on stage in front of a large group had never been Annie's strong point. She could handle a classroom-size gathering, but larger crowds brought out the insecure youngster who stood out because she was different from her classmates but didn't know why. Once her condition was identified, her understanding of how she saw the world and how she functioned in it, Annie began to make strides. She rejoiced in knowing she wasn't alone.

"Here." Char slid a fresh drink in front of her. When had she finished the first one? "Promise me you'll get out of your head long enough for at least one dance."

Annie practically snorted her drink. There was no such thing as one dance where Char was concerned. That was okay. Char's "Let's give it hell" attitude regarding predicaments was a welcome distraction. Not everything had a clear resolution and that's where Annie's struggles had always been. Hence, the gray area surrounding the quasi-relationship with Harlen.

"Thanks." The tartness brought her back, though the ever-present thoughts of Harlen remained. Since confronting her at the office, there was still no contact, which was okay. Harlen had to process the news of her involvement with Chloe. Annie still needed to hash out their future because she still believed there was one. Before they got there, Harlen needed to admit she still loved Chloe. If Annie was reading her correctly, Harlen continued to walk away from Annie because it was easier than walking away from Chloe.

Then, like a flash of lightning that at another time might have foreshadowed the onset of a migraine, Annie knew what she needed to say. Harlen didn't need to walk away from Chloe, she needed to walk toward Annie. The epiphany reassured her. A familiar tune keyed up and she bopped along in her seat before hopping off.

"Let's get out there and show them what two single women can do." There wasn't anyone else on the dance floor when she and Char began with their free dance style, laughing as they gyrated along. Soon others followed. Annie smiled. Dancing was like that. Everyone was too self-conscious to break the ice. She had apparently blown off the hesitancy that had plagued her the preceding weeks. Annie thrived on having a plan. All that was left to do was see it through. Easy.

❖

Harlen took off her drug store cheaters and rubbed her eyes. She'd been avoiding her semi-annual exam because she didn't want to acknowledge she needed glasses. Every day when she worked on the computer, read, or did a detail-oriented project, Harlen found she was squinting. The magnifying glasses were a temporary fix to get her through until then. Yup. Right after she made the appointment.

She looked in the refrigerator searching for something to drink, but nothing appealed to her. Having a cocktail sounded really good. If she had one she wouldn't think twice about having another. Harlen snagged a room-temp bottle of water with a sigh. When her doorbell rang, she cocked an eyebrow. Who would be ringing her bell after eight? When she swung the door open, her mouth dropped.

"Yes, I know. It's rude to show up unannounced, but I couldn't chance you not opening the door. The only thing worse would be if you ran away." Annie's smile looked tentative.

"You aren't wrong." Leave it to Annie to make the necessary move to end the charade and Harlen smiled. The collar of Annie's Verdun green wool coat was held up by a scarf in a beautiful shade of chartreuse. "Come in."

"Thanks." Annie's cheeks were rosy. The cold air from outside had followed her in, and brought the scent of impending snow. She stood awkwardly, their eyes locked. "At least you let me in"

"I'm a jerk sometimes, but I'm not cruel."

"Good," Annie said as she untied her scarf before unbuttoning her coat. Harlen hung them in the closet.

When she turned back, she forgot to breathe. Annie wore a soft-looking striped sweater in shades of green and blue that she'd paired with black knit pants, tucked into midcalf, low-heeled boots. Her makeup was flawless, and her wind-tossed hair was sexy as hell. Harlen wondered if she'd worn the outfit to work or if she'd changed for her surprise visit. Annie again waited. Harlen was at a loss for words. Saying good-bye to Chloe had taken a lot out of her mentally. She hadn't fared much better physically. Her sleep was still haphazard. Annie must have gotten tired of waiting and sat on the couch. Not knowing what else to do, Harlen sat in the adjacent chair.

"We keep having a tug-of-war." Annie pointed between them. "I don't want to land in the mud, do you?"

Harlen shook her head in agreement. Her scalp tingled. "I don't want you to, either." It was true. Harlen didn't want either of them to end up regretting the dynamic pull they shared.

Annie's gaze softened. "That's kind of you. I came to tell you…" Annie's voice faded, then she took Harlen's hand. "It's alright that you still love Chloe because I understand you always will. It's also okay that you want more. You might think it's a stumbling block to any relationship we might have, but it's not. Your love for Chloe doesn't make me jealous."

"It doesn't?" Harlen was in short-circuit mode and she was only able to respond with a couple of words. She *had* thought she had no right pursuing Annie when, at the end of the day, her thoughts always returned to Chloe's lifeless form. The unfairness of that reality had kept her from acting on her desires. All she'd done since meeting Annie was react. When Annie mimicked a gesture of Chloe's, Harlen didn't celebrate the memory. Instead, she'd viewed it negatively, but why? Annie squeezed her hand.

"I do worry what visiting her will do to your soul. Watching someone die can leave scars." Annie kissed her palm, then held it against her cheek. The intimacy of the gesture wasn't missed. "Scars do heal. What's left are the reminders so you don't forget."

Harlen swallowed around the knot that had formed. "I won't forget."

"I imagine not. You're the type of person who doesn't give her heart easily. It's part of you, just like your loyalty and the depth of your love." Annie let go, and the disconnect was instant. Painful. "I want to know more of that part of you. I want you to tell me how you found the woman you dropped your guard for. Tell me about the fun times and the discoveries you found together. Tell me all of it. Let me in." Annie reached for her long-time companion,

Carly's Sound. For a second, Harlen panicked, then relaxed. This was Annie. Annie held the book face up. "Write the book, Harlen."

Could she actually tell Annie the story of her life with Chloe? If she did, would Annie change her mind? How many blows could their relationship take before it fell apart, like her and Chloe's? Annie wasn't Chloe, and Harlen was a stronger person with Annie than without her. Harlen took the book, rubbing her thumb over the cracked cover. She met Annie's imploring eyes.

"I don't know where to start."

Annie stood. "I've found having coffee is a good ice breaker."

Harlen smiled. "I'm in." Maybe all wasn't lost. Whatever came out of tonight's conversation, at least she was opening the door to her heart, even if it was only ajar.

CHAPTER THIRTY

"Where did you first meet?" Annie asked. Harlen had acted willing enough to share her story until they sat facing each other from opposite ends of the couch. A little nudge couldn't hurt. Right?

Harlen's eyes brightened. "The third year of my degree was packed with a full course load." She shook her head. "I'd been on an architectural design degree track until the prior year when I lost interest in drawing blueprints and all the red tape involved with building codes and inspections."

Annie thought about what little she knew about architecture, which left her wondering why Harlen had chosen architecture to begin with. "That's when you decided to focus on interior design?"

"Yes. They were both four-year majors. It meant having to take fine art, sketching, color theory, and a few more fundamental courses in order to make the switch. That decision added condensed summer courses and an entire year for my degree."

"And that's when you met Chloe?"

Harlen nodded and set the mug she'd been holding on the coffee table. "She was majoring in journalism and doing a minor in art. We met in a color theory course."

"Were you able to use some of your credits when you changed your major?" She couldn't imagine starting over from scratch.

"Some. I had a lot of catching up to do and took what I needed over two years. It also meant taking a couple of evening and summer courses." Harlen laughed without any mirth. "At twenty-five, I thought anything was possible." The positive outlook ebbed when Chloe left. "The schedule nearly killed me."

"I can't imagine what your days were like."

"If it were just days, my future might have been very different, but what did I know? I was in class from eight in the morning until ten at night, four days a week."

"How did you fit in time for a relationship with Chloe?"

A sigh escaped as Harlen stood. "I didn't. It was more a fling" She pointed to Annie's mug.

"I'll go, too. I need to stretch my legs." The little white lie was her way of keeping the momentum of their discussion going.

Harlen poured steaming brew into their cups. "Chloe finished her degree and left before we really had a chance to connect." Harlen leaned against the counter and blew across the top of her mug, and Annie noticed the words "Keep on keeping on," in red letters on the black enamel. "I knew we were attracted to each other since we texted every day, but Chloe had landed an apprenticeship at a newspaper in Michigan, so that was that."

"Did you keep in touch after she left?"

"At first, we did. Then her job demanded more and more of her time and I was cramming to keep my GPA up and we lost touch." Sadness clouded Harlen's eyes.

"But that's not the end of the story." Annie was there for answers and she wanted to hear the whole story.

"Four years later, I got a text from an unknown number. I don't usually look at those kind of messages, but I did. It was from Chloe. She had to change her phone number after her purse was stolen." Harlen stared into space. "She was moving back to the area and wondered if I still lived here. We made plans to meet up." Harlen's smile was the kind Annie saw on faces when the ending overshadowed the joy.

"What happened to your design career? Were you working at Forrest then?" There were so many more question Annie wanted to ask, though she was afraid Harlen might shut down if she asked too many.

"I was so overwhelmed with having given up everything else during college, I just wanted to do something that wouldn't be full of demands. The family business had been going for almost fifteen years and growing in leaps and bounds. My grandparents offered me a position in acquisitions while I took a mental break. It was an easy choice because I could start earning a decent income." Harlen looked into her empty cup. "I think I need something stronger than coffee."

"Do you want to stop?" She wasn't beyond having empathy, especially for someone she cared about. "I don't think you were expecting to have to retell your life history."

"I wasn't, but it's okay." Harlen went to the sidebar and chose a bottle of bourbon, turning it so she could see the label. Annie nodded.

"Neat, please."

Harlen returned, sitting closer than before, and tapped her glass. "To memories."

"Cheers." The heat bloomed in her stomach and warmth spread outward.

"The years passed so quickly, I got caught up in the family dynamics and stayed. Then, when Chloe returned, we started dating. We were going to move in together and I had a nest egg for a down payment on a home. It wasn't the best time to start a venture on my own." Harlen drank, then winced. "I don't know why I drink this stuff other than liking the buzz."

"I think that's why people drink." Annie set hers down. She didn't want to miss a word.

"Chloe was thrilled with her job. There was a lot of celebrating and meeting the family. We settled into a house. Chloe did a lot of traveling, which she loved. The idea of working in interior design fell by the wayside. I was content with life, and I thought Chloe was, too. A few months before the accident, she told me she wanted more."

Annie witnessed Harlen's pain. Had Chloe wanted more than Harlen could provide? Were there outside influences that interfered with their relationship?

"She wanted to become a freelance journalist and travel the world. I was shocked."

"What did you want, Harlen?"

Harlen sat still for a few minutes. "When I was forced to look at my life, I realized I wanted to put my degree to work and start my own interior design business. We talked once about having kids and taking family vacations." Harlen broke eye contact. Annie pictured the discussion that followed, but she didn't know either of them well enough to know if there was shouting or tears or silence. "Chloe had changed her mind about wanting children. She didn't want to be responsible for anyone but herself. She wanted adventure and exposure to different cultures and the opportunity to write about the frailties of humanity."

She didn't believe for a minute that Harlen would let Chloe go that easily. Even with how little she knew of Harlen's personal life she didn't doubt family meant a lot to Harlen. Did she still want children of her own? For fuck's sake, Annie didn't even know how old Harlen was. Annie waited for Harlen to keep going.

"I thought we'd be together forever, that's how good we were at the start." Harlen finished her drink. When she looked up, her eyes glistened with unshed tears. "My suggestion of seeing a counselor wasn't well received. Chloe said we didn't have issues that could be resolved by talking to a stranger."

"How long ago did she tell you she wanted to end the relationship?" It was a hard question and she needed to know the answer.

"Two months before the accident. Chloe started looking for an apartment while she transitioned to a new position at the paper. I…I said she could stay. That we'd make our living arrangement work. She thanked me for the offer but said continuing to live together wouldn't be good for either of us." Harlen shook her head. "I knew it was a bad idea. I just couldn't let her walk away while I was still in love with her." She scrubbed her face. The motion might have been to take a much-needed break or to hide the threatening tears. As much as she wanted to know everything, she wasn't about to push her beyond her emotional limit. For the first time since their talk had resumed, she took Harlen's hand.

"Saying the words out loud can't be easy. How about we stop for tonight."

Harlen studied their joined hands before letting out a shaky sigh. "I never thought I'd say talking about Chloe was exhausting, but it is." Beneath her smile was a layer of sadness. "I think I'm done."

As much as she wanted to know how Harlen ended up dedicated to Chloe after being told it was over, Annie wasn't going to have all the answers tonight. Harlen had shared a lot, and she had a lot to process. She slid her hand away, hoping there would be other opportunities. They stood at the same time. "Thank you for letting me understand how important Chloe is in your life."

Running her hand through her hair, Harlen's cheeks colored. "There's more. I'm sorry—"

"No need to apologize." Annie shrugged into her coat, glad for its weighted warmth. The chill was from more than thinking about going out in the cold. "Get some rest. We'll talk again soon." She placed a kiss on Harlen's warm cheek and wished they were heading to bed instead of saying good-bye.

"I'll call you." Harlen shoved one hand in her pocket while the other held the door open. She stood gazing at her for a long minute. "Thank you for not judging me, Annie."

She pulled in a breath. "It's not my style. I want to understand you and what motivates your actions, that's what's important." Annie turned away. If she stood there any longer, she'd ask to stay out of selfish desire. That would not have been fair to Harlen.

Chapter Thirty-one

Harlen stared at the color swatches and charts scattered across her worktable. She was supposed to be working up ideas for a single-family home that Forrest had obtained through foreclosure. She wasn't keen on sketching out the remodel part of it because waiting until the buyer had a voice in the reno would have been the ideal situation, but waiting was also a double-edged sword.

Prospective buyers wanted to be able to envision themselves living in a home before buying it. Some of those same buyers weren't capable of forming pictures of what the space would look like when it was remodeled. That left the company with the choice of renovating before putting it on the market at a higher price and knowing there would be customers who weren't thrilled with the design, no matter how beautiful. Alternatively, trying to sell at a lower price as is and showing them examples of what it could look like after they put their "personal touch" on the design was a gamble.

Either way, Harlen was left with the task of making mock-ups and letting the sales department decide which option to go for. With a click on the folder named by the address of the home, Harlen found the blueprint document and the schematic that displayed the square footage, including the dimensions of each room, and the outdoor space. Some designers didn't include the outdoor space in their drafts, but she believed it was an integral part of every home.

After strategically placing the open documents between the two oversized monitors, she sat back and took a drink of her lukewarm coffee, sighing.

"I need an assistant."

"Doesn't everyone?" Jane asked as she took one of the seats in front of Harlen's desk.

"Hi, sis. What's shakin'?"

"Oh, you know. Same old, different day." Jane smiled. "What's up with you and the assistant?"

"Wishful thinking on my part." She turned. "What news do you bring?"

"Mom's birthday is in two weeks." Jane usually took charge of getting the family together for their parents' birthdays and the five-year anniversary celebrations. After the first few anniversary parties, their mother had sat them down. The conversation came as a bit of a shock, but Harlen was glad her mother had spoken up, saying they loved everyone wanting to celebrate their marriage, but having a party every year left no room for intimate plans of their own. Between Pete's embarrassment and Jane feeling unappreciated, Harlen had been the one to smooth things over. That's when they agreed on the five-year plan. Everyone walked away satisfied and her parents didn't have to cancel trips at the last minute. Jane was big on surprises.

"Same date every year." She smiled, knowing Jane had a dry sense of humor and would likely make her pay…at some point.

"Funny. I've run out of ideas."

Harlen leaned forward. "Say it isn't so." Her sister was notorious for coming up with unique gifts, themes, and locations. This was a huge revelation.

"I know. Next year is Mom's seventy-fifth birthday and it's going to be an affair to remember, so I have to keep it low-key this year, and I'm stumped. Next year is also their fiftieth anniversary."

She hadn't given much thought to either occasion since she wasn't the family event planner, but both deserved special attention. "I can't believe you don't have any ideas."

Jane looked down at the notebook in her lap. She met Harlen's gaze, but she could see the hesitation. "There's only one thing I could think of, but everyone would have to be on board." The key word there was everyone, meaning Pete would have to do his part, and they both knew what a curmudgeon he could be.

"Tell me your idea and I'll get Pete to do his part."

Excitement lit Jane's eyes. "Okay, so, you know how Mom always talked about opening up the dining room?"

Uh-oh. "Yeah." Years ago, when the family was still fairly small, their mother had "suggested" to their father that a bigger table and open floorplan would make it easier to have family gatherings. Dad had grumbled it would be a waste of money since they didn't have "the crew" over except for Sunday dinners and celebrations. That was right before Jane got married to Jason. The following year, Peter and Marie had their first child, Mark. From there, their immediate family continued to expand, and aunts, uncles, and cousins they'd rarely seen since childhood moved back to the area after being scattered across the country.

"What do you think about giving Mom what she wants?"

Disbelief coursed through her. With everything going on between not seeing Chloe, things with Annie being better though still not great, and her trying to get the design department up and running at full steam, Harlen couldn't even think of another project. "That's a big ask, Jane."

"I know, but it's for Mom and Dad. You have to agree after all they've done for us, they deserve having something they can use and appreciate every day."

Harlen snorted. "Mom will definitely like it, but what about Dad? Don't you think he'll feel cheated?" She could see it now. Her father might have the louder complaints, but her mother had always had the upper hand when it came to family stuff.

"I'll think of some way to placate him." Jane tapped her chin with her index finger several times. "What about the big screen TV he's mentioned? And a new recliner?"

"That would be good. I know he's having trouble seeing the one he parks in front of." Dad loved to watch sports and movies were a close second. "What's my part in all this?"

Pale pink shaded Jane's cheeks. "That's what I wanted to talk to you about. Would you be willing to design and decorate the new space?" She waited for an answer as she leaned closer.

Harlen wasn't surprised by her request. Jane was busy with work, the kids, and taking college courses. Lord knew Pete didn't have a lick of fashion sense, and his wife had hired a decorator to revamp their outdated home furnishings.

"What are you suggesting?"

Jane went on to explain her ideas and they discussed the timeline of taking on a project that would include removing the walls between the dining and living room, as well as incorporating the smallest, first-floor bedroom. It made sense since there were five bedrooms and they were empty except when the grandchildren slept over. To make up for the lost space, Jane suggested a convertible couch. Harlen knew from experience they were hard to set up and uncomfortable to sleep on. She'd research high density sectionals that could be reconfigured to accommodate children or adults. Jane left twenty minutes later, all smiles.

Great. One more project on my never-ending list. She didn't mind helping her parents, though someday soon she hoped to have the time to work on her own relationship. That was, if Annie didn't lose patience and move on before Harlen found a way to spend more time together. Sad truth was, she was scared they'd get on track only to run off the rails without having a clue things between them were going sideways, like with Chloe.

Even more daunting was having to tell Annie about having severed ties with Chloe and the harder truth that Harlen missed the connection. She hadn't been to see Chloe since she gave the video card to the Williamses. The obligation Harlen had carried since the accident eased a little more every day. Annie deserved to take center stage if they had any chance at a real relationship, and that was all on her. Wasn't it always?

Harlen sighed and turned to the screens in front of her. She was only one person and she had a laundry list of tasks to complete. For now, she had to stay focused. Work. Annie. Reno for parents. That was the order of items to accomplish. All she could think about was how much she was dreading telling Annie she'd taken a back seat in Harlen's life. Again.

❖

"I don't know what to think, Maise." Annie lay on the floor with her chin in her hands while Maisie watched her wide-eyed, her tail flicking as Annie talked.

The heartfelt discussion with Harlen helped her understand why there was hesitation to get involved with Annie. But seriously, to go MIA for the enth time was a hard pill to swallow. Mostly because there'd never been anyone that Annie worried about where they stood, until Harlen.

"The thing is, do I trust my gut like I have my entire life, or do I drop the idea that Harlen could be 'the One.'"

She didn't bother with air quotes since Maisie appeared to get it when she tipped her head in response. Annie had done well training her to understand words she used repeatedly. That did not mean the princess in residence was always an angel. There were times when all she wanted to do was get in loungewear and have a drink. Those were usually the same times when her fur baby tried her patience by doing everything she wasn't supposed to do until Annie gave up and held her while she napped. Granted, she only weighed eight or so pounds, but still. Maisie was dead weight like a sack of potatoes in Annie's arms.

"And." She began before rolling onto her back, looking at Maisie upside down. "I've mostly been the one to initiate contact."

Annie couldn't help chuckling when Maisie flopped over and rolled to her back. She flipped over to do Maisie's bidding for belly rubs.

"It's times like these I wish you could talk, Maise."

The cat chortled and wiggled back and forth. Annie's phone rang and her heart picked up speed. Aside from Char or her parents, there wasn't a list of people dying to talk with her. She scooted to the coffee table hoping it was Harlen calling her. Her stomach dropped when she saw the Spam Risk on her screen and she let it ring.

"So much for hoping, my good girl." She couldn't help treating Maisie more like a child without the expense of one, rather than a pet. From the first day she brought Maisie home, she had claimed Annie as her momma. "How about I get you some treats and a cup of tea for me, then we'll play." Maisie followed her to the drawer that held her goodies. She picked out her allotted number, broke them in half and laughed when Maisie beat her to the spot designated for eating the special morsels.

While her tea cooled, Annie dragged the cotton ribbon, one that had gotten considerably shorter over the years, back and forth until Maisie flopped, mouth open and paws swatting. She was a ball of energy for short bursts of time, but Annie knew playtime was coming to an end when she tossed the ribbon in the air and Maisie watched it fall to the floor without any effort to catch it. She dropped into her chair and reached for her tea. The lavender and honey brew was the perfect temperature. Sipping her drink like a fine wine, Annie thought about Harlen's Houdini act. Sometimes it was smarter to leave well enough alone.

Chapter Thirty-two

"Hi, Annie." Harlen finally had the mental acuity to face the inevitable and made time to contact her.

"May I ask who's calling?" Annie's voice was cool.

"It's Harlen." She swallowed down the bile that threatened to rise. Annie's reaction was understandable considering the long periods of ghosting that happened.

"No kidding." The line was eerily quiet while Annie paused. "Are you going to jerk me around more by disappearing again? If you are, don't bother. We're either going to address our issues or move on, Harlen. I'm not a play toy for your amusement."

This was the Annie she admired the day they collided. Just like her heart, Harlen was unable to avoid the emotional and physical attraction that she'd been distracted from.

"My behavior is inexcusable and I'm sorry you were on the receiving end." She'd practiced her plea a dozen times, each attempt sounding more pathetic than the last. Frustrated, Harlen decided on jotting a few key words to keep her on track, and she referred to them. "I'd like to finish my story, if you'll let me."

Annie let out a breath. "Your absence has hurt, Harlen. I'm not impervious to emotional pain. If I give you another chance, how do I know you won't fuck me over again?"

"I'll try my damnedest not to." Harlen was encouraged by their ongoing conversation, knowing Annie held the upper hand.

"Please." The noise she heard on the other end might have been tapping.

"Three strikes and you're out."

In Harlen's excitement, she started rambling. "I might have already hit that ceiling." Panic rose when she realized she was throwing herself under the bus.

"That's not a great way to move forward." A sigh could be heard from Annie. "Are you serious about wanting to work on us?" Her voice was soft but her tone was unyielding.

"I really do. Definitely." She was horrible at talking with Annie and she jotted it down to examine the reason later.

"Fine. My terms, no excuses." If she wasn't mistaken, Annie sounded excited at the prospect.

"Understood. When can I see you?" She didn't care if she sounded desperate since she was.

"Coffee is Life's Blood Café at six." Voices in the background meant Annie was still at work. "Hold on a sec."

While she waited, Harlen jotted key words. In her heart she knew this was the last time Annie would be willing to give her another try and she couldn't blame her.

"Harlen?"

"Yes."

"Don't be late. Good-bye."

"See you then." The silence on the other end was followed by the call ended screen. Had Annie heard her? She hadn't said what day and she didn't have a chance to ask. Harlen would go tonight in the hope that she got the details right. One more fuck-up on her part and she wouldn't get another chance. Harlen glanced at the scribbles on the paper in front of her. She had to decipher them and have a clear conversation with herself. She'd said good-bye to her first love, but hopefully she would be seeing her second soon. Harlen sent out a silent prayer to whatever entity watched over her that it wasn't too late.

❖

"Hi." Harlen slid into the seat across from her. She appeared shy or embarrassed. Maybe both. At least she was on time.

"Hello." Annie took a breath. "Today is a clearing the air meeting. No excuses for past behaviors and no judgment." She needed to make it clear she would not be manipulated while the tingle of seeing Harlen returned.

"Got it." Harlen fidgeted with a piece of paper she produced from her coat pocket.

"What's that?"

Harlen blushed. Though her cheeks were already rosy from the cold, Annie had no problem seeing the change. "It's all the things I want to talk about."

"That's quite a list. You might want to get a drink before we start."

"Good idea. Can I get you anything?" Harlen's gaze spoke volumes. She was focused on Annie, her gaze moving from her eyes to her mouth and back again.

"I'll never refuse another cup of oolong tea with a packet of honey crystals, please."

Harlen smiled. "I'll be sure to get it right."

While Harlen was gone, she played with the notion of Harlen being an attentive partner. If her ongoing dedication to Chloe was any indication, Annie didn't think she'd have to worry about much, but they were far from being in a committed relationship. She wasn't about to give in to her libido again without having reassurances, as much as anyone could, that Harlen would remain open and honest with her.

"Here you go." Harlen set the steaming mug in front of her. "I brought a couple of extra packets, though I think you're sweet already." She glanced away nervously when Annie caught her gaze.

"Flattery is nice, but it won't get you brownie points." She blew across the liquid, liking how the steam swirled in response. It was still too hot to drink, but the flavor of the tentative sip she took was satisfying. "Are you going to pick up where you left off when we last spoke?" She wasn't in a hurry to get away, but she was vulnerable to Harlen's charms and she needed to stay on point.

Harlen cooled her coffee with the same technique before quickly setting it down. "Damn, that's really hot."

Annie raised her brow.

"Right." Harlen cleared her throat before continuing. "Before the accident, Chloe and I talked about healthcare directives. She was emphatic about not wanting to be a vegetable. I promised I would never let that happen to her." Harlen smiled wistfully. "Unfortunately, she never completed a proxy form."

For a moment, Annie's breath froze in her chest. This was why Harlen couldn't give up on Chloe. Not being able to let her go due to love was part of it, and certainly understandable, but this new piece of information was what jarred Annie to her core. Harlen refused to give up because she'd promised Chloe she wouldn't leave her to linger. If Harlen couldn't force the issue, then who had the power to overrule her?

"For all her good intentions, Chloe was terrible at following through on a lot of them." She shook her head. "She also hated authority of any kind telling her what to do, and that included the seat belt law."

"That's how she ended up in a coma." Annie didn't ask Harlen to confirm what was plain.

"Yes." Harlen reached for her hand and she let her. "The day of the accident wasn't the first time she hadn't worn a seat belt. I asked the ER doctor if…" Harlen swallowed hard, and Annie instinctively knew she was choked by emotions. "If wearing one would have made a difference. Of course, he said he couldn't guarantee it, but he'd seen enough accident victims that he could say Chloe's odds for recovery would have definitely improved."

"Have you been fighting with the hospital to turn off life support?" There were a lot of stories Annie had read about medical and ethical battles and the right to die issue, knowing very few patients ever got what they wanted without legal directives in place.

Harlen's features changed from melancholy to pinched. "Without the document I have no say in decisions about Chloe's medical treatment. None."

Annie wasn't about to let Harlen continue to face the issue alone. "Who does have legal say?" Then it dawned on her. "Her parents," she said at the same time as Harlen, who managed a tiny smile.

"I've told them of Chloe's wishes, but they said they would never give up on their daughter recovering. More than once, they pointed out that miracles happen every day." Harlen shrugged. "What could I say? At the beginning, I shared their hope of Chloe waking up." She stared ahead.

"Do you still think that way?" Annie's heart thudded in her chest as she clicked her tongue, a habit that sometimes appeared when she was unable to take control of a situation. What if Harlen had been using her as a distraction from the duty she was bound to by a promise?

"No. To what end? Even if by some miracle Chloe woke up, she'd never be the woman I knew and loved. She'd be a shell of herself, forced to live a less-than life that wouldn't be the real Chloe. I'm done waiting for her corpse to rise." Harlen's shoulders lowered. Whether it was in defeat or resignation, Annie had no way of knowing.

"I'm sorry you've suffered through the wait." She squeezed Harlen's hand before she slipped away.

"Thank you. Part of what I wanted to tell you is that I've walked away."

She hadn't expected to hear the news. "What does that mean?"

"I've visited Chloe for the last time. A coworker from the paper sent a holiday video they found. It was the last one Chloe attended. I gave it to her parents and told them to watch it because what they'd see is how Chloe wanted to live her life. Kind, fun-loving, and bossy. Not lying in a hospital bed covered in a white sheet."

"Wow. What did they say?"

Harlen took her time and drank the cooled beverage. "They threw me out and threatened me with an order of protection."

Annie's hackles rose and she sat forward, ready to fight in defense of Harlen's obvious love for Chloe. "Can they do that?"

Harlen hmphed. "When you're rich you can do almost anything regardless if it's for the wrong reason."

Forrest Enterprises was a rich company. Annie had done a lot of research and had dug deeper after she and Harlen had dinner together. That night at the restaurant when she disappeared felt like a long time ago. The company gave a respectable percentage of their earnings to worthy organizations and provided scholarships based on merit to local students. They were one of those families that she was happy their success resulted in giving back to the community. Annie felt the same way about Dolly Parton and the likes who consistently shared their wealth with others.

"Are you going to let them?"

"I don't think I have to worry. It was an idle threat, just like the ones Chloe heard growing up when she didn't bow to their every whim." This time Harlen's smile looked genuine before she leaned forward. "I owe you an apology. I wasn't ready for a relationship before."

"Why did you let me think otherwise?" She wasn't about to turn all soft and gushy just because the hot woman sitting close had changed her story.

"Because I was—am—really attracted to you, and there were things you did that reminded me of Chloe. They were endearing." Harlen took a breath. "I got scared though, and thought if I let you in too far, my love for Chloe would disappear, and it crushed me."

Annie rolled her eyes. "So you ghosted me?"

"It was wrong. I know."

"You think?" Annie looked off. If she kept her eyes on Harlen, she wouldn't be able to process, because she was about ready to say, "Fuck it", and ask her home. She replayed all she now knew, weighing the pros and cons as she did. Then she went over possible scenarios and her response to each. She didn't want a decision this important left to a "being in the moment" kind of response. "Tell me where we stand today."

Harlen's eyes lit up as she straightened in the chair. "Dating and daily communication like people who are dating do, but without the ghosting part." She smiled that killer smile, and for the first time, Annie recognized real hope in her gaze.

"Only if it's on my terms."

"Yes. Fine." Harlen nodded vigorously.

"We'll have an in-person date at least once a week, more if we can, with most of them being at home. I don't need fancy. It's spending time with you that I want most. So, yeah, daily communication is the goal. Even a short text would be okay, but don't make a habit of it." Annie waited before she went on, giving Harlen a chance to take it all in.

"Yes, to every stipulation. Are there others?" She was blown away when Harlen didn't hesitate to agree to her terms. Did that mean this time Harlen was all in?

"We spend at least all the holiday eves or the actual holiday together. And I need an escort to my work gala, and I want you to take me." Annie's requests were reasonable since she'd taken into account their already busy lives, but she wouldn't settle for being second or third string. "If you haven't disappeared and I haven't ignored your calls or texts by New Year's Eve, we make it official."

"Whatever will make you happy, Annie."

Harlen closed the distance between them until she caught the scent of chocolate on her lips before she slipped her hand to cup the nape of her neck, keeping her close. Annie didn't breathe—couldn't in the few beats that passed as she waited. She watched as Harlen's lips grew larger, and disappointment swept through her when they bypassed her mouth and stopped at her ear.

"You forgot one very important item, Annie. We're going to do a lot of fucking, or it's a deal breaker."

Harlen's lips pressed hers in a soft, almost too gentle kiss. As Harlen moved away, she caught Annie's lower lip and tugged just enough to let her know who would be in charge in the bedroom. A gush of wet heat dampened her panties.

"I had to leave something for your list," she said, surprised she could get the words out.

"No worries. It was the only thing on mine. I knew you'd take care of the rest." Harlen stood. "It's one of the reasons you're so fucking hot." She threw her cup away. "I'll call you tomorrow and you can let me know when and where you want our date to be, Annie."

How long she sat with her right hand around the empty cup while her other touched the spots Harlen had kissed was anyone's guess. There'd been so many reasons why their relationship could go sideways.

"Huh."

Annie stood, pressed the remote start button for her car, then tossed her cup. In the car, she glanced into the rearview mirror and admired the smile plastered on her face.

"Have I got news for you, Maisie."

She laughed out loud, like a weight had been lifted from her entire body. When she was focused enough to drive, Annie headed home, all the while thinking about her impending date and the promise of steamy hot sex. A promise she knew Harlen would keep, no matter what.

Chapter Thirty-three

"I can't believe you're giving Harlen another chance." Char swung her arms like pendulums.

"Don't judge." Annie's legs were burning with fatigue. "Harlen's agreed to my requirements for the relationship." Steam clouded her vision. Just a few more blocks and their walk would be over, thank goodness. She hadn't been taking care of herself lately, and it showed by being winded and having to push hard for the last half mile of a four-mile walk.

"I can only imagine how demanding the list was." Char laughed as they slowed down for the bench she considered theirs.

After stretching, Annie dropped onto the worn, comfortable wood and took a drink from her water bottle. She ignored the cold beneath where she sat. "I'm not that bad. Besides, if you count how many times Harlen pulled a Houdini, she's lucky I didn't make her sign a contract."

"Tough-as-nails Annie has gone soft." Char did a few squats and hamstring stretches. If she wasn't mistaken, they should have done the stretching *before* they walked.

"I can't help it. Harlen's the only person who makes me feel…" Annie caught Char's gaze.

"What?"

She turned her gloved hand, not sure of the word she was searching for. "Normal?"

Char stared at her. "You say that like you think feeling normal is a bad thing." Char did air quotes around normal. "We just deal with things differently is all." Char's experiences were vastly different from Annie's.

On the one hand, Char knew that slowing down and taking the time necessary to develop a solution was important, but another part of her brain demanded immediate action. Sometimes she lost the battle, but that was okay. Annie wouldn't have her be any other way.

"That hasn't changed for me. It's being with someone who sees me as I am and still wants to be with me that matters."

Char pulled her legs up and wrapped her arms around her knees. It was a self-preservation technique she used when she felt vulnerable. "Tell me how Harlen treats you."

"It's hard to explain."

"Try." Char softened her tone. "Please?"

Annie would do anything to help Char understand how she felt whenever Harlen was around. "You know how dates act like they're waiting for you to go off the deep end and start yelling or whatever?"

"Yeah." Char hugged herself tighter.

"With Harlen, there's none of that."

"Damn, girl. You really did find someone special."

She nodded. "Then you can understand why I'm willing to give her, and us, another try."

"Of course." Char put her feet on the ground, then bumped shoulders. "Doesn't mean I can't be jealous, but you deserve it." She kissed Annie's cheek. "Let's get a drink to celebrate your on-again infatuation with Ms. Studly."

Annie rolled her eyes. "I am not going anywhere in sweaty clothes." She wrinkled her nose at the idea.

"Fine, Miss Hoity-toity. I'll shower at your place."

"Fine." Annie chuckled. Char always had an overnight bag in her car. When asked about it, she said, "A girl can still dream of getting lucky, can't she?" Annie was lucky to have met Harlen and the way she felt in Harlen's presence wasn't easy to ignore. She hoped her instincts were right and they were meant to be together. Otherwise she might spiral into a state of morosity she might not recover from.

❖

"This is nice." Harlen internally winced. Being with Annie was more than nice.

Annie tipped her head, studying her as she drank her mango lassi. "What's going on with you?"

Shit. Annie would see through a lie. "I'm worried I'll do or say something that will ruin the vibe." That wasn't quite right, but Annie would decipher it. She always saw through to her core, and her keen awareness would keep Harlen from pretending things between them were okay if they weren't. Like she had with Chloe.

"Do you think our situation is that fragile?" Annie dipped a vegetable samosa into ketchup and took a bite.

"You're always so inciteful." Harlen ate chicken tikka masala without tasting it. The air between them crackled, and she was convinced it wasn't in a good way.

"Stop avoiding the question." Annie leaned against the foot of the couch. Dinner was spread across the coffee table and they sat on large pillows on the floor.

Making Harlen own up to her feelings was something Annie was good at. "When you say it, my worry sounds foolish." She smiled. Annie continued to wait for an answer. "No, we've been through enough to prove it can weather storms."

"Then let it go, Harlen." Annie set her empty glass down with a thud. "You're overthinking. It happens, but you don't have to worry with me. I've never left you guessing, have I?"

There it was. The in-your-face blatant truth that Annie had no problem saying out loud. "No, you haven't."

"Then stop worrying." Annie went back to eating. Apparently, the issue was solved.

Harlen made a concerted effort to do as Annie suggested, although she was fairly convinced in Annie's mind it wasn't a suggestion at all. She smiled. "What's going on with work?"

Annie told her about Michael's sixth sense and his uncanny ability to anticipate how he could help her find work-arounds in sticky situations. He was also her right-hand man for all the details regarding the fundraising gala she had planned. Harlen wasn't threatened by their congeniality. In fact, she was glad Annie had someone she could rely on to have her back at work.

"How's the design work progressing? Have you stepped away from acquisitions?"

"There's a lot going on, though training someone to take over my position was easy. Everything else turned into a cluster fuck." Harlen's faced burned. She rarely swore around Annie. "Promotional ads and flyers went out last month. I'm so busy with renovation and design projects at Forrest I don't have time to get my own business off the ground." She didn't want to sound ungrateful for the chance to do what she loved, but being stretched across a half-dozen projects at once was taking a toll. "It's not an excuse, but it is responsible for some of our scheduling issues."

Annie wiped her mouth. "But not the only reason."

"That's true. The others are non-issues now." Harlen watched for a reaction. She could tell Annie was working through the information.

"Right. Let's clean up. I bought a Turkish coffee blend I'm keen to try." Once the food was stored and the dishwasher started, Annie moved to the coffee maker. Harlen caught her mid-stride.

"The coffee can wait." She started the kiss slowly on purpose. Annie didn't resist her undisguised meaning. Somehow she ended up pinning Annie between her and the counter with nowhere to go, and she moaned into Harlen's demanding mouth. By the time the kiss ended, they were breathing hard. Annie's eyes were lust filled, her hard nipples poking the material of her blouse.

Annie touched her swollen lips. "Damn, you can kiss." She stayed leaning against the counter with her hand wrapped around the edge, like she was afraid she'd fall if she let go. Letting go was what Harlen wanted, too.

"Thanks." Her entire body tingled. "There's always room for improvement."

"We better lie down before I pass out." Annie chuckled weakly.

Harlen nuzzled Annie's neck. "I don't mind you passing out as long as it's after I make you cum." Annie crumpled in her arms. "I've got you."

"Good thing you do." Annie held onto her shoulders until she could stand on her own. "Let's go."

Chapter Thirty-four

"Where's Maisie?" Harlen asked as she practically ripped off each piece of Annie's clothes.

She moved her mouth from Harlen's while she fumbled with Harlen's zipper. "How the hell should I know?" After her initial greeting and apparent disinterest in what Annie was doing, her fur baby had disappeared, like she often did.

"I'd like to have you all to myself until tomorrow."

"You will." Naked and wet, Annie flipped down the covers and glanced at the closed door. Unless Maisie was asleep under her bed, they wouldn't be interrupted. She climbed in, shaking her ass in invitation.

Harlen growled and pinned her down with the weight of her body. "Do you know what happens when you tease?" She licked Annie's tight nipple, making it harder.

"No. What?"

"This." Harlen bit down and a jolt of painful pleasure shot to her already soaked center. "And this." She pushed two fingers inside with ease, filling her.

"Fuck." She did her best to meet Harlen's fingers before they were gone.

"Not yet." Harlen appeared to regain control, letting her know who would be leading their lovemaking.

The idea they were lovers wasn't new, but lovemaking was intimate, and she wasn't sure they were there. Later. *I can sort out what it means later.* Annie thrust her hip, flipping them both. "That's so wrong." She slid her wet center against Harlen's, the friction moving her closer to the orgasm she needed so desperately.

"Baby. What you do to me." The words came out breathy and Harlen reached for her breasts, hefting their weight.

Annie liked when Harlen acted on her desires. "Mmm...I like what you do to me, too." She slipped her fingers between Harlen's slick folds, then tasted her. "I want more of this."

Harlen rolled her to her back. "Oh, don't worry. You'll have your fill of me." A slow, passionate kiss with tongues and the combined heat of their mouths followed. "I've had so many wet dreams about you I can't wait for the real thing." Harlen entered her again and she opened to welcome her deeper.

"Yes, yes. I need to cum so bad." She didn't care if she sounded needy. Harlen made her want the kind of sex in romance novels. The kind she knew Harlen was capable of giving. Her desire to find out if their first nights together were flukes, or that this was how sex with Harlen was destined to be, set off an inferno inside.

"Can you let me watch you, baby?" Harlen kissed her softly as she slowly moved in and out. "Will you let me see you cum?" Harlen asked as she rubbed her thumb on Annie's clit.

The tight knot between her soaked folds was so hard she thought it might literally explode. She'd fight the natural reaction to close her eyes when she climaxed. If Harlen wanted to see the moment happen, she'd do her best. "I'll try." She bit her lip, hoping it was a promise she could keep.

"It's okay if you can't."

"I want to." Annie's insides clenched. She was almost there. "Remind me."

Harlen smiled. "That's my girl."

The term of endearment sent her into orbit. Her body convulsed and she had to fight against closing her eyes until she saw the pure joy in Harlen's gaze, making it easy to give her what she wanted. The contractions went on and on while the struggle to keep her promise continued. When the spasms stopped, Harlen kissed her cheek.

"Close your eyes and relax while I hold you," Harlen said softly. When she withdrew, all Annie could do was whimper at the loss. "It's okay, honey. There will be more. As many as you want." Harlen kissed her forehead.

For a second or two, she fought the euphoria that followed her orgasm before giving in. As many as she wanted. That sounded like a dream come true.

Harlen watched Annie doze off, her face relaxed, and she smiled. She was content knowing she'd given Annie pleasure, but it was more than that. Annie had opened herself to Harlen in ways she didn't think were easy for Annie. For all her bluster about speaking her mind, Annie kept her guard in place, aware people might misinterpret things she did or said.

Annie shared what she felt when she felt it. Maybe there were people who pooh-poohed her for being insensitive or egotistical. That wasn't it at all. People failed to recognize when someone was speaking their truth. Harlen hoped to conquer her fear of rejection from speaking hers. Whether or not she loved Annie was no longer the question. However, instead of telling Annie how she felt, Harlen kept her feelings secretive. Annie was too good for *her*. How could Annie love her when Harlen still loved Chloe? Annie deserved better. Admitting her fears was scary shit. Annie stretched beside her.

"Mmm," Annie said as she moved onto her side. "Why is it I'm always knocked out after I cum?" She rubbed her hand over Harlen's stomach and abdomen, stopping short of her hairline.

Concentrating was hard when Annie touched her. "You were very relaxed." There could be worse reasons.

"True. I usually bolt after sex and relax when I get home." Annie's finger circled her nipple, making it pebble. Annie stopped moving. "Except when I'm with you." Her eyes were stormy.

"I'm glad you can be you with me." Harlen lightly kissed her mouth. Intimate moments didn't always revolve around sex. Sometimes sex lacked intimacy. That's when she realized her relationship with Chloe had changed.

"Me, too." Annie reached for the glass of water on her stand and gulped down what was left. Her gaze met Harlen's and she batted her lashes. "Oops. Let me refill this while you get comfy. As sweet as that mouth is, I'm ready to taste other parts of you." Annie threw the last sentence over her shoulder as she opened the door. A speeding bullet few in. "Damn it, Maise."

"It's okay. She's probably wants to know what's going on in here."

Annie put her hand on her well-shaped hip. She had no clue how sexy she was. Or maybe she did. "Are you always going to side with the little fur bag?"

Harlen rubbed under Maisie's chin before moving to the top of her head. "Not always but she's cute, so it will happen a lot." She chuckled. Annie left the two of them in bed. "Your mommy is special." She listened as Maisie purred loudly, the sound soothing. "You're smart and already know that, right, Maise?"

"She doesn't know shit except how to aggravate me when she *does* know better." Annie chuckled as she set two glasses down and waited until the love fest ended. "Out, Maisie." She pointed to the open doorway. Maisie chortled. "Don't make me get the spray bottle." Maisie pawed the sheets for a beat, trilled, then jumped down before sauntering out the door. Annie closed it soundly. Their exchange might have looked contentious, but she knew how much Annie loved Maisie and there was no doubt Maisie loved her back, though who was the boss in their relationship remained up in the air.

Annie made a show of climbing into bed along Harlen's spread legs and straddled her hips. "Are you ready for me to amaze you with my talents?" Annie waggled her brows, clearly enjoying the role reversal.

"You amaze me all the time, Annie. In and out of bed."

The comment made Annie briefly pause. "I'll take that as a compliment," she said before pressing their lips together. There was no mistaking what Annie wanted and Harlen was more than ready to oblige. Annie worked on her nipples, squeezing her flesh and sucking the tip in a way that made her wet all over again. By the time Annie settled, putting a pillow under each knee, Harlen prepared to explode the second Annie's tongue touched her swollen clit. "You look good enough to eat."

Annie's eyes locked onto hers as she opened her mouth and closed around her. She used her tongue like a lethal weapon. Each swipe more maddening than the one before. Harlen did her best to be present, focusing on the way Annie's hot mouth encased her throbbing clit between sucks and licks, swirling the moisture around the tip and coaxing her into growing longer and harder.

"Babe, I'm not going to last."

Annie hummed her approval and the vibration tipped her over the edge. Her legs stiffened, her core shook, her muscles strained. For a second she thought she'd break a bone. A deep roar was torn from her and juices flowed from her center, pooling under her ass and coating Annie. Her heart had to be in tachycardia, pounding so fast and hard, her only thought was there were worse ways to die.

"No more, baby. I can't." She pushed Annie away. Overstimulated and out of breath, Harlen wondered if Annie's orgasms were similar in intensity.

"Wow. You were amazing." Annie sat up, her chin and chest covered in Harlen's wet heat.

"I've made a mess." She could only imagine what the bedding looked like. If she were with anyone else, Harlen would be mortified, but not with Annie. Annie was her judgment-free zone.

"Don't worry about it. There's a waterproof pad." Annie kissed her thigh and got out of bed. A few minutes later, she returned from the bathroom with an oversized towel and an orange chamois. "We can change the sheets later. Until then, these will do." Annie had dried her face. "Lift."

"I need to clean up." Harlen rolled away from the spot, cognizant of not leaving a wet trail.

"Do you want to take a shower?"

"That sounds wonderful." Making love to Annie hadn't been physically demanding, but a sheen of sweat had covered Harlen. Annie turned up the heat after dinner and now she knew why. Making love in a freezing house wasn't romantic unless that's how it was supposed to be.

"I'm joining you."

Harlen waited at the doorway. "It will be my pleasure to wash you."

"No, it will be mine." Annie winked and a shiver of excitement coursed through her. She couldn't wait to see what the rest of the night would bring.

Chapter Thirty-five

"I'm going to my parents' for Thanksgiving. My younger sister, Laura, is flying in from London." Annie hadn't been this excited about a family holiday in a long time.

"My entire family will descend on my parents' for an early brunch, then my siblings will go to their in-laws' for dinner," Harlen said. She looked both happy and annoyed.

"Why don't you sound excited?"

"I am, but it's a lot. There's a crowd of relatives, and the kids are rambunctious."

"Are you afraid I can't handle being there?" Annie would be upset if she didn't know Harlen was giving her a heads up on what to expect. Their dating was going great. Even with both having a busy schedule, she was happy they managed to make time for each other, which was paramount to a successful relationship. Meeting each other's family was the next logical step and she was more than ready.

"Maybe?" Harlen smiled. "Sometimes it's too much for me."

Annie chuckled. With her family being relatively small by comparison, she could sympathize with Harlen. "It'll be fine." She wrapped her arms around Harlen's waist and looked up to meet her gaze. "If it will make you feel better, we can both drive. I can meet you there, then we can drive separately to my folks' where there will be a quieter celebration."

Harlen kissed the tip of her nose. "That's a good idea." The kiss on her lips began softly until Harlen slipped inside and the heat began to build. Pushing Harlen away was the last thing she wanted to do.

"Babe, we don't have time." She had to leave for work soon. Harlen had the luxury of a very flexible schedule which came in handy when they stayed together. Annie couldn't function well without her routine.

"There's always time." Harlen turned her around and pulled her against her firm body. "I can't help wanting you." Her breath tickled the sensitive skin beneath Annie's ear as she lifted her skirt and slipped beneath her lace undies. Harlen moaned. "I love how you're always ready for me."

Annie leaned against her. "You make me wet." Spontaneous moments like these were part of the reason she didn't protest in earnest. She began to grind against Harlen's hand.

"That's it, baby. Take what you want." Her encouragement drove her need higher and she grabbed Harlen's wrist, pushing her deeper. When her blouse slipped from her shoulder, Harlen bit the exposed flesh. Annie trembled. "I won't let you fall. Give me what I want."

All the threads of pleasure coursing through her congregated in her center and she tightened around Harlen's fingers as they filled her over and over. "Yes, yes." Annie's body jerked as the blood-filled knot turned to stone. She was going to cum and Harlen would take all she had to give. Harlen circled her clit, then filled her one last time before she closed her eyes. The bursts of starlight obscured the darkness.

"Oh, God."

"Ride it out, baby." Harlen's movements slowed, coaxing the contractions to continue well past the point of her ability to stand.

"I can't." Annie panted out. "I need to sit."

Harlen guided her to a chair and held her on her lap, careful to keep her skirt out of the way. She was glad Harlen had understood her frustration at having to change from an outfit she'd picked the night before. "You're so beautiful." Pressing her lips to Annie's, Harlen conveyed how much she enjoyed giving Annie pleasure.

"I'm a mess." She laughed weakly.

"It doesn't matter. You're still beautiful." Whenever Harlen said words like beautiful, lovely, amazing, or any of the dozen adjectives she used when referring to her, Annie's heart melted.

"So says you." She stood slowly. On a similar occasion not long ago she got up too fast, and the room had spun. If Harlen hadn't been there to catch her, she would have had a nasty fall.

Maisie strode in, sleepy-eyed. She sat, curled her tail around her feet, and looked between her and Harlen. She'd gotten used to seeing her there. After her customary greeting of a chortle and flopping on her back for a belly rub, Maisie only returned when she wanted attention.

Harlen fixed their coffees and brought them to the table while Annie toasted muffins. The ease with which they work together felt so natural Annie enjoyed sharing her space, an outcome she hadn't expected.

"Do you want to go for a drink after work tomorrow?" Annie crunched on her slightly dark muffin. "Rumor has it the office is closing at two."

Harlen's eyes lit up. "Great. We can grab a bite before Mom sends me her laundry list of things to pick up."

"What will be on it?" Annie didn't have a clue how other families functioned since she'd only been involved in relationships that lasted less than a few months.

Harlen shrugged. "It's different all the time. Every year, she goes shopping on Tuesday, swearing she got what she needed, and every year, she texts me the next day with a list of things she forgot." Harlen smiled. It became clear to Annie that she didn't really mind.

A plethora of thoughts roamed through her brain. Annie was a little overwhelmed with all the changes happening in her life, but she found a way to quiet the cacophony. Harlen rinsed dishes before placing them in the dishwasher while Annie finished her coffee.

"I gotta run, babe. I have a client meeting in an hour and a bunch of emails to sort through." Harlen bent to kiss her.

"Have a nice day."

"Thanks. You, too." She bent to pet Maisie. "Be a good girl for Mommy." Maisie chortled. "Bye." Harlen called out before she closed the door.

"You've successfully managed to wrap Harlen around your paw." Maisie wandered over and snaked around her calves. Annie scratched her head. The deep purr helped quiet the chaos inside and was the reason Annie considered her a therapy cat. "It's going to be a roller-coaster ride for the next month, so try not to annoy me too much, okay?" Maisie lightly pawed her hand for more loves. "Is that a yes?"

Maisie trilled.

"Uh-huh. That remains to be seen." Annie stood and made a hand signal. "You better check your dish for food so you don't starve." The cat trotted to her bowl and started eating. Annie shook her head and glanced at the clock. She had enough time to freshen up before heading out. While she primped, all Annie could focus on was the upcoming introduction to Harlen's family and the butterflies that batted her insides. She glanced in the mirror one last time. "This is the kind of relationship you've always hoped for. You've got this."

Chapter Thirty-six

Harlen opened the door to find Annie holding a bag in her gloved hand and a smile on her face. "Hi." Once inside, Harlen kissed her rosy cheek. "How are the roads?" she asked while she hung Annie's coat and purse.

Annie added her low boots to the pile amassed by the front door, then slipped her feet into slippers. "Not too bad."

"That's good." Laughter floated into the foyer. Harlen assessed Annie's demeanor but didn't see any reason to think this was a bad idea. "Are you ready for the family circus?"

"Don't worry so much." Annie placed her hand on Harlen's chest. "You've got my back."

"Always," she said, while holding Annie's shoulders. She slid down to take her hand.

"Welcome," her mother said. "It's so nice to finally meet you, Annie." Her mother gave Annie a hug, her usual greeting. Harlen tensed, but she needn't have worried. Annie relaxed into the motherly arms.

"It's so nice to meet you, too, Ms. McGhee." She held out the bag she brought. "I made an apple pie, and there's vanilla ice cream to go with it."

"It's Lennie." Her mom took the offerings. "This was very thoughtful of you." She turned to the rest of the family behind her. They'd gone quiet during the meeting, and Harlen's anxiety rose. "You know Jane, of course."

"Hi, Annie. It's good to see you again. Come meet the crew."

As the introductions ensued, Harlen followed her mom to the kitchen. "Let me put those away, Mom."

"I've got it, dear." Her mom stowed the ice cream and set the pie with the three other desserts sitting on the counter.

Harlen glanced at the scene unfolding in the dining room and the members who stood in the living room doorway.

"Why don't you see if Annie would like something to drink. She's going to need one after meeting everyone."

"Good idea." Harlen turned, her mom lightly clasped her arm.

"She's simply lovely, honey. I'm so glad you invited Annie." Love poured from her mother, settling her unwarranted nerves.

"Thanks, Mom."

"Go on before your brother starts with the third degree," she said.

"Right." Harlen joined the throng and wrapped her arm around Annie's waist. Based on the look on Annie's face, she was confident Annie wasn't the one who needed reassurance. Harlen guided her to the living room and introduced her father.

"Call me Harry. We're not much on formality here."

"It's nice to meet you, Harry." Annie looked at the children seated on the floor playing a board game. "Are these your grandchildren?"

"Yep. We're a prolific group." Harry chuckled.

Oh, God. Harlen hoped her father didn't go into his usual spiel about reproducing like rabbits. "Would you like a drink?"

Annie perched on the edge of the couch and watched as the children took turns at the game. "White wine if you have it."

Harry chuckled and slapped his knee. "We're Irish. There's always alcohol." He turned to Harlen. "Give Annie the good stuff. Not that cheap shit your uncle brings."

"Grandpa said a naughty word!" Charlie, Jane's youngest child, yelled.

Harlen's mom held out a large plastic container labeled "Cursed Presents." Her father grumbled and pulled a wad of cash from his pocket, then dropped a dollar into the jug. Harlen handed Annie her wine and sat next to her. "Not swearing around the children is enforced with monetary penalties." She held up the bottle of beer she'd settled on. "Happy Thanksgiving," she said as they touched beverages, then drank. Without forethought, Harlen leaned in to kiss her cheek. Her mother caught her eye and smiled. Her father winked at her when Annie turned her attention back to the children. Harlen often missed the family Sunday dinners when she was with Chloe and being told to go without her, using a number of excuses to leave her behind. Being MIA hadn't been on purpose, but Harlen understood the importance of their family bond after the accident, vowing never to abandon her loved ones again.

Dinner around the makeshift tables was the usual boisterous affair. Through it all, Annie seemed to be enjoying the family antics of animated conversations that looped around the group. With the exception of a tray of burnt dinner rolls, the food was particularly tasty, and Harlen attributed it to Annie's presence.

Chloe always chose to join her parents on a European vacation for Thanksgiving. It was the one time Harlen refused to leave her family, saying it might be the last time she got to see her grandparents. Chloe took the news in stride and never forced the issue. In fact, Harlen had the distinct feeling she was happy to spend time away from the family Harlen loved with all her heart. Looking back, Harlen recounted all the celebrations with her family that Chloe missed for one reason or another. Maybe the signs their relationship was in trouble were there long before Chloe shared the news with her.

❖

Annie glanced at her watch. She leaned close so Harlen could hear her. "I have to get going, babe." Her parents were sticklers for being on time.

"Sure. We can go." Harlen started to rise and she held her in place.

"It's okay if you want to stay." She looked around the table, smiling at the scene. If this was what being with family meant to Harlen, she understood how important it was.

"I can't miss meeting your family." Harlen pecked her lips and stood. "We need to go." Moans and cajoling followed. She was going to chime in, but Harlen had the situation in hand. "I promise Annie will be back on Christmas Eve." Cheering ensued. Amy, Jane's eldest daughter, approached her as she slipped her boots on.

"Are you going to have a stocking, too?"

She glanced at Harlen who shrugged. "I'm not sure."

"Everyone has a stocking for Christmas." Amy's forehead wrinkled. "Except for Chloe. She never came for Thanksgiving or Christmas."

"Amy," Jane said as she put her arm around the child's shoulder. "Maybe Annie doesn't share our traditions." Jane looked uncomfortable.

"It's nice of you to ask, Amy. I think I'll leave that up to Harlen." The child's face brightened.

"Then you'll definitely have one. See you Christmas Eve."

Amy ran back to where the children were playing yet another game. She was amazed at how well-behaved the brood was. There hadn't been one disagreement between them. The only time she'd heard one of them yell was for Lennie to get the jug two additional times when Harry swore. After more good-byes, Harlen held her while they walked through the couple inches of snow on the ground. She was glad the weather had cleared. Driving in snow still made her gut tighten.

"Are you okay to drive to your parents'?" Harlen brushed a piece of hair from her eye. "We can come back for your car if you want to leave it."

This was one of the many reasons Annie knew what was growing between them was love. "I'll be fine. You have the address in case we get separated?"

Harlen nodded. "I put it in the GPS this morning." She smiled. "Besides, I've got my eye on you, and I don't plan on losing sight of you."

Annie's breath froze. What did Harlen mean? Had she missed a crucial bit of conversation? "I'll see you there." She got in the warm car and took a breath before taking the lead, and Harlen pulled behind her.

While she drove, Annie talked herself down from the threatening spiral. Harlen was being Harlen is all. She was thoughtful and caring. The snow had probably reminded her of the accident that took Chloe from her. She glanced in the rearview when she stopped at a light and Harlen waved enthusiastically. She laughed and waved back, intent on enjoying the rest of their time together. An hour later she pulled into the driveway next to a car that must have been her sister's rental and shook off any residual worry.

Harlen met her as she opened her door. "Are you ready for round two?" Harlen asked.

She took her hand as she got out. "The more important question is are you?"

"This will be a piece of cake after the McGhee whirlwind."

She slapped Harlen's arm. "Stop. You have a wonderful family. I can see why spending time with them is important to you." Annie studied Harlen's face. There was a sadness in her eyes that she attributed to Chloe's lack of involvement with Harlen's family.

"Yeah, well, sometimes it's a bit much. Everyone was on their best behavior today."

"Oh, why is that?" Annie asked as she went to the trunk to retrieve the taco dip she'd made for her family's traditional football feast.

"The threat of bodily harm."

She laughed. "You're so bad."

Harlen's teasing attitude sobered. "I thought you liked when I was bad." Harlen's brow rose.

Annie felt her cheeks heat. "Your delivery could use some work." Shock formed on Harlen's face. "Kidding. Let's get in there before all the munchies are gone." They held hands as they walked side-by-side, and not for the first time, she was certain this was how her life was meant to be. Only time would tell if she was right.

Chapter Thirty-seven

What happened to the days between Thanksgiving and today?" Harlen lifted two heavy shopping bags and headed to her parents' front door.

"I have no idea, but I'm exhausted."

That might have been true except her enthusiasm for shopping, wrapping, and cooking told a very different story about how Annie felt about the holidays. Annie was on her heels carrying homemade cookies and a special mac and cheese for the kids. Harlen had accused her of sucking up to the "in-laws."

Annie had stopped Harlen in her tracks to ask if sucking up was something she needed to do. Harlen assured her it was only a joke. Annie smiled, then slapped her. Her timing continued to be off, but she thought of it more as not yet fully on board with where Annie found humor.

Harlen had no holiday rituals. She watched the people she cared about all year and made notes of likes, dislikes, and ambiguous things. The week before Christmas, she took her list and advantage of the huge sales, shopping late in the evening when crowds were tolerable and employees didn't mind the extra pay. She wrapped as she bought. Each person had a designated Christmas paper and Harlen made a chart with a sample of each, leaving empty space to write in what she purchased.

For some reason this year, she was more generous than usual with her family. The same was true for Annie's gifts, though instead of an expansive number of boxes, she'd decided on three special items. Annie wasn't impressed by ego-driven spending.

"Merry Christmas Eve," Harlen called out. She was met with a rush of similar greetings and a crush of bodies, all wanting to hug her and share the love that permeated her family. Growing up, her friends enjoyed coming over. She often wondered what their home life looked like.

Peter hugged her before pushing her aside. "Merry Christmas Eve, Annie."

Harlen stood in awe. The few times Chloe had joined her for a family function, Peter had barely said two words. Annie seemed to have brought out her brother's better side.

"Happy Christmas Eve, Peter." Annie set down her bags and let him take her coat, opting to keep her scarf. Funny how Harlen was still carrying the bags and wearing her coat.

The dining table was pushed against the wall she'd designated to come down, and another had been placed under the decorated windows. A spread of dozens of dishes included appetizers, casseroles, snacks, and sweets. Annie added her dish to the mix, along with a large plate of decorated cookies.

"Merry Eve, Harlen," her mother said in their special greeting. Then she hugged her tight enough to break a rib and whispered in her ear. "I'm so happy for you, darling."

Harlen was choked with emotion. "Merry Eve, Mom."

Her mother let go and turned to the throng behind her. "Don't just stand there. Help Harlen with her things." Her mom turned to Annie next. "It's wonderful having you here for our Eve celebration. I see you brought goodies."

Harlen watched while Annie talked with her mom. Someone removed her coat, and her brother and sister each carried a bag to the tree. The whole family knew the deal and they set out the presents according to their paper while she wondered if Peter was playing Santa this year.

"Oh my goodness, there's so much food," Annie said as she took a slice of bruschetta from the small plate she held before trying it. She couldn't help but smile.

"It's like this every year." Harlen watched her father for a minute wondering if he was feeling okay. "Do you want something to drink?"

"An alcohol-free one would be good."

"You got it." Harlen went in search of her mother, locating her in the kitchen where she was sliding yet another tray of appetizers in the oven. She took her opportunity while they were alone. "Mom?"

"Yes, dear?" Her mother stood against the counter with a mitted hand on her hip. There were some new lines on her face, but the sparkle in her eyes remained and she relaxed a bit.

"Is Dad okay?"

She tipped her head. "What makes you ask that?"

"I don't know. He looks pale and his hand shook when he handed a book to Charlie."

Her mother's smile faltered. "He's getting older, Harlen. We both are." Her mother turned away and Harlen went to her.

"Mom, what's going on?" She snuck in front of her in time to see a tear fall. When her mother cried, it was never good news.

"We're not talking about this tonight," she said before trying to turn away again.

"Mom, please don't make me wait." Dread filled every corner of her mind. Cancer. Heart failure. Alzheimer's. The list went on and on.

"He has the beginning stages of Parkinson's. The doctor caught it early, but the medication is causing tremors until his body adjusts." She put on her brave face. "He's going to be with us for a long time yet." She squeezed her arm and went to the fridge.

Harlen had so many questions, she didn't know what to ask first. Parkinson's meant limited mobility, shaking, falls…didn't it?

"Stop making up scenarios in your head. We're going to enjoy the rest of the holidays before anyone else knows. Promise me,

Harlen." Her mother's eyes pleaded that she understand there was time.

"Okay, Mom. I promise."

The relief on her mother's face was instantaneous. "Good. Now wipe the worry off your face and go be with that amazing woman of yours."

She kissed her mother's cheek. "Yes, Mother." That earned her a swat on the ass. She was almost to the door when she remembered Annie's drink. She grabbed a can of seltzer from the fridge and joined the crowded living room. Annie was perched on a corner of the hassock and smiled when she saw her.

"Is everything okay?" Frown lines appeared on her forehead. Harlen opened the can and handed it to her.

"Not great, but well enough," she said in a whisper. "I'll tell you later." Annie continued to scrutinize her for a minute.

"Thanks for this," she said. After she drank, she held the can out to her.

Harlen straddled the seat and she took a drink, wishing she had something stronger. Annie leaned against her and turned her head so Harlen could hear.

"Whatever it is, I'll be at your side."

"I know. Thank you." She kissed Annie's cheek and set the can down. Her father wasn't the only one who had the shakes. Luckily, Peter took that moment to appear.

"Ho, ho, ho." The kids squealed in delight. "Merry Christmas." He sat on the hearth. "Who will be my helper this year?" Five small hands and several adult ones went in the air. Peter picked Amy for elf duty, clearly making her day. She sat near the tree next to Santa, read the tag, and handed him the gift.

With the tradition under way, Harlen read the names on the stockings hung from the mantle. Her mother insisted the adults in the family were never too old for a stocking. Warmth spread through her when she saw "Annie" written in script across the cuff of a new stocking.

"There's no doubt you're part of the family now."

"How can you be sure?"

Harlen pointed. Annie followed where she gazed. Her eyes grew large and her mouth opened in a silent exclamation. She blinked several times.

"Thank you for letting me in."

Harlen wrapped her arms around her. This charming, smart, amazing woman had somehow found her, and Harlen wasn't about to let her go. "Thank you for opening the door."

"Ugh…I'm stuffed to the gills." Annie laughed weakly. Lennie had insisted she try a little of every dish on the table. Her only saving grace was the foods that included cherries, which she politely passed over. Her mother had packed up her favorites, too, and everything was stowed in a cooler in the back.

Harlen laughed. "I warned you."

"True. I wasn't prepared for my family going all out, too." She groaned as she tried to sit straighter. "They probably wanted to impress Laura with their expanded palate by ordering from a number of restaurants."

"Your parents didn't make the food?"

Annie laughed so hard she thought she might burst. "Are you kidding?"

Harlen glanced at her after they exited the highway. "But you cook all the time."

"Thank the powers that be I had a grandmother who loved to cook and bake." Grandma had died almost twenty years ago and she still missed her. "Before I found out I was autistic, Grandma kept me from being overstimulated by helping her cook for the family." She took a shaky breath. "Grandma understood me."

Harlen closed the distance between them with her hand and gently squeezed.

"I was one of the lucky ones, and I'm grateful for her love."

"Hearing you talk about her makes me think about the times I haven't appreciated my family."

"It wasn't all wine and roses with mine." She squeezed Harlen's hand then let go. It was dark and slippery out, and she needed Harlen to have both hands on the wheel. Annie diverted her attention to the conversation. "Mom threatened to lock me in my room when I told her school was boring and I refused to go. Dad wanted to send me away to a special school 'for gifted children.' I heard them arguing one night and discovered the so-called school was actually an institution for mentally ill children. My thoughts took a while to process and I'd get frustrated because I didn't know why, but I wasn't sick in the head."

"I'm sorry you had to go through that." Harlen pulled into the driveway a few minutes later.

Annie was lost in flashbacks of her youth. The world was a much grimmer place back then. After high school, she sought the opinion of a neurologist. She'd scared her father into thinking she had a brain tumor that he'd let grow because he didn't care about his daughter. She threatened him with a public scandal and he caved. She was nineteen before she confirmed there wasn't anything "wrong" with her brain. It was simply wired differently.

"We're here, Annie."

The engine was silent. How long had she been reliving those hard times and what had brought it on? "Okay." She wasn't going to dwell on her temporary absence, confident Harlen understood her better than anyone, except Char.

"I can get these, babe." Harlen held out her keys, then opened the hatch. "Get inside before you freeze."

Annie looked down. All she wore was a sweater and her leggings. She'd taken her coat off and thrown it in the back before getting in the car. "Are you sure?" She chewed her lip.

"Certain." Harlen's gentle smile was full of empathy.

She nodded and grabbed her coat and purse from the back seat, along with the cooler. She could use a few minutes alone to gather herself.

Harlen took her time bringing their things inside. Annie stood in the kitchen with a glass of water, staring out the back window into the darkness that lay beyond. Laura didn't come into the picture until Annie was almost twelve, about the same time she was heading to high school. For all her challenges, Annie had tested high on the required acuity screening and was placed in an accelerated program when she entered middle school. Laura had been the perfect baby, toddler, and teen. No wonder seeing her again was throwing Annie into an emotional tailspin.

"Hey," Harlen said before wrapping her arms around Annie, and she sunk into her warmth. "What do you need?"

Could it really be that simple? Was Harlen the one who would always hold space for Annie to be herself? Love her for who she was…who she'd always been? Wait. Did Harlen love her? She hadn't said the words, but that didn't mean she didn't. Annie loved her, and she hadn't told Harlen either. She wasn't sure what she was waiting for, but she trusted the time would come. She turned in Harlen's embrace.

"I need a kiss, a glass of wine, a shower, and you holding me for the night."

Harlen covered her mouth with soft lips. She didn't slip her tongue inside, sensing that Annie didn't want sex when she needed intimacy and being cared for. Harlen stepped back, pulled down wine glasses, and poured out the deep purple liquid a third of the way.

"Merry Christmas, darling." Harlen touched her glass to Annie's and the ring sounded like hope.

"Merry Christmas." For tonight, she would let Harlen take care of her and made a promise to herself of never taking Harlen for granted.

A little while later, Harlen lay in bed waiting for her. She turned out the overhead lights on her way, knowing the bathroom night-light would be plenty once her eyes adjusted to the dark. Harlen held up the covers.

"Curl in next to me with your head on my chest."

Annie did as told, sighing when Harlen tucked the cover in around her and held her close.

"Are you concerned about Maisie being alone?"

She could picture her perched in the tree. "No."

"Try not to worry about whatever's bothering you. You're here with me, and you're safe. I won't let go. I promise."

Promises were something Annie knew Harlen would keep. "Thank you."

"You're welcome." Harlen's voice rumbled in her chest. Annie focused on being warm and comfortable in Harlen's embrace. She needed to shut her mind off and Harlen was the switch. The last thing she heard before drifting toward oblivion was Harlen's voice.

"Good night, love."

She could have sworn she heard the word love, but that couldn't be.

Chapter Thirty-eight

"Mom, we're not going to chance the drive." Harlen was only a little disappointed that her plans had changed. She'd come to Annie's New Year's Eve day and they'd spent some of the time making love between errands and the grocery store. She enjoyed the connection they shared so much, she didn't hesitate when Annie asked her to spend a couple of days with her. After waking to a white wonderland, Harlen asked Annie if she'd mind staying home. She didn't miss the twinkle in Annie's eye at the idea of having three uninterrupted days together.

"I'm sorry to hear you won't be joining us, but being safe comes first. I'm sure our numbers will be down due to the storm." Her mother hesitated. "I imagine you have everything you need?"

Last night after a fabulous dinner they fixed together of chicken and chorizo paella with garlic bread, they snuggled on the couch with Maisie and watched random shows on streaming channels. To make it more fun, Annie devised a game with a scoring chart ranging from one to five, giving each show a score. To make it fair, she used a randomization app to pick a number between one and the highest possible combination. Just before midnight, they tallied their scores and the person closest to the randomized number won anything they wanted to ring in the new year. Harlen had won. Annie didn't seem the least bit upset at losing, and she suspected Annie knew what she was going to ask for.

Annie chose that moment to strut through the door with two steaming cups of coffee. Maisie darted in front of her. Annie stopped in time to avoid tripping over her, and Maisie zoomed across the bed before disappearing. When Harlen mouthed, "What was that?" Annie responded in like.

"Morning calisthenics, Maisie style."

Harlen laughed, nearly spilling the scalding liquid. "Yes, Mom. I have everything I need." She was about to hang up. "How's Dad doing?"

"He's tired from all the excitement, but he's fine." She lowered her voice. "I think the medication is taking hold and the tremors have just about disappeared.

Relief flooded through her. "That's good. We'll talk next week."

"I know, honey. Happy New Year to you and Annie. I love you."

"Same to you and Dad. I love you, too. Bye."

Annie somehow managed to not spill a drop from her cup as she climbed into bed and settle next to Harlen. "How did your mom take the news?"

"She fine." Harlen took another sip and sighed. "I think she thinks we'd rather spend the day in bed than with family."

"She's not wrong."

Harlen chuckled.

"How's your dad?"

She'd told Annie about her father's diagnosis the day after Christmas. While Annie prefaced what she said next by saying she was no expert, she did confess she'd done a ton of research on neurologic disorders and diagnoses after the riddle of her own condition was identified. Parkinson's disease was well researched with a ton of information available. Annie had asked a few questions to help clarify how advanced her father was. After they talked, Annie sent her an article from a renowned clinical trial on the medication her father had been prescribed. Harlen felt somewhat relieved after reading it.

"Tired, but otherwise good. Mom thinks the medication has started working." Harlen pulled Annie closer. "Thanks for the coffee." Maisie jumped on the end of the bed and sat watching them. "Does she do that every morning?"

Annie smiled. "Pretty much. Right, little shit?"

Maise chortled and flopped on her side, Harlen heard the low rumble.

"If you want loves, come up here. I'm not moving." Annie pointed to a spot beside her. Maisie got up and flopped in her appointed spot. Annie began to scratch and rub in places that made Maisie purr louder. "Even if we spend most of the day in bed, you aren't. Don't get too comfortable, Maise."

Maisie looked at Annie upside down. Harlen had seen them interact enough that she believed Annie when she said Maisie had a handle on vocabulary.

"Do you mind if I turn on the news? I want to find out how much more we're in for." Harlen asked.

"Does it matter?"

Harlen thought for a moment. "Not unless we're getting another foot. If that's the case I want to shovel before it gets any heavier." A little apprehension crept in. "Do you have a shovel?"

"I'm not a Neanderthal," Annie said straight-faced.

"Sorry."

"Get down before you get your fur everywhere." Annie pointed. Maisie ignored her. "Out." Annie pointed toward the door. Maisie made a point of moving slow, complaining all the while. Annie set her empty cup down. "In fact, I have a snow blower." She smiled sweetly.

"When were you going to share that tidbit?"

"What difference would it make? You're not going anywhere." Annie straddled her. "In case you haven't noticed, you're my sex slave for another day." Annie lightly scored her nails over her exposed stomach, causing gooseflesh to rise.

"Funny," Harlen said before flipping Annie onto her back making her scream in delight before pinning her down. "I thought you were my sex slave." She took possession of Annie's lips, then her mouth, and her desire flared. Out of breath, she rose up.

"Win, win situation in my book." Annie wriggled one hand free. "Sit up for me." Annie slipped her hand between them and unerringly found her hard clit. "Ride me."

Whether Annie knew it or not, she'd do anything Annie asked. "Like this?" She slid back and forth against Annie's fingers.

"Whatever feels good to you."

Harlen leaned forward. She wanted to taste Annie's mouth as she rode. As soon as Annie opened to her, Harlen knew the battle to keep control was lost. A few minutes later, Harlen pressed firmer against Annie, holding her shoulders as she thrust against her.

"Yes, baby. Just like that. You're going to cum for me, aren't you?"

Her entire body trembled as the universe converged where Annie touched her. "Annie," she cried out.

"Keep going."

Harlen's thrusts became uncoordinated as her muscles contracted to the exquisite build-up until her body froze and every tendon felt like it would snap before her clit exploded. "Fuck," she roared, torn between the intense pleasure and the pain of knowing it would soon end.

"Mmm. I've got you." Annie milked her clit until she had nothing left to give.

She needed to get off of Annie, but she was boneless, unable to move.

"Hang on. I've got you." Annie held her tightly and used leverage to roll them onto their sides. Harlen lay trembling beside her. "Are you okay?"

"I think so. Am I alive?"

"As far as I can tell."

"Good. Then I'm okay." She let out a sound that might have been a chuckle, but it was weak, so she couldn't be sure.

"Still worried about the weather?" Annie rubbed her back in soothing circles. Her eyes grew heavy.

"Nope."

"It will be there when you wake up."

She was about to protest, but her body had other ideas. She couldn't think about snow when she was wrapped in the safe cocoon of Annie's arms.

Chapter Thirty-nine

The big day had finally come. Annie hoped to prove her skills as a fundraiser tonight. The final head count of one hundred twenty-five was better than she'd hoped for. Of course, the advertising campaign she'd insisted was necessary had done its job, too.

"How excited are you?" Michael asked, while he boxed up the last of the plaques that would be presented to the attending corporate sponsors. For those that declined the invitation, a thank you note of appreciation had been included and sent via mail.

Annie took Michael by the shoulders. "I'm depending on you to help keep my anxiety level down. If anything happens that you can take care of, do it, then let me know when it's no longer an issue. Okay?"

"Got it." He folded the flaps of the marked box. The seating chart was tucked on top and each individual gift had a discreet label with the sponsor's name and table number. "I'm going to put these in my car." He'd proven himself worthy of the responsibilities she'd assigned him for the evening.

"That would be great." One less thing for her to think about. Annie was doing her best not to get caught up in the uncertainties that she had no control over.

Allison appeared at her door. "You should be home getting ready instead of working." She told the office staff to leave by noon. Annie looked at the clock, surprised it was already one. Her plan was to be at the venue by three. An hour before guests started to arrive. If she didn't leave soon, she'd be late to her own party, so to speak.

She forced a nervous smile. "I know. There were a few last-minute things that needed my attention."

Allison strode in and held her hands. "You're meticulous in everything you do. It's going to be fine. Some things are beyond our control, and I hope you're okay with that." The director had given her accolades during the last staff meeting. She disliked being in the spotlight, but the praise she received and the applause from the staff was a nod to her accomplishments.

"Thank you. I'm leaving now."

"Good." Allison smiled warmly. "I'll see you there."

Annie checked her email one more time, tossed her tablet in her bag, and practically ran to her car, checking the trunk for the items she'd placed there that morning. Why she thought they might magically disappear was ridiculous, but that didn't stop her from looking. Time was dwindling before she had to be at the elegant hall she'd rented, and she was going to have to hustle. On the short drive home, she recalled the message Harlen had sent.

You're going to be the most beautiful woman at the gala and I'm honored to be your escort. Remember to breathe. I'll see you there.

Harlen had asked if she'd like her to pick her up, but Annie declined. Harlen was a distraction. A wonderful one, but a distraction nonetheless, and the last thing she needed was to get caught up in her alluring persona when she needed to focus. She yanked her car into the driveway and sprinted to the door. Maisie trotted out of the spare bedroom that she'd claimed as her own.

"Today's the day, Maisie."

Maisie chortled while Annie headed to the bedroom and began to strip. She'd showered that morning and considered a refresher, but time wasn't on her side. She sat at the vanity counter and began selecting products. Annie wasn't big on a lot of makeup except for special occasions. If this didn't count as one, she'd wasted a lot of money on the designer dress she'd bought. After applying the basics, including a complementary blue eye shadow, Annie tackled her unruly hair. She used mousse to get it under control and was pleased she'd been somewhat successful in taming the waves.

The shoe bag held the gold pumps she'd found marked on sale along with navy blue flats that would give her feet a break when she felt blisters start. There were always blisters with dress shoes and the reason she brought extra shoes and Band-Aids. Navy stockings were next, followed by the off-the-shoulder dress that showed just the right amount of cleavage. The cut was such that every bra she'd tried on looked unseemly, so she'd decided to go without. Once the dress was on, doubts formed about her choice. When she stood, things were fine, but if she bent over too far, she was afraid she'd fall out. At the last minute, she went with adhesive cups. It wasn't perfect, but at least if she leaned over her breasts would be covered for the most part. Maisie lay on the bed watching her every move. She glanced at the clock.

"That's enough primping. I have to go, Maisie." She grabbed the clutch she'd prepared, stuffed her phone and ID inside, and snagged her shoes on the way. She hated having to wear boots, but the short suede ones she liked had a good sole for slippery weather. Thankfully, it hadn't snowed in almost a week, so most of the roads were clear. Being proactively cautious was how she kept anxiety at bay. Her black scarf and black wool swing coat finished the ensemble.

She gave Maisie a pet. "Be a good girl."

The last thing she needed was her keys. The car was running and so was her mind. She closed her eyes. It wouldn't do any good to become frantic. After a few breaths, she put the car in gear and turned toward the main road. She allowed herself to picture how Harlen would look in a tuxedo. Big mistake. Fantasizing would have to wait. Once she arrived, she'd be working and there'd be no shenanigans with her date until the party ended.

"I've got this," she said out loud. All she had to do was believe it.

Chapter Forty

"Hello?" Harlen didn't recognize the number displayed on her car screen, but that wasn't surprising. She'd been handing out electronic business cards for months and customers called all the time.

"Harlen?"

She could swear she knew the voice. "Yes, this is she."

"It's Jason Williams, Chloe's father."

What the hell was he calling her about? "Go on."

"I know we didn't part on good terms and that was my fault. I know you loved our daughter and I should have listened to you. We watched the video New Year's day. Chloe was doing what she loved and—" Jason's voice cracked and he cleared his throat. "She looked so happy and so full of life. Not like she is now."

Harlen wanted to be angry with him, but what purpose would it serve? She drove into her garage and turned the car off. "The holidays were her favorite time of the year." Memories flooded in. Mostly they were good ones, but not all. Chloe had chosen to spend them apart. The signs had been there all along and she could see that now.

"Since the time she was a little one she would for ask for months when it would be red and green time. That was the Chloe we were reminded of."

"Is the video why you called?" Harlen didn't want to rehash the past if she could help it.

"Yes, and to tell you we're ready to let her go. I thought you might like to be there when we do."

Annie's gala was today. Harlen had been running errands, packing an overnight bag. She was short on time and couldn't talk much longer. "When?"

"We're driving to the hospital now and should be there in about forty-five minutes. They assured me everything would be ready, but there's no telling how long it will take for her to be gone."

Chloe was already gone, but she wouldn't argue semantics at this point. Harlen rubbed her face. It was almost two. She promised Annie she'd be there at four when guests started arriving. Today was a big day. Their first public event to attend as a couple. Her promise to Chloe had stolen time she could have spent with Annie, and she wouldn't let her down again.

"I have a prior engagement at four that I can't miss."

"We decided on the flight back and knew there was a chance you wouldn't be able to be there."

"No…I…I'll meet you there."

"Thank you, Harlen." Jason ended the call.

Shit. Harlen thumped her palms on the steering wheel. Of all days they had to pick from to finally end Chloe's state of limbo, of course they picked today. "Get your shit together." She typed out a short message to Annie, saying she might be running a few minutes late, hoping she'd understand.

Harlen darted inside, jumped in the shower, tended to her skin, then dried her hair. She was grateful she didn't wear makeup or need to fuss with her hair. Another ten minutes and she was in her tux minus the suit coat, then pulled on her wool overcoat. Back in the car, she sent a silent plea into the universe asking that Chloe would go quickly. She would keep her promise to Annie no matter what.

❖

Annie stood near the entrance to the grand ballroom with Allison and greeted their guests. She tried not to panic. Harlen had promised her, though the text she sent had her wondering what was so important that she was late in arriving. It was almost four thirty. Annie had to check on the caterers and the DJ. Michael had done his part setting out the place cards and plaques.

"I need to check on the kitchen," she said to Allison while there was a break in arrivals.

Allison studied her. "Of course. Is everything alright?"

Was it? Annie had no idea. All she knew was that tonight was the culmination of her and Harlen's dates and the time they'd spent getting to know each other. She was supposed to be Annie's escort. Instead, Annie was beginning to feel like a bride left at the altar. The comparison was a bit over the top, but she couldn't help feeling rejected.

She strode with purpose toward the kitchen. She had a job to do. All the months of planning were coalescing tonight, and she wanted everything to be perfect. The only way that would happen was if Harlen was by her side. Annie should have known better than to trust Harlen to keep her word. Why the hell did she pick tonight of all nights to break it?

The kitchen was in high gear. Appetizers were being plated and a line of wait staff stood at the ready with piles of cocktail napkins in one hand. The head chef saw her and rushed over with a small tray.

"Ms. Dawson, these are for your tasting before I send them out." He put the tray at the end of the counter while they continued to fill the larger ones. The last thing she wanted was food. Annie nibbled on the four types she'd chosen, not tasting any of it.

"Thank you, Mark. They're wonderful." Her insides tightened. "You may serve the guests." She watched while a string of servers moved among the guests. After the cocktail hour, dinner service would begin. She'd been looking forward to the food, but even more than that, what she wanted most was to sit beside Harlen. Annie felt queasy and turned for the ladies' room when she heard someone call her name. She turned to find Harlen closing the short distance between them, and her disappointment evaporated. She should have never doubted Harlen.

"I'm so sorry, babe." She kissed her lips, making them tingle.

"What happened?" Annie searched her face for the answer.

"I'll explain everything later." Harlen stood back and slowly twirled her in a slow circle. "I told you I'd be with the most beautiful woman here, and I was right. You look amazing." The wide smile and sparkling eyes conveyed her sincerity.

Annie thought about pressing her for answers, but there wasn't any need. Harlen was here now and that's what mattered. With her emotional crisis avoided, Annie was able to appreciate how dapper Harlen was in a striking black tux and white pintuck shirt. The royal blue bow tie at her throat matched the blue flowers in Annie's dress. "I'm not the only looker. Dare I say you're the handsomest person in a tux I've seen."

Harlen gave a small bow.

"I want to introduce you to someone." She took Harlen's hand and led the way to the entrance and stood next to Allison. "I'd like to introduce you to my partner, Harlen McGhee." Annie turned to a shocked Harlen. "Harlen this is the director, Allison Goldberg." After they shook hands and exchanged pleasantries, Annie moved to the table that displayed place cards for her and Harlen. Allison wanted Annie and her plus-one at her table, but Annie had declined, leaving the seats for another couple who were platinum-level sponsors. She was fine being out of the spotlight. Harlen held Annie's chair, then bent next to her.

"Would you like a drink?"

"God yes." She laughed softly. Harlen smiled brightly.

"You've got this, Annie. You always do."

Annie opened her mouth to protest and stopped. Harlen was right. Whatever bumps in the road developed, she'd find a way to smooth out the ride. "Thank you."

"Thank you for being you." Harlen kissed her cheek. "I'll be right back." Heat filled her cheeks. Harlen had that effect on her.

The rest of the night went smoothly except for a slight snafu with the podium speaker that was quickly remedied by Michael. The photo booth was a hit. For a donation of one hundred dollars, couples could have their picture taken at the smartly decorated trellis. Harlen had insisted paying though Annie was sure the photographer wouldn't have charged them. With the last of the guests leaving, Allison told her to go home. She protested she needed to make sure the caterers had cleaned the kitchen and the DJ packed up her equipment.

"I know this is your baby, but you've done enough. Michael and I can handle the rest," Allison said.

Annie glanced where Michael stood talking with the head waiter. He gave her a thumbs up. She had no idea how much was raised, but if the nonstop dancing and the number of photos purchased were any indication, it had to be a tidy sum. Guests had made a point to find her throughout the evening, telling her what a spectacular job she'd done. Her head swelled with pride, but her feet were killing her.

"I am tired." She barely had the energy to smile one more time.

Allison squeezed Harlen's arm. "I think your partner is ready to be swept away, Harlen."

"I believe you're right." Harlen turned to her. "May I please escort you home, Ms. Dawson?"

"You most certainly can, Ms. McGhee." She took Harlen's arm, glad for the support.

"I don't want to see you in the office tomorrow." Allison's voice carried to where she stood at the coat check.

Harlen helped her with her boots. When she stood, pain shot up her leg and she dropped onto the bench. "What's wrong?"

"Ugh…damn shoes. I have a blister and I can't wear these." She pointed at her feet. Harlen got on one knee and removed them. Adding them to the two pair she'd stowed with her coat.

"Easy fix," Harlen said. She handed the bag to Annie as she stood. "Ready?"

"I can't walk outside barefoot." She could deal with a lot of discomfort, but frozen toes weren't one of them.

Harlen handed her keys to the valet before joining her on the bench. "Ye of little faith. Do you honestly think I'd make you walk?"

Annie was too tired to think. "Unless you have a wheelchair for me, yes."

"Wouldn't be the first time you were wrong." Harlen rose, then picked her up, making her gasp.

"You can't carry me." Even as she said it Annie wrapped her arms around Harlen's neck.

"I already am."

When they got outside, Harlen's vehicle was there. The valet opened her door and Harlen set her down gently. Heat engulfed her feet. She couldn't help sighing.

"Better?" Harlen asked once she was behind the wheel.

"Much."

"Good. Let's get you home and out of that gown."

Annie groaned. "Babe, I don't think…"

"I'd love to ravish you after being so close to you all night and not being able to touch you, but I'm not. I'm going to bathe you, massage your feet, and tuck you in." Harlen turned onto the freeway.

As much as Annie loved the plans Harlen had, she couldn't really relax yet. "There's one more thing you need to do."

Harlen glanced over at her. "Anything."

"Tell me why you were late."

Harlen moved to the far left and put on the cruise control. "Chloe's father called me. They watched the video of her last Christmas at work. They'd decided to turn off Chloe's life support. He asked if I wanted to be there."

Of all the reasons Annie had imagined for Harlen's absence, an end to Chloe's existence wasn't one of them. She reached for Harlen's hand. "I'm so sorry, for you and the Williamses." She let the news sink in. "You could have stayed."

"No, I couldn't. I didn't want to. Chloe drew her final breath and I felt nothing except relief." She glanced over once more. "I'd said good-bye months ago and the promise I'd made was honored."

Annie couldn't fathom how difficult it was, no matter what Harlen said, she had to be grieving for the love she'd lost.

"Mainly, I'm grateful that Chloe is free to be at peace." Harlen's lack of tears was unexpected. Perhaps she was done with tears. "I can finally admit the reason I hoped she'd wake up for so long was to find out if she recognized me." Harlen shook her head. "It was a selfish reason. I'd almost sold my soul to satisfy my ego." Harlen took her hand again, the way she did when they were side by side. "But the hardest question I had to answer became how can I do better for you?"

Annie pressed her palm to Harlen's chest, the way she had whenever Harlen was being vulnerable with her. "Oh, baby. All I've ever wanted was what you had with Chloe. That's the kind of love I want to experience...*with you*."

"You showed me I'm not losing Chloe's love. I'm gaining yours."

Annie waited until they were safely parked in the garage. She ran barefoot around the car, not caring how cold the concrete was. When Harlen emerged, she kissed her tenderly and let intuition guide her. The heat built slowly. It wasn't long before the flickering flame flared into an inferno.

"I've wanted you to let me all the way in from the start. Tonight you have."

Harlen's eyes glistened as they held hers. "There's no one else I'd rather let in than you, Annie Dawson. I love you and I promise to not give you a reason to doubt it's real."

Until that moment, neither of them had spoken the words out loud. Annie had held back to protect her heart. She understood Harlen's hesitation. Tonight confirmed breaking a promise wasn't in Harlen's DNA. Chloe was gone, never to return. Her promise had finally come to fruition, and she was free to love again.

"Harlen McGhee, I love you." Her vision blurred as joy filled every fiber of her being. "Even if you did make it hard at times." She smiled.

"My bad." Harlen chuckled.

What else would they discover as their relationship deepened was uncharted territory. Declaring their love had been inevitable. Keeping that love alive would be the real test. Annie, in her ever-optimistic way, was certain the ensuing years would be some of her happiest. She'd been upfront about being different, and how finding love can be hard for neurodivergent people, but no harder than for anyone else. Annie had almost given up, until she found the perfect person to love her. Isn't that what everyone wanted?

"I want to show you how much I love you."

Annie smiled. "Does it have anything to do with your list?"

Harlen pulled her into her arms and kissed her until she couldn't breathe. "It definitely does."

Annie was led to the bedroom where Harlen began taking care of her by bathing her and massaging her sore feet. She even kissed her blister and put an antibiotic cream with an adhesive strip on it. When she joined Annie in bed, she held her in the shelter of her arms and Annie snuggled in.

"This is nice."

"Uh-huh," Harlen said as she drew lazy circles on her back.

"Could you do one more thing for me?"

"All you need to do is ask." Harlen kissed the top of her head.

"Make love to me?"

"Are you sure?" Harlen asked as she caught her gaze. "What about your feet?"

Annie chuckled. "As long as there's no standing involved, I'll be fine."

Harlen gently rolled her onto her back. Then she began kissing every inch of skin, including the ticklish spots, earning her a playful slap. Annie believed she'd found her forever person. The one who never made her feel less than. The one person whose promise she put her faith in. She wasn't going to worry about tomorrow since she couldn't predict the future. For now, she was happy. Wasn't that the most important part of living in the moment? Harlen was here, and at this moment her heart overflowed with love. The rest would work itself out. They'd already proven their connection was too strong to resist.

"Annie?" Harlen's voice centered her.

"I'm here."

"That's good. It would be a shame if you missed what I'm about to do." Harlen settled between her thighs.

She was ready for Harlen to show her how being loved felt in all its forms. Annie wasn't afraid to let Harlen in because she'd already taken up residence in her head. Little did she know when their cars tangled, their hearts would also collide in a most unexpected way.

About the Author

Renee Roman lives in New York's capital and loves the change of seasons (mostly). Much like the characters in her books, Renee is rediscovering herself through living a passion-filled, adventurous life and spending time with her loves, friends, and family as often as her busy schedule allows.

Her works include *Escorted,* the Golden Crown Literary Society (GCLS) 2023 Erotic Novel category winner, *Chance Encounter*, and *Stranger in the Sand*. You can reach out to Renee at reneeromanwrites@gmail.com, through social media platforms, and at Bold Strokes Books.

Books Available from Bold Strokes Books

Experts Only by Kel McCord. Torn between comforting solitude and the irresistible pull of connection, Michelle and Cas begin to wonder if the life they thought they wanted is enough. (978-1-63679-944-5)

Never Say Die by Meredith Doench. Detective Rory Scott's personal and professional lives converge as she races against time to find the connection between two crimes and bring a killer to justice. (979-8-90035-051-6)

Swept Away by Radclyffe. When ER physician Sloane Marshall is called in as a last-minute replacement for a federal outreach mission in the remote mountain town of Coulter's Gap, she doesn't expect to fall in love with a sharp-edged helicopter pilot. (979-8-90035-050-9)

When Hearts Collide by Renee Roman. A car accident isn't a likely way to meet the love of your life, but when Harlen's and Annie's hearts collide, they may not have a choice. (978-1-63679-922-3)

Yes, Honey by Claudia Parr. Four sexy couples break stereotypes about committed sex to explore lust and love when the honeymoon is over. (978-1-63679-992-6)

Hurricane Season Hustle by Greg Herren. Scotty must catch the killer to protect his nearest and dearest, before they strike again. (978-1-63679-882-0)

Royal Rush: 75 Days to Fall in Love by Lissandra Rowe. When a royal matchmaking scheme leads to a chance encounter with Isabella Acosta-Ramon, a slow burn sparks that neither can deny. (978-1-63679-965-0)

The Moon to Me by Ana Hartnett. Sometimes it takes traveling thousands of miles to discover what's been yours all along. (978-1-63679-918-6)

To Love Violets for Their Thorns by Rachel Sullivan. Forced to face the heartbreak they never quite got over, Elly and Sonia must decide: breathe fresh life into an old love or try again with someone new? (978-1-63679-928-5)

Virtually Perfect by Melissa Sky. If your AI flirts better, listens harder, and never ghosts you…does that count as love? (979-8-90035-005-9)

Brooke Takes Queen by Alaina Erdell. Brooke Staley faces personal and professional upheaval when Elizabeth Bettancourt, the emotionally scarred new owner of the resort she works for, considers selling. (978-1-63679-886-8)

Coda by Anna Gram. Parker is intriguing, magnetic, impossible to ignore—and completely wrong for Hannah. But sometimes love's melody refuses to end. (978-1-63679-926-1)

Secrets Under the Junipers by Suzie Clarke. Who killed Hallie Lynn Peeples? Cecilia McConnel needs to know. Bitsy Hanover holds the key. Can love uncover secrets? (978-1-63679-845-5)

The Debutante Dilemma by Jane Walsh. Two debutantes are engaged to wealthy and titled brothers…but discover they only have eyes for each other. (978-1-63679-896-7)

The Love Book by Gun Brooke. When literary agent Rowan Cross receives an anonymous manuscript that deeply resonates with her, Verity realizes she has accidentally sent her own manuscript, complete with her very real feelings for her boss! (978-1-63679-850-9)

Traveling Toward Forever by Erin Dutton. When almost-strangers take a road trip through America's national parks, love may be the final destination. (978-1-63679-894-3)

Beautiful Things by Emma L McGeown. A warmhearted romance of missed chances, undeniable chemistry, and a stubborn love that maybe, just maybe, can find its way back. (978-1-63679-934-6)

Love Takes a Village by Karis Walsh. As Lena Preiss struggles to manage a busy restaurant in the Bavarian Christmas village of Leavenworth, Washington, chocolatier Devin Meyer brings an unexpected richness into her life, along with her delicious desserts. (978-1-63679-902-5)

Secrets of the Heart by Jenny Frame. When a beautiful stranger starts asking questions about Nikki Sharkey, head of an infamous crime syndicate, Nikki will stop at nothing to protect her daughter Isla. (978-1-63679-653-6)

Talon and the Songbird by Julia Underwood. In a world where survival depends on strategic alliances, Makayla and Talon must navigate not only complex politics but also the dangerous territory of their hearts. (978-1-63679-970-4)

The Great Popcorn Romance by Georgia Beers. Opposites attract, and Riley Shaw stands no chance of resisting Hannah Kramer's magnetic pull. But opposites know just how to drive each other crazy… (978-1-63679-910-0)

Three Blissful Days by Dena Blake. Kendall Jackson attempts to make her ex regret dumping her by announcing she's dating beautiful park ranger Ivy Patterson. But there's nothing fake about how attracted Ivy is to Kendall. (978-1-63679-707-6)

Chasing Her Scent by MJ Williamz. When Sheridan Rousseau walks into Lisette Mouton's charming little bookstore in Quebec City, she unknowingly holds the key to a mysterious box hidden in a secret room. (978-1-63679-900-1)

Heart's Run by D. Jackson Leigh. Hoping to recover an escaped racing mare, stock transporter Tobie Mason locks horns with local wild horse advocate Maggie Wilkes. (978-1-63679-825-7)

Scandalous by Kris Bryant. When a Hollywood actress trades places with her twin sister, everyone's in an uproar about getting duped, but Lindsay's more concerned about finding out which twin she made out with. (978-1-63679-874-5)

The Art of Love by Ali Vali. When Mimi and Bianca both set their sights on Jolly, sparks fly, loyalties are tested, and hearts collide as they navigate the unpredictable nature of their hearts (978-1-63679-719-9)

The Other Side of Forever by Kel McCord. Will Kenzie and Rachel be able to make love work when Rachel's cozy suburban dream feels like Kenzie's worst nightmare? (978-1-63679-812-7)

The Secrets of Rhydian Hill by Ronica Black. A doctor in need of a new start. A woman running from a killer. A love story that could end in tragedy. (978-1-63679-880-6)

Bold Strokes Books
Quality and Diversity in LGBTQ Literature

www.ingramcontent.com/pod-product-compliance
Lightning Source LLC
LaVergne TN
LVHW091024080826
845145LV00002B/352

* 9 7 8 1 6 3 6 7 9 9 2 2 3 *